Praise  Debut,
The Go ances

"*The Gods of Second Chances* is emotionally charged family drama, but it's never sappy or sentimental—it's Alaska, where Hilda's Pharmacy has a selection of birthday and sympathy cards but nothing of the Hallmark variety. You could try faith and forgiveness in a few lines of canned poetry, but it won't hit anywhere close to home. *The Gods of Second Chances* is another story."

– Brian Juenemann, *Register-Guard*

"His debut novel, *The Gods of Second Chances*, is the story of a man overwhelmed by the things beyond his control: a granddaughter on the verge of adolescence, a daughter returning from prison rehab, a frivolous lawsuit, and falling for the one woman he can't have, all while trying to fish his living out of a fickle ocean in the mercurial weather of southeast Alaska. It's no wonder that one god isn't enough for him."

– Leigh Anne Kranz, KBOO's "Between the Covers"

"Can I just say… I loved this book. Rarely have I come across a novel that blends story-telling, drama, and great writing quite as well as *The Gods of Second Chances*. I confess—I bought this book for my husband, but when he fell asleep, I snagged it, and couldn't put it down. There are moments of sadness, well-paced reveals, lush landscape description, fantastic and honest character sketches—all the things I look for in a stay-up-all-night read. Also, the book itself is beautiful. You want this one on your shelves."

– Suzy Vitello, author of *The Moment Before*

"I love this story of a grandfather seeking help from any god or goddess who will step in, as he raises his granddaughter. When the child's mother returns from prison, the fragile family ecosystem Ray has established is shaken to its bedrock."

– Néna Rawdah, St. Johns Booksellers

"Rituals, deities, and folklore are another strong theme sprinkled throughout the novel, from Tlingit legends to Christian saints and maritime superstitions."

– Ashley Swanson, *The Columbian*

"What a page turner! I could not put *The Gods of Second Chances* down, and could totally relate to the need to fight passionately for family and the life one has chosen."

– Laurel Rain-Snow Sandone, *Rainy Days and Mondays*

"The book moves at a beautiful clip, depicting how we can get hurt in family, using this hurt to defend ourselves against the world."
– Christi Krug, author of *Burn Wild* and founder of Wildfire Writing

"Dan Berne's *The Gods of Second Chances* could be a long-form entry in the FisherPoets fest; the book's protagonist, Ray, is an Alaskan fisherman struggling to make a living and care for his granddaughter, Sitka, who's been his ward since his meth-addicted daughter disappeared years before."
– Alison Hallett, *Portland Mercury*

"Second chances abound throughout the story, from Ray raising his granddaughter in a second crack at parenthood to Jenny's attempts to get clean and Ray's multiple attempts to date a local therapist. Faith plays a strong thematic role as well, with Ray's sailor superstitions (the Buddha statue he rubs every time he takes the boat out, and the collection of deity statues he keeps around his home) and the conflict all this creates when his daughter returns as a born-again Christian."
– Jeff Fleisher, *Foreword Reviews*

"It's the kind of book that pulls you through to the end with that feeling of 'I've just got to know what happens next.' The Alaska setting is vividly depicted in Dan's lucid prose, and his understanding of the family dynamics involved in the return of an errant daughter from prison to a family that is suspicious of her every move makes for a compelling read."
– Stevan Allred, author of *A Simplified Map of the Real World*

"*The Gods of Second Chances* is a poignant and sad first novel, and we can look forward to more from the compelling Dan Berne."
– Norman West, *The Portland Book Review*

"What I love about this story is its unassuming premise, and the humble characters that live ordinary lives in the unforgiving Alaskan landscape. Ray's story is one that could happen to anybody, and I was rooting for him from the opening scene."
– Gwen Stephens, *The 4 a.m. Writer*

"Author Dan Berne brings the Alaskan scenery to life effortlessly as he weaves the tale of a broken family trying to reunite, missing one of its members, and struggling to fit the pieces back together."
– Valerie Lawson, *Barbies on Fire*

"The greatest strength of this novel is the exploration of relationships among members of a fractured family."
– *The Book Binder's Daughter*

The Gods of Second Chances

The Gods
of Second Chances

a novel

by Dan Berne

illustrations by
Reid Psaltis

FOREST
AVENUE PRESS
PORTLAND,
OREGON

ISBN 978-0-9882657-4-5

Library of Congress Control Number: 2013951720

Printed in the United States of America
by Forest Avenue Press LLC
Portland, Oregon

2 3 4 5 6 7 8 9

Distributed by Legato Publishers Group

Cover design: Gigi Little
Illustrations: Reid Psaltis
Interior design: Laura Stanfill
Copy editors: Annie Denning Hille and Tracy Stepp

Forest Avenue Press LLC
6327 SW Capitol Highway, Suite C
PMB 218
Portland, OR 97239
forestavenuepress.com

For my daughter, Aiyana,
whose creative voice and dedication to her craft
are always an inspiration to me

Chapter 1

MUD AND RAIN INVADED my dreams after Donna's death. In southeast Alaska, where I've lived for half my life, we have precipitation 310 days out of the year. All those nights with the skittle-skattle of wet pellets against the windows, you'd think that rain would have formed the base molecules of my sleep a long time ago. And the mud. It's everywhere up here, omnipresent and brutal.

Until my wife died, my dreams were somehow waterproofed, sealed against the elements. Maybe it was feeling her back scrunched against my chest as we lay in bed, her leg draped over my thigh. My arm around her waist, breathing in the scent of her skin, listening to her breathe. Twelve years she's been gone, and I seldom sleep without the rain beating on the walls of my subconscious, the sludge seeping up through the decks of my memory.

Standing on the aft deck of my crabbing boat, I read the letter from my daughter for the third time. She wants to come home. Jenny, who together with the rain and the mud, murdered my wife.

"Ray!" Sitka's voice hollers from the bow of the boat.

Last year, on her eleventh birthday, she decided to call me

by my first name. Fine by me. I was only thirty-eight when Sitka was born—too young to be a grandfather. During the summer and on the weekends, if the weather isn't too bad, she goes out on the boat with me and Felix.

The two of them are on the foredeck, emptying the last of the thirty-inch octagonal shrimp pots. I can bring Sitka along with us when we go shrimping because the pots are small and we can manage with just the three of us. Different story with crabbing, though. Too dangerous for a kid her age, with the huge pots and the wintry-tough weather conditions. Not that we couldn't use an extra hand. Crabbing brings in a lot more money, and the gods know we could use that, too. I had to get the boat's engine overhauled up in Ketchikan last March, something I'm still paying off.

"Ray!" Sitka shouts again. "You'd better come here!"

I stuff the letter from her mom into its envelope and then hide it in my pocket before making my way forward. Sitka stands beside one of the pots, her arms folded. Her sandy hair, tied in a ponytail, sticks out the back of her baseball cap. She's thin, but tall for her age. Genes from her good-for-nothing-but-fish-bait father.

"You're not going to like what's in here," she says.

"Not a bit." Felix is half-Tlingit, half-Russian. Most people can't place the clicking sound his voice has, and assume that he's from Norway or Sweden.

The sun glints off the metal bars of the pot, making me squint. Sitka plunges her rubber-gloved arm into the pile of shrimp. They fidget and tumble over each other as she pushes them from side to side. When she wriggles her arm free, she holds up a small brown crab. Its shell is no more than four inches across. The frantic front claws are covered with a soft, tan bristle. They remind me of the mink muff Geraldine Chaplin wore in *Dr. Zhivago.*

"That's all we need out here," I say. "Chinese mitten crabs."

They came over from China like the Mongol Horde. They're usually close to shore and spend their time being little bulldozers, burrowing into the muddy banks of streams and marsh channels. They keep digging and digging until the whole river bank collapses. They get into everything: pipes, drains, traps, not to mention our nets. The little bastards love to steal bait from fishing lines and pots. They're bottom feeders to boot. Eat them and you're getting a meal of bio-toxic soup.

"Why ain't they up in the estuary?" Felix says, lifting up his Greek fisherman's cap. He has been my business partner and best friend for the past twenty years, and he knows as well as I do that mitten crabs are already established all around Blind Slough. Where they should have stayed. "If this keeps up, they're going to be all over our fishing spots."

"There's at least another three in there." Sitka pitches the crab in her hand overboard. "Fuck you," she shouts, as it spins head over claw into the water.

The boat is the one place she's allowed to swear. I don't like it in the house and her teachers tell me they hold it down in the classroom, but out here sometimes it just seems to fit. And I'd be hard-pressed to set a good example myself.

"Hang on, let's not throw them overboard," I tell her. "These might be females getting ready to overwinter. If that's true, they're probably carrying eggs. We'll separate them out and drop them off at Fish and Game. See what they can learn."

We need this crabbing season to be a good one. We tapped out early with the summer Dungeness back in August. They were running low on account of the warmer ocean currents, and the Fish and Game department shut the season down three weeks early. The sea lions only made things worse, munching on the Dungeness like they were snack packs. I wish I had a dollar for every time I wanted to take my rifle and shoot one of those puppy-faced scavengers.

Seals are just as bad. F&G caught Terry Meeks last month when he shot up a half dozen of them. Fined him $10,000, suspended his crabbing license for six months. Meeks didn't think they'd nab him because he was doing his herd thinning at two in the morning. Idiot. Didn't he realize that would be the perfect time for patrol boats to hone in on him? Now he's pretty well screwed for the rest of the year.

"Not much we can do about Chinese mitten crabs," I say. "Besides reporting them."

"Wait a minute, wait right here, the both of you." Felix goes into the pilothouse. We can hear him banging open drawers.

Sitka peers in his direction, as if she can see through the bulkhead. "What's he up to?"

I shrug, although I have a general notion of what he might be looking for. Sitka's hazel-green eyes remind me of her grandmother's, set wide near the nose and tapering down to a slit. Her nose that hooks up slightly—*It's big! It's ugly! I hate it!*—and her mouth that turns down at the corner, she gets from me and her mother.

Felix is back on deck, holding a small glass jar. He unscrews the lid and sniffs at the contents. "This should still be good."

"What is that?" Sitka's nostrils flare at the musky scent.

Felix pulls a light brown root out of the jar. "Jqa'tuJ tcin naku." He unsheathes the boning knife that he keeps on his belt and uses it to slice off a small chunk. "The medicine that makes things humble."

Sitka rolls her eyes. "And this is supposed to protect us from the mitten crabs?"

"Hey," I tell her, "a little respect for the maritime beliefs of your elders, young lady."

I can see that she's ready to make another wisecrack, but she stops herself. She knows that Felix and I take these things seriously. There's too little control one has over life, especially out at sea. So I'm with Felix—get all the help you can get, whether it's from saints, Hindu gods, Tlingit spirits, or rituals handed down from sailor to sailor since the beginning of time.

Felix chews on the root, then spits the brown gunk into the shrimp bucket, and onto the deck, and for good measure, he walks over to the port rail and lets some fly into the cove. "That'll teach those buggers some manners."

"Maybe. We'll still take these into dock and report them."

I stretch up my arms, trying to work out the kinks in my back. "I'm bushed. Let's get the last of these pots emptied and stacked while I'm still awake."

It takes Felix three tries to get the winch going. The motor shudders against the casing, then stops again.

"I don't know how much longer this old winch is going to hold out," he complains. "It's a wonder the whole thing just doesn't crack apart."

With a flathead screwdriver from a small toolbox we keep on deck, I turn the intake valve a quarter inch to the right. "Yeah, well, if I had the money to repair everything that needed fixing on this boat, I'd be a rich man."

"If you wanted to be rich, you would have taken that captain's job up in Bristol Bay years ago."

"And leave Sitka down here alone for months at a time? I don't think so."

I signal and Felix turns the crank. The motor coughs out gray vapors and dies. I kneel down and whack the butt of the screwdriver onto the engine casing. Readjust the input valve. This time, Felix cranks the engine and it clunkers to life.

"There you go," he says. "You can thank the jqa'tuJ tcin naku for that as well."

"As long as I don't have to chew it," I tell him.

Felix uses the winch to haul up the last pot, and Sitka and I help settle it onto the deck. We find four more mitten crabs and dump them into their own five-gallon bucket, then Sitka unhooks the cable from the pot.

"Don't get your hand caught in the door latch," I remind her. "And mind your feet around those lines!"

With her back to me, Sitka waves her finger in the air, as if to say, Why are you being such an old biddy? She knows what she's doing. But I find it nearly impossible not to give her the wisdom of my years anyway. Hell, I've been doing it since she was a baby. I have no regrets about staying here and raising her. If I had gone over to Bristol I would have probably drunk myself to death.

I go aft and finish securing the pots and stowing the lines. Then I allow myself a break at the railing. I catch the milky translucence of a lion's mane jellyfish and the swirl of pink anemones amid the brown sea kelp. Across the cove, the shoreline of Foxglove Island is lined with birch trees, whose leaves are already turning red under the late September sun. At the top of a hemlock, a pair of white-crested eagles fortifies their nest. Autumn has arrived. This time of year the black-ringed geese disappear to the south. Near our house on Yatki Island the pink flowers of the sundew have withered away. The purple blossoms of the salmonberry have been replaced with small orange and yellow orbs of sticky fruit. In a week or two the rains will be almost unceasing. And the darkness will circle like a shark around the corners of the day, taking out chunks of sunlight, until all that remains are thin strips of gray.

I shuck a Camel out of its pack and light up. There's something moving on the island, toward the back side of the beach, behind some alders. Brown bear most likely. Yeah, there they are—a mother and two cubs scrambling over a pile of bleached driftwood. They sniff along the logs and foxglove before heading into the forest. No sign of the father. Mama Bear knows to stay well away from him after the cubs are born. He's just as likely to kill his unprotected offspring as look at them.

Foxglove Island has more brown grizzlies than any place around here, which is why I never camp there. You're supposed to have a special permit to even hike on it, but every year a few kayakers wander into those woods with their backpacks full of food and a string of bells on their walking sticks, announcing that dinner has arrived.

"You shouldn't smoke, Ray." Sitka has her hands on her hips. As if she were the grandparent.

"Yeah, well, I shouldn't do a lot of things. You just make sure you don't smoke these cancer sticks. And if I ever find you using drugs—"

"Sheesh, I've heard it a hundred zillion times. You'll feed me to those bears."

I stub out my smoke in the sand-filled coffee can nailed to the bulkhead and give her a good long stare. "Don't think I won't."

Sitka ignores this. "You want to stop at Sumner Strait on the way back in?"

"Nah. I want to see if F&G has a lowdown on these mitten crabs before we sink any more pots." I put my hand out to rub the top of her head, but she ducks away.

"Stop it! I'm not a little kid anymore."

As if I don't know that. As if I can do something about it. "All right. Go ahead and hose down those last five pots, then we'll stack them."

Sitka pulls her cap tighter before heading along the starboard side to the bow. She's singing to herself, but I know she's focused on the task at hand. I've taught her to be that way. A boat is a good place to get seriously hurt if you don't keep your mind on what you're doing.

The wind picks up, blowing south from the Icy Straits, bringing a peppery scent to the air. Low stratus clouds move in, blocking the afternoon sun. It's enough to make me zip up my jacket and reach for the thermos. I unscrew the cap and pour some coffee into it, listening to the water slapping against the sides of the boat, the red salmon leaping, and the intermittent cacophony of sea gulls. I never tire of these sounds. I raise the cup to my lips just as someone raps me on the shoulder. Hot coffee slops onto my hand and sleeve.

"Damn it!" I yell to the coffee gods.

Felix squats next to me and laughs. "Hah! That's what you get for not telling me it was officially mug up time." He takes off his Greek fisherman's cap and rubs his left hand over his bald scalp. He loves that hat. Dark blue, genuine leather, with braids that look like rope strands across the front. "It's going to be rough if we have another season like last year. I've already got that second mortgage on my cabin."

I swill some of the coffee down my throat. "Mickey Dobbs has been swamped with late-season tourists. Maybe we can take on some of his leftovers."

Dobbs runs two of the larger charter boats out of Yatki Island, offering fishing, whale watching, trips up to the glaciers, the whole bit. He's even got a website. It's not unusual for him to get overbooked, and he's pretty good about throwing some of that business our way—for a small finder's fee of course.

"I don't know, Ray. You know I don't like turtles all that much." Turtles is how Felix refers to tourists. "They make me jumpity."

I throw the rest of my coffee overboard and start another cigarette. "So what the hell do you want to do, Felix? Wait and see how the season turns out or try and take advantage of whatever we can in the next few weeks?"

This comes out faster and meaner than I intend. The muscles in Felix's jaw twitch, a sign that he is struggling with how to respond. For his sixty-third birthday last January, Felix got new seat covers for his pickup from me, the Greek fisherman's cap from Sitka, and a stroke from whatever combination of bad genes and good living. He was lucky, so the doctors say. He can get around pretty well, except that his right hand shakes from time to time, especially when things get stressful. There's this part of the brain called the ventromedial area. Right behind the nose. Felix's got all fucked up with his stroke, and now he's basically incapable of making a decision. He's perfectly rational. He can memorize and rattle off every line on the tide table and recite the weather forecast for the next eight days, but he can't tell you if you should take the boat out or not. That's why it's so easy for me to slip up with him. You don't realize how many conversations wind up asking someone to decide something, until they're no longer able to do so.

"Tell you what." I flick ashes over the railing. "Let me go ahead and talk with Mickey. I'll keep the turtles in line and we'll make a couple thousand for a day's work. Okay?"

Felix's hand slows its quivering. "Sure, Ray, we can handle it. But are you all right? You've been doing more staring than working ever since we started out this morning."

"This was waiting for me at the post office yesterday." I

reach into my back pocket and pull out the letter from Jenny.

He opens the crumpled envelope and unfolds the paper, carefully smoothing the creases against his leg, as if it were a telegram from the Red Cross. "When did she get out of prison?"

I turn around to make sure Sitka is out of hearing distance. "Six months ago. She's been in some kind of rehab program for her parole."

Felix nods his head several times, as if he's counting the number of rehab programs Jenny's been in before. "So what's she doing coming here after all this time?"

"I don't have a clue."

"She clean?"

I stare at Felix a good long minute. "You remember a time when she was?"

"Here and there," he reminds me. "Here and there."

Felix didn't blame Jenny for Donna's death. Neither did the sheriff or anyone else. It was an accident, they said. I'm the only one who can admit the truth.

"How is Sitka taking the news?" Felix asks.

"She doesn't know yet." I grab the letter from him and stuff it back in my pocket. Sitka looks so much like her mom did at this age. There'd be no comparison now. Not with what the meth has done to Jenny's face and skin.

"Oh, man. That's going to be some kind of reunion. How you going to manage it?"

I don't have an answer. This is one time I could really use Felix to help me decide, because every time my daughter Jenny spins herself back into my life, it's like I get whacked on the nose and my own ventromedial thingamajig gets all fucked up.

I crush the cigarette in the coffee can. "Let's get on in and unload what we've got."

Before we haul up anchor, we make sure everything is secure. On the foredeck I pick up the bucket that holds the mitten crabs. I reach in and take one out. On its back, it looks harmless enough, clickity-clacketing its claws in the air.

Chapter 2

CREOSOTE, DIESEL FUEL, AND gutted fish are heavy in the air as we motor into St. Innocent Harbor. The water changes from the blue-gray of the strait to a murky olive, with small brown slicks of spilled fuel floating on top like camouflage. The gulls, flitting between our V-shaped wake and the canneries, crane their heads to spy the best opportunity for a quick snatch of fish. Felix tosses a handful of shrimp overboard. The gulls go crazy diving after them. We do this each time we come back into port, a way to thank the sea gods for what we've taken.

We dock at the north end of the fishery to unload and weigh the shrimp. It's nearly impossible to carry on a conversation, because of the whine of conveyor belts and canning machinery. Felix attaches the cables to the pots while I work the crane. Sitka steadies the pots as I hoist them up and over the rail of our boat. The dock crew dumps our catch into the weigh tank. Halfway through, the winch starts shaking violently and I have to stop, get out a wrench, and smack a T-bolt into submission. The vibration settles down to an acceptable hum and we carry on. I'm going to have to re-weld the base over the winter.

When we hoist up the last pot, I latch the boom while the dock master weighs and records our load. The paperwork takes a while, so I light a cigarette and look up inside the building's open doorways. It's dark, with a few shafts of sunlight illuminating sections of conveyor belts and tanks. I can see the upper halves of bodies in black aprons, hunching over, slicing, sorting, and discarding the crabs. Listening to the loud drone of the conveyor belts, I can almost feel the vibrating wood floor underneath. I worked the slime line the summer after I graduated from high school. My job was to process red king crabs. In other words I butchered them. First I would cook them alive, then I'd break off the long legs, wrapping them in groups of four. I'd pitch the body shells into a trashcan. There isn't much demand for the bodies of kings. I used to wonder how the crabs felt about that. And then I wondered whether our own lives come down to that. The parts of ourselves we value so much: our minds, our hearts—how often these were discarded in favor of what someone else wanted from us.

Back in the seventies and eighties, the king legs were favored menu items in white tablecloth restaurants from Seattle to St. Louis, though most of what we processed got shipped to Japan. The place was humming back then. I could work a twelve-hour shift and they still could have used me for another twelve hours. Even though I wore a black rubber apron, the slime line stench stayed on my clothes and seeped into my skin. In my one-room flat, everything reeked of raw crab.

One day, the steel mount holding the cauldron of boiling water cracked and the whole thing tipped over. I was young enough and fast enough to leap back in time. Even still, the scalding water splashed and burned me. I still have the white scar coursing from my left knee down to the top of my foot. I was out for two days, then came right back on the job. A sane person would have quit, but I needed the money. Donna had just had Jenny. We were flat broke, living with her parents back in Seattle. We wanted our own place, to start our own life. Alaska seemed the best place to make a lot of money fast. Of course I was just a nineteen-year-old cheechako back then, a newcomer. Growing up just outside of Seattle, I knew nothing of the realities of living north of the Lower 48s. But cannery wages were good and I was confident that I could make a decent life for my new wife and baby. As if I were an actual adult. As if I had a clue.

But since moving here, I've never wanted to live anywhere else. Our town is the sole community on Yatki Island, population 1,475, not counting tourists. Yatki is the Tlingit word for children. According to the legend, a small clan of warriors set out for the island in search of a new home, one that offered better fishing grounds. They brought their women and children with them. Just as they were within a mile of the island, a violent storm arose, sending twenty-foot waves to crash over the small boats. They capsized and the adults drowned, but the ocean gods took pity on the children and sent orca whales to carry them on their backs safely to the island. Wolves and ravens took care of that first generation, giving them food and shelter. Wolf showed them how to hunt. Raven taught them how to talk and make tools. Children born here are protected from danger, especially when they go out to sea. So says the legend.

Most of the people living here fish, cut and process fish, have something to do with tourism, or more often than not, do a bit of all three. Yeah, there's a few rich so-and-so's here and there, but most of us eke out a season-to-season kind of existence. People settle here because this is where they were born or this is where they want to be. Making a living is secondary to that. You go to a wedding or a barbecue around here and I promise you that you won't hear "What do you do for a living?" No, we're going to talk straight on about the weather, about the ocean, about hunting and fishing, about the kids, about the husbands and wives. And hockey of course. We're as bad as the Canucks when it comes to hockey. What we really want to know is if you're the kind of person someone can count on when they've got a busted propane tank and it's thirty-three degrees out and raining torrents. Are you going to come over and lend a hand or not?

WE WAIT ON THE boat while the dock master completes the paperwork. I log our trip. Sitka sits on the deck rail, winding and unwinding the ends of her ponytail, then zipping and unzipping her jacket. She pouts her lips in and out as if she were popping bubblegum while waiting for a school bus. Felix pours himself the last cup of cold coffee. Finally we get the weigh-in papers. The numbers are not good. We're a third below our seasonal average. And prices are down thirty cents a pound from last year. At this rate, there won't be a dime to add to Sitka's college fund this year.

Sitka and I are back at the house by four o'clock. It's a three bedroom, 1940s bungalow, just up the hill and three streets over from the pier. The foundation is going. The whole house leans to the left and you have to sort of swagger up the steps to the front porch. I should level it and put in a French drain before it gets any worse. But that's a huge job.

The 122 inches of rain this island gets every year keeps creating sinkholes in the driveway. Half of the blue-gray siding shingles need replacing and much of the white trim paint has worn away. I've fixed the roof leaks, most of them anyway. The two window boxes are still in good shape. They have that Norwegian rosemaling pattern carved into them: brightly painted flower stems and petals, and more curlicues than should be legal. They're supposed to be the hallmark of a good Scandinavian abode. I always thought they were ostentatious and I wanted to whitewash over the stupid things, but for some reason Donna loved them even though her parents are German and from the Midwest. She bought stencils with similar patterns that she used throughout the inside of the house, making the walls a tribute to Norwegian folk art. The stencils are still stuffed in the bottom drawer of the hutch in the living room. I was going to get rid of them, but didn't get around to it, and then when Sitka was about five, she found them and started making drawings with them using her crayons. Maybe someday she'll have kids and they'll play with them as well.

You can't see the house from the wharf because of the sharp

angle of the hill and the dozen spruce trees clustered along the street. But that suits me fine. I like to keep my home and the sea separate. Unlike my neighbors, I don't have a bunch of nautical knick-knacks in my front yard—anchors, carved ropes, or cartoon replicas of skippers—nothing like that on the inside either. I do have a pretty large collection of gods and goddesses, statues that I've picked up since Donna died. Sitka thinks the odd assortment of Christian saints, Buddhas, Hindu gods, and Chinese and Japanese deities take up way too much of the available counter and tabletop real estate in our house. But they give me some measure of comfort, a visible reminder that there are forces to call upon when so much is out of our control.

As soon as I unlock the door, Sitka sprints around me and up the stairs to her room to pack her duffel bag. She's spending the night at Sarah Poulson's house, where she often goes if I'm out with the boat overnight. I wander into the kitchen and put on some coffee. Just as it's done, Sarah and her mom knock at the front door.

"Come on in. It's open!" I yell.

The hinges squeak as the two of them come in, Sarah looking expectantly up the staircase.

"Sitka's finishing packing. You can go on up if you want."

Sarah doesn't waste any time, taking two stairs at a time, and soon there's a burst of giggling and a gaggle of "Oh my Gods" streaming out of my granddaughter's room.

"Thanks again for having Sitka over, Julie." Like most of the parents of Sitka's friends, Julie is about fifteen years younger than me. With streaked-blond hair, breasts that tip a bit forward like water-filled balloons, and hips that push on the seams of her faded jeans, she's attractive enough that I would try a little flirting, if Sitka and Sarah weren't around. If she weren't married. If her husband Phil wasn't such a nice guy who lets me borrow his sea kayak. And then there's the sloppily done green and blue orca tattoo on Julie's right forearm, but still. "You want any coffee while you wait?"

Julie shakes her head. "We've got a pizza on order and I

still have to pick up some Coke and chips." She looks toward the stairs. "Girls, let's get a move on, please!" The girls yell back, "Okay! Okay!" but there's no movement down the stairs. Julie looks at me and shrugs. "I'll drop them off at the Marine Museum tomorrow. Can you pick them up there around five?"

For their first major biology project of the year, Sitka and Sarah are making a PowerPoint presentation on the giant Pacific octopus, complete with photos and an embedded video. The Marine Museum keeps a couple of the pink and purple creatures in a tank near the back. They're fairly common around here, so they're easy to research. And they're a good draw for the tourists, who stand in front of the tank with their mouths open when they see the size of them. To me, they make pretty good cut-up bait for crab.

"The Marine Museum, eh? That wouldn't have anything to do with Connor Davis working there on the weekends, would it?"

Julie confirms this by cocking her head to the side and smiling. Connor Davis, a high school sophomore, is already a starter on the Penguins football team. Tight end, I think. He also plays guitar and sings in a garage band. Sitka and Sarah, together with half the girls in the seventh grade, believe Connor to be our island's natural choice for the next American Idol.

"We always love having Sitka over," Julie tells me. "She's a really sweet girl."

"Thanks. It's been awhile since Sarah's spent the night here. You know she's always welcome. She's a great kid, too."

"We'll see," Julie answers.

"Tell you what. Why don't we plan for next Saturday? We can swing by your house after we bring the boat in."

"Um, I don't know, Ray." She looks around at the walls, and there's such hesitation in her voice that I push for an explanation.

"Julie, is something wrong?" Did she notice that I was admiring the arc of her high-bridged nose, the way it complimented her pecan-brown eyes? "Is there a reason you don't want Sarah to stay over here?"

Julie leans forward and whispers back at me. "It's not you. It's just that Sarah . . ." She stops and looks up the stairs, making sure that the girls are still in Sitka's room. "Sarah got her first period last month and now she's—oh, girls at this age can be so sensitive. You probably went through all of this when Jenny hit adolescence."

I shake my head no. "That was Donna's department."

"In that case," Julie offers, "when that time comes for Sitka, maybe you should let me take her shopping."

"Ooh, shopping for what?" Sitka interrupts, as she and Sarah come downstairs, each with a hand on Sitka's heavy duffel.

"If you behave yourself," I tell her, "something for your birthday."

It's still three months away, but that doesn't stop Sitka from bringing up the topic every couple of weeks. She clasps her hands, swinging her arms in front of her. "The new iTouch?" Her eyes open wide as a fawn's in a morning meadow.

Julie points to her watch. "Girls, the pizza was ready five minutes ago. Other people are waiting for us to get home."

"Say hi to Phil," I tell her.

Sarah frowns at her mom. "Can't we stop by the video store first? I don't know why we can't stream movies from the satellite like normal people."

"There goes my night." Julie shifts the purse on her shoulder and opens the front door. "Watching these two watch a bunch of boy-band videos."

I nod over to the DVD player. "What about all those Justin Bieber videos?" Sitka begged and begged me for them last year. In response to my suggestion, she and Sarah roll their eyes to verify just how clueless I really am.

"Night, Mr. Bancroft," Sarah sing-songs out the door.

"Night, Ray." Sitka sashays out the door on Sarah's heels. She's not about to give her grandfather a hug in front of her friend.

"Remember to help Mrs. Poulson with the dishes tonight," I remind her.

Julie pats my arm as she turns to leave. "We'll talk about that little subject later, Ray. You let me know. I'll be happy to help out."

I nod my head in acknowledgment as I close the door behind them. It's true that underneath Sitka's bulky sweatshirt and jeans, the outline of a young woman is beginning to take shape. Any day now she'll ask me to buy her some special female items at the Moose Market. Or a training bra. Where the hell do you find those? Maybe it would be easier to ask Julie for help.

I go into the kitchen and dump out the coffee that's gone sludgy and cold in my mug. I open the refrigerator and take out a bottle of Alaskan Amber, twisting off the top. Sitting at the kitchen table, I consider the other implications of Sitka's soon-to-be adolescence. I'm not ready for her to be boy crazy yet, but do I have a choice? Going on twelve, it's only natural for Sitka's sonar to start tracking the opposite sex. But is she starting out way too early like her mother?

I reach into my pants pocket and pull out the note from Sitka's mom. Jenny. My drugged out, ex-con, now-I'm-ready-to-come-home-and-be-forgiven-once-again daughter. The envelope has no return address. The letter's on powder-blue stationery, the kind with darker blue lines that don't go quite all the way across the page. The words are written in purple ink, with large, circular letters.

Dear Father,—yeah, when did she ever call me that?
I am writing to you and hoping you are well. I know this is probably a surprise for you, since it's been so long since we've communicated or seen each other—try five years. *I am happy to announce that I have completed my rehabilitation program here at the New Ways House in Kalispell. I know you must be almost as proud of me as I am of myself. Now with the support of the staff here, and with God's help*—yet another twelve-step program, how many did this make? Three? No, four—*I am ready to reclaim my life. I will be arriving home to see you and Sitka, whom I miss so dearly*—that explains all the times

you've never called her on her birthday or Christmas. *I will be arriving on the afternoon ferry from Juneau on Friday, October 4.*

Your loving and newly empowered daughter,
Jenny

The writing has all the style and sincerity of a con letter. I imagine some ex-druggie counselor sitting down next to Jenny and encouraging her. Go ahead. You'll see. This note will mean so much to your dad and to your daughter. What it means to me is acid in my stomach.

I don't feel like cooking. Not in the mood to be by myself, not in the mood to be with other people. I put on an old sweatshirt and my hooded jacket, stick Jenny's letter in my jeans pocket, and go outside. The evening air has cooled. I'm not exactly sure what I want to do, but I still have to eat. I walk a few blocks down to the Blind Dog Tavern, an old clapboard building that used to be a brothel, before it became a store-front church, before it changed back to a brothel, before it became the Blind Dog. The floor is rough boards, sawdust, and peanut shells. It's comfortably dark and warm inside. A jukebox plays a Clint Black love ballad.

"Waa sa iyatee, ya yaa koosge daakeit, Ray."

"Hey, Muskeg."

Muskeg Sally's the owner/bartender and she is full Tlingit, Eagle clan. She always likes to shout out the traditional native greeting. It shakes up the tourists something awful.

Muskeg flicks her bar towel at me. "Don't call me that in front of the customers, you furry marmot."

When she was in her younger years, Sally was one of the first people to go out and study the muskegs, those grassy, swampy bogs that populate the islands around here. This was before everyone and his brother threw around the word ecology. Sally just had a natural interest in the muskegs. She'd snip away at the dark green Labrador tea plants or gather the dank leaves of the swamp birch, and document where she found them. Over the years she recorded all of the various grasses, flowers, ferns, and toads that inhabited the muskegs. Sheldon Jackson College published some of her work, and she gave a few lectures to very small audiences up in Juneau and Anchorage. That's when someone dubbed her Muskeg Sally, a fan of Wilson Pickett no doubt.

"Somebody's not getting enough loving," I tease. "I'll call Felix and tell him to come over and meet you after work."

Muskeg and Felix have been dating each other for as long as I've known Felix. Muskeg refuses to get married, but they may as well be. They go out to movies and dances, stay over at each other's cabins, and, most importantly, they fish and hunt together. Even though Muskeg is pushing sixty, she can beat any woman and half the men in town in arm wrestling. And for a woman her age, Muskeg does okay in the looks department. Unlike some of the older women around here, her face isn't so lined it looks like the bark of a hemlock tree. Muskeg keeps herself in shape, and though I've never seen her in anything close to approaching a skirt or dress, she's nearly always presentable. Two large silver earrings in the shape of salmon dangle from her ears. The copper outline of them matches the henna in her hair.

She and Felix are Sitka's godparents. They've treated her like a favorite grandchild since day one, and Muskeg watches her during my overnight boat trips whenever Julie can't.

There are a few other folks I recognize and we grunt hello to each other. Dave Rifkin is in the far corner booth, snuggled up with Wendy Canter. They're married, each to other people. They somehow act like the rest of us don't have a clue what's been going on, like Yatki Island is as big as Seattle, where they could mess around in private.

I pick a bar stool with no one on either side, wrapping my ankle around one of the legs. I take out Jenny's letter and put it on the bar without unfolding it. As if I could decide what to do by studying the crumpled paper. I've thought about taking Sitka off-island with me, maybe heading over to Kodiak for an extended fishing trip. But wouldn't that just delay the inevitable?

"Goddammit, Jenny." No one hears me say this, which is probably just as well. I should have my head on straight to figure out what to do when she arrives. But I've had twenty-eight years to come up with a game plan for how to deal with her and I haven't succeeded yet.

Muskegs swipes the bar with a damp rag, making her way down to where I'm perched. "Ready to order?"

I rub my hand on my chin. "What's in the pot tonight?"

"It's on the board behind me." She tosses the rag into a bucket behind her. "Same as always. Can't you read?"

"Too damn dark in here." I squint at the chalk scribbling.

"Elk stew," Muskeg says. "My sister made it this morning from that big buck Earl shot last week."

"All right. That and a beer."

It takes less than two minutes for Muskeg to draw an Alaskan Amber and slop some stew into a bowl and set them in front of me. I have to ask for a knife and spoon, and oh, yeah, a couple of buttermilk biscuits. The stew needs salt and some green vegetables, and it tastes gamey, though nowhere near as gamey as caribou, which even we locals avoid when we can. I lift my glass and give a silent salute to Latis, the Celtic goddess of beer and water. The beer and the biscuits cut back on the hunted beast flavor. Halfway through, I order another beer, then finish the bowl, holding it up and licking the bottom.

Stew and beer, I should feel content, but I don't want to feel content. I'm itchy and restless. I want to smash the tidy rows of liquor bottles. Between them, there's a muddled dark reflection of my face. Just another bachelor fisherman, alone at the bar.

"Muskeg," I yell, "a whiskey."

Muskeg stops wiping a beer glass and squints at me, then grabs a shot glass and sets it on the counter. "I thought you were a beer man." She takes two bottles from the shelf behind her and holds them up in front of me. She tilts one bottle toward me, then the other. "Preference?"

"Whichever one brings enlightenment the quickest."

She frowns and pours from the bottle she's holding in her right hand. I'm expecting it to be caramel-colored with glints of gold. Instead it looks muddy, like something you'd bottle straight out of Little Coffee River. I hold the shot glass up to the light but it doesn't help the appearance any.

"Here's to empowered daughters, Muskeg."

She lifts her eyebrow. "Felix told me you were acting odd today. Said Jenny was on her way back here. You want to talk about it?"

My answer is nothing more than a grunt as I pour the liquor into the back of my mouth. It's warm, almost hot. It makes the muscles in my throat contract and it burns my esophagus and stomach. Just what I want. I point to the shot glass and Muskeg refills it.

"Suit yourself. But go easy with that. I don't want to have to drag your sorry ass out the door just so I can close up tonight."

The whiskey roils in my stomach and feeds that line of twitchiness all the way into my bone marrow. The yammering voices prick at my skin like nettles, especially that group of tourists. Eddie Bauer sporting jackets, clean fishing hats, and those godawful duck shoes. They're the noisiest bunch in here and someone is saying something about Alaska Airlines that sends the rest into fits. One of the women in the group has a raucous laugh, spraying out her beer as her head juts forward. Fucking turtles yapping away like ill-bred puppies.

"Muskeg!" I raise the shot glass. "You gonna keep this filled or what?"

She refills my whiskey, then settles the bottle on the bar top. "You sure you're okay, Ray? It ain't like you to sit all by your lonesome and just drink. I haven't seen you drunk since . . ." She doesn't say since Donna died. "You want me to call Felix? Have him come by?"

I wave her off and drink. I'm beyond the whiskey buzz,

nervous and prickly, the remnants of the elk stew scratching like spruce bark inside me. There's some woman singing from the jukebox now. Reba McEntire or LeAnn Rimes or some other country western type.

"Jesus, Muskeg! Can't you play anything but backwoods music in here?"

She doesn't even move from the other end of the bar. "Most folks like it. More importantly, I like it, so just lighten up."

"I think I'll do just that." I wrangle the whiskey bottle, fill up the shot glass, drain it, and fill it up again. I get off the stool and address the crowd in general. "Christ, it's not like we're Wyoming." This is very clever. I give myself a laugh. "We've got more hard times, alcoholism, and two times the broken hearts per capita than any state in the union, so why can't we come up with our own music? Look at Hawaii. They've at least got hula music. Why can't we have something like the Eskimo blues?"

No one answers. Fuck 'em. I help myself to another whiskey and drink it more quickly. I don't like that touristy crowd in the corner. All dressed up in their fancy touristy clothes. What do they know about an honest day's work is what I want to know. Which one of them had to tell his wife there'd be no vacation or birthday gifts because the price of salmon dropped? Man, I could really go for some blues right now. Seattle has a lot of blues bars. Everywhere does but this dump.

"Muskeg! You're Tlingit. Your people got a lot to sing the blues about." I slap my hand on the bar in what must be a pretty good Tlingit-Blues rhythm. Bah, bah, bah, bah, boom. She-bah, bah, bah, bah, bah she-boom.

Muskeg slaps my hands with her wet towel and moves the whiskey bottle back to the shelf. "Time to go home, you."

This place, there's another thing about it. In Juneau, I could get as drunk as I want, when I want. But this is a small town. People look out for one another. Bunch of nosy buttinskis.

"C'mon, Muskeg. The party's just getting started!"

No one seems to be laughing with me, least not that tourist

lady. What's her problem? I'm woozy now. Almost completely nauseated. Mission just about accomplished. I reach toward the shelf of liquor bottles behind her to give Muskeg a hint. She grabs my sleeve.

"Ray, get your butt on home now or I'll call Earl and he'll sit your skinny ass in his patrol cruiser and then you'll have to spend the night in the county jail, and Earl tells me the heater is broken over there."

"All right, goddammit, let me go." I get up and stumble a bit as I make my way gracefully to the door. "Gunalcheesh!" I make such a deep bow that I almost fall face forward. I stagger back up. "Gunalcheesh!" Thank you. A Tlingit thank you, ladies and gentlemen, and goodnight. This bow, this exit is remarkably charming and funny, and I yell it repeatedly as my marshmallow legs somehow get me all the way home. See that, Jenny? This is what you do when life gnaws at you. You get drunk, like any red-blooded American. Then you walk, goddammit, you walk home. You don't drive. You walk and you sing out your thank yous to the night. "Gunalcheesh! Godspeed! Gesundheit! Gunalcheesh!"

MY HAIR AND CHEST are soaked and my stomach is turning and stopping like a band saw with a bad switch. The bed seems to be shaking underneath me. My head is hot and my feet are icy cold. I still have my clothes on, except for one boot. There's an insistent scratching noise, an iceberg scraping against the sides of the house. Maybe it's a bear. Maybe I should go check. I go downstairs, my feet tumbling over the last three stairs. It takes a couple of tries to get the door open and stumble outside. I'm standing in the light of a three-quarter moon. The air is sharp. I turn my head this way and that, looking for moose or bear, but have no idea what I'd do if I saw one. I left my rifle inside and I can barely focus. Maybe my stink would drive it away. That's funny too, and I laugh before I have to bend over and retch out the elk stew and liquor, the hot bile running up and down my esophagus. I slump onto the grass and lay back, the moon and stars making zigzag dog sledding tracks across the sky. I have to close my eyes to make them stop. But then I have to open them again.

As the sky spins, I try to make out the constellations, but they look unfamiliar, skittering around up there. But that one, over to the west—it sort of looks like a woman. Like Donna. Her head and arms and shoulders, the pelvis and legs. A beautiful woman made out of starlight and darkness. Beautiful, beautiful, beautiful. But what the hell can she do for you? Nothing, that's what. She's cold and empty.

I want the flesh and blood woman. I want the warm body breathing next to me in bed, waking up with me and drinking a cup of coffee with me. The woman I can talk to, with skeleton and skin and nerves that tingle when you brush her neck. The woman who will rub my shoulders just because I've had a hard day. I want to take her feet when she's sitting on the couch and massage them for no other reason than that she likes it. I want the woman who tastes like a perfectly ripe pear when I kiss her. The warm hands that will massage the inside of my thighs and move up onto my balls. The woman who will kneel in front of me and offer her backside because she likes to feel me scrunch up against her. I'd move inside that woman because I know exactly the right angle she likes, and when she wants to move onto her side or climb on top of me, I don't have to think about it, but just flow with that rhythm we know so well, but is as fresh and startling as a jazz riff. I want the woman who will just hold me when I don't know what the hell I'm talking about.

Come down from that goddamn night sky, Donna. Come down. Come down. Come down.

Chapter 3

"MAN, OH MAN. YOU look like you stuck your head in a patch of devil's club and swirled it around in the toilet." Felix carries two thermoses filled with coffee into the pilothouse. He takes down two coffee cups from the dozen that are on safety hooks above the mounted GPS unit on the starboard side. The cups are spaced well apart for safety and all of them face forward, for luck.

"Don't even start." I slump further down in the captain's chair and massage my temples. The array of controls reminds me that I have to get my act together. I've already checked the navigation system, the communications deck, and the radar. Charts are laid out on the console on the port side behind me. Wish I could afford one of those dynamic positioning systems like the big boys use. That would make life easier.

Outside it's late September drizzle. Everything on the docks looks slippery cold. Our paying guests will be here in an hour.

"How about you cutting up the bait this morning?" I ask Felix. "I don't think I can handle it right now."

He grunts but doesn't move, while I take the lid off the vanilla milkshake I bought on the way to the boat. I dump a packet of salt into it, then sprinkle Tabasco sauce on top. The canteen that serves the cannery is located at the end of our pier. Over the years they've learned to offer various hangover concoctions in the morning; otherwise, the slime lines would never start on time, and fishing vessels would stay docked. If Felix had come in five minutes sooner, he'd have seen me downing one of their greasy burger and fried egg sandwiches, which actually helped to settle my stomach. I take a gulp of the shake. It's cold and heavy, and dampens the burning in my gut, while making my chest feel like it's a baby berg. I slap my chest trying to get out a good burp. It doesn't work.

Felix fishes a pack of cigarettes out of his shirt pocket and offers me one. "Muskeg said you had your own personal pity party going on last night."

I take the cigarette and light up, fighting down the bile clawing up my throat. I hack a dry cough before I can say anything. "Jesus, you'd think this town wasn't so full of drunks that I couldn't have a night of drinking now and then."

"That's just it," Felix says. "That's why Muskeg called me. You're not one to do that sort of thing."

"Yeah, well nice to know Muskeg cares about me so much."

I wish Felix would have a seat in the co-pilot's chair and relax, but he stares at me as if my face is a pile of bark shavings that he can poke around in with a stick.

"There a particular thing eating at you or is this gonna be a habit? I'm just asking because I've got to have my sorry ass out on this boat with you and I don't want to wind up on the bottom of Icy Straits just because you fall asleep at the wheel."

I struggle out of my chair. "I've still got to bring the groceries and beer and wine onboard. They're in the back of the truck. And that bait isn't going to cut itself up. While you're aft, go ahead and double-check the life rafts, ditch bags, flares, and MOB poles. I'll tape over the deck fills and hawseholes, and make sure the chain is pulled back into the bilge. I've already tested the SSB radio and sonar."

"All right," Felix says. "I'll check the emergency pump and GPIRB."

We've done this routine a million times, but we never leave dock without ticking down our checklist. The sea gods have a mind of their own and that's all the more reason to make sure you have your act together before you leave port.

When I go out on deck, the drizzle is refreshing on my scalp, but I still feel rocky. My legs want to uncoil like loose rope, while the back of my neck is as tight as a rusty hinge. I lean over the edge of the boat, fighting the urge to throw up. The camouflage-green dock water marks a ragged salt line along the outer bulkhead.

In the slip on our port side, Ed Thompson and his three boys are lashing down their anchors with double lines. Ed waves and I nod back. He points to the sky. The paying customers aren't going to be pleased with the weather. I hold up my hand like I'm downing a bottle of beer—don't worry. We'll have plenty of booze onboard to keep them happy.

Saturday mornings are a busy time on the docks. Thirty or more vessels are preparing to get under way, especially for tourist fishing. There's a crew of anywhere from two to five for each boat, checking engines, untying lines, clearing the decks of clutter. On the dock, early rising tourists are milling about and pointing out to the sea, in anticipation of landing a record-breaking halibut. Three men are practicing how they will pose with their catch suspended next to them.

The noisiness of the harbor—percussive engines starting and restarting, crews hoisting and dragging gear onto decks, checking winches, yelling orders and jokes to each other—is a communal sound that is usually comforting to me. That stuff Hemingway wrote about the old man facing the sea on his own? Romantic bullshit. I like having my fellow fishermen around me in the morning. I don't want to face those fickle sea gods all by my lonesome, thank you very much. But right now all that clanking thumps against the back of my neck. I have to squeeze my eyes to focus.

I get busy with the duct tape and deck fills. After securing the hawseholes, I load and secure the groceries and booze on the aft deck. The drizzle has subsided and yellow light is spreading out from beneath the clouds.

Felix comes up to me and points to the pier. "Finished just in time. Those must be our turtles."

A man and three women. That's what Mickey Dobbs said. "Time to turn on the mariner charm," I say.

"You still look like you should be rolled up under a tarp," Felix says. "You sure you're ready to play captain?"

I run my hand over my face, dotted with stubble. "Maybe they'll think I'm authentic." I sniff at my chest and armpits, but honestly, I can't really tell if I smell decent or not. Fortunately the cannery provides plenty of aromatic distraction.

We stand by the gangplank as our turtles wander down the walkway. A man and a woman lean into each other as they talk; they must be the married couple. He's in his late forties, but the woman holding his hand can't be any more than twenty-two or twenty-three. She's got the build of a short cheerleader, with bangs the color of carrots sweeping just below the rim of her cap. He looks like a one-time college football tackle gone overweight.

Behind them are two women, maybe in their late thirties. A petite, attractive blonde whose frizzy hair jumps out from her head like that of an unbrushed poodle, flaps her hands as she talks, so that she constantly has to readjust her shoulder bag. Her taller friend is a pretty brunette. A pair of sunglasses is perched just above her forehead, ready if the sun decides to come out. She tilts her head as she listens.

"At least they got on their Yatki sneakers." Felix is referring to the calf-high brown rubber boots that we wear up here most of the year. The man and his wife and the poodle blonde are toting rod and reel carrying cases. There's advantages and disadvantages to turtles bringing their own gear. It's easy to show them how to use yours, but they'll often bitch about how cheap the loaner equipment is. If they do bring theirs, they're usually more self-sufficient, but they'll be ready to sue your butt off if they fumble and drop their favorite rod and reel into fifty feet of water.

The tourists stop, searching for our boat. The man turns and says something to the others. They seem to have formed that loose bond of strangers starting off on an adventure together. We don't wave to them. That's the thing about turtles. It takes them time to get their bearings, but it's important not to rush in to help them. Otherwise you're spending all day picking them up and moving them around. Finally the brunette sees us and motions to her companions. The man steps out ahead of the others. Gripping his gear in his left hand, he proffers his right one.

"You must be Captain Bancroft."

"Just call me Ray." I extend my hand in return. The man pumps it like he's going to get well water out of me. He's going to need the XX-large size life vest.

"I'm Walt Francke and this is my wife, Cindy." He says my wife like I say my boat. Cindy lifts up her rod and reel case, the tip of it nearly hitting Walt in the face. She squeaks out a "Hi ya."

She and Walt are wearing jeans, matching green sweatshirts and identical orange REI all-weather jackets. Their caps are different though. Each has Terre North Lodge embroidered in canary yellow, but his is blue-green with a dark brown brim, while hers is red with a powder-blue brim. Terre North is an expensive hunting lodge up near Prince William Sound, the kind of place for people who want to experience the great outdoors and leave none of the luxuries behind. Extra thick mattresses and fancy sheets. Dining room with waiters and white tablecloths. Wine served on the oversized porch. That kind of thing.

The blonde steps around Walt. "I'm Alison French." But my friends call me Ali," she adds quickly, her green eyes flitting back and forth as she talks. "This is my friend Nicole Harris, that's with two ars and one es, but her family still calls her Nicki, which she hates. We've been up here for five days and it's just been beautiful, except for the rain, but we're from Seattle so we're used to that, but it looks like you get even more up here, which I hope isn't too bad for Nicole, because she's actually moving up here and I'm helping her get settled."

Ali and Nicole are both wearing water-resistant slacks, wool sweaters and rain-proof jackets. Smart choices when you're go-ing out on the water in this weather. Nicole has a Nikon camera case strapped over her shoulder. Ali holds her fishing gear com-fortably in her left hand.

"I see you brought your own rod and reel. You know your way around a boat?"

Ali leans the rod a bit forward. "This was my dad's. I grew up in a little town in western Oregon and he used to take me salmon fishing."

"Over at the mouth of the Columbia River?"

"Up near Ilwaco, Washington. You know it?"

"I've caught my share of Chinook at buoy 10."

A harbor seal barks and our guests rotate to see where it is. Nicole turns all the way around. She has a lovely shape. Her hips press out just slightly against the fabric of her slacks. The seal flips under the gray water and everyone turns back to me, so I motion for Felix to step forward.

"This is my partner Felix. He'll be helping you catch some great fish today."

Walt extends his hand, but Felix sidesteps, as if he has to check the starboard fenders. Walt looks insulted, but I explain to him that Felix considers shaking hands with strangers before we leave dock to be bad luck. I tell him that Felix is part Tlingit, and that's good because his grandfather has handed down a list of secret fishing spots. Walt nods and I think he may actually be buying this. The part about believing it's bad luck is true. Once we're under way, Felix will do better with the turtles than I will. And if all goes well, he'll be the first one to offer a hearty shake when we dock.

The group follows me onboard to the foredeck, where we've laid out the personal floatation devices.

I pick up one of the vests. "I have to go over some safety in-formation. The first thing you will each want to do is to put on your PFD. Please take one you think will fit. Try it on and we'll help you adjust it if necessary."

"I'm not wearing any goddamn life jacket just to go fishing,"

Walt declares. He holds up his rod and reel in testament to his prowess. "Hell, I go up to northern Lake Michigan every winter and this isn't near as bad as that can get."

The muscles around my neck and forehead constrict, making my headache worse. "I can't force you to wear one, Walt. But Coast Guard regulations do demand that you try one on that fits you and that you know where we assemble in case of an accident. We don't leave dock until you do." I reach over and pick up our sixteen-foot boat hook. It has a titanium handle and a supposedly unbreakable polyurethane head with three prongs. "Besides, if you go overboard without a PFD on, then I've got to drag you out with this."

Walt harrumphs, but doesn't protest more than that. After we get through the fittings and the emergency drill, we're ready to go. Felix unhitches the hawser lines from the moorings, while I give the passengers the last of my spiel.

"We've got bagels, coffee, and fruit for breakfast and plenty of snacks and sandwiches for lunch. Don't hesitate to help yourselves, particularly if you start feeling queasy. There's also Alaskan Amber and some wine from Washington if you want something stronger." I point to the coolers stacked on the port side. "We'll use these to store any fish you catch. Felix and I will be happy to fillet and pack your catch in ice for shipping or taking back on the plane home with you. The sea's a little rough today, but we'll try to keep it as smooth as possible. We'll be heading to Frederick Sound for the king salmon, then on up to Thomas Bay for the halibut. Any questions?"

I'm hoping there's not because sweat is breaking out across my forehead and I'd just as soon take my seat in the pilothouse and get under way. The breeze on the open strait would sure feel nice right now. But Walt folds his arms across his chest and nods out to the Sound. "We're staying at the Indigo Lodge and the manager there said we'd be guaranteed to catch a hundred-pound halibut."

"And lots of salmon," Cindy chirps. "Don't forget the salmon, Walt."

The last thing I want to do is get into a one-on-one pissing contest with a client, so I address the entire group. "Well, folks, I can't guarantee we'll catch anything, just like I can't guarantee the weather. The kings are running a little slow right now, but the halibut are doing pretty well. We may stay in one spot for a couple of hours or we may move around. It all depends. This is only a six-hour trip, so Mother Nature will have to be on our side today is all I can say. Anything else?"

"What's this?" Nicole asks. She's pointing to a little statue fastened to the ledge just outside the pilothouse. A squat, round figure sits with its legs jutting out, hands plastered to its sides. Its arched eyebrows accentuate a head that is carved into a sharp peak. The mouth is set in a wide, mischievous grin. "It looks like a Chinese Buddha statue."

"That's our Billiken." Felix has returned to the aft deck.

"What's a Billiken? I mean, what's it for?"

He steps up to the figurine and pats the belly. "He's the god of the way life ought to be." Felix brought the statue onboard years ago and always makes sure he strokes it whenever we head out. "If you rub his belly and he keeps smiling, then you'll be safe from harm."

"Jesus," Walt says. "I always knew sailors were superstitious, but this is ridiculous."

"Is it okay if I rub it?" Nicole asks.

Felix slips his calloused fisherman's hand around Nicole's wrist, guiding her fingers gently across the Billiken's soapstone stomach.

"Thanks," she says quietly. Felix beams.

"What did you wish for?" Ali asks.

Nicole drops her hand to her sides and mumbles something, her mouth turned down. I'm too far away to hear what her answer is. Walt lays his hand on my shoulder, steering me starboard, away from the rest of the passengers.

"Say, Bancroft." His voice is hushed, like we're a couple of Wall Street broker types ready to make a secret deal. "See if you can help me out here. I don't mind telling you that my wife has a big appetite, if you know what I mean. And I'm not saying I can't take care of her needs, no way. But, you know, it doesn't hurt for guys our age to add a little booster to the rocket, know what I mean? I've heard about that great stuff you guys use up here that keeps you going all through those long winter nights."

Maybe it's my hangover, but I have no idea what great stuff this guy is talking about. "I'm sorry, Walt. You're going to have to be more specific. What exactly are you asking for?"

He turns his face sideways, leaning in toward me, as if speaking the words out of the corner of his mouth will tighten whatever conspiracy is supposedly going on here. "Gall bladders," he whispers. "You know, from grizzly bears."

"Gall bladders," I repeat, shaking my head. They're rumored to have great powers of sexual potency. There's a whole black market for them, especially in China. But it's not only illegal to hunt bears for their bladders, it's cruel and wasteful, because the other parts of the bear, except for the paws, are discarded.

"Can't help you out in that department, pal. And you ought to know, and I think you do, that it's illegal and you could wind up in jail."

"Look, if it's a matter of money, I'm willing to pay." Walt places his hand on my forearm. "And you would get a finder's fee. We can work that out."

I let out a sigh. "It's not a matter of a finder's fee. I'll say this as clearly as I can. It's illegal and even if it weren't, I would have nothing to do with it because it's just a plain wrong thing to do."

"Just my luck," Walt mutters. "I come all the way out to Alaska and wind up with some kind of tree-hugging bear lover. Forget I even fucking mentioned it."

I can tell from his tone that he's half worried I'll turn him in to the authorities. "No worries, Walt," I reassure him. "Just wanted to set the record straight. I'm sure you're going to enjoy the fishing we have today."

He turns and slides past me, heads to the cooler, and helps himself to a beer.

The rest of the trip up to Frederick Sound goes well enough. The clouds open up, dappling the sky with large patches of white. The waves settle to less than a meter, and even the overhauled twin engines decide to behave. Along the way, we catch sight of a pod of orca whales and sea lions in the water, and mountain goats and black bear on the islands. My head and neck muscles finally start to relax. Cutting through the strait with the open air on my face calms my stomach. Even still, I'm feeling a bit busted so I ask Felix to take the wheel and I go aft to check on the turtles.

Walt and Cindy are portside, taking their rod and reels out of their cases and assembling them. Nicole, stationed at the railing on the other side of the deck, points her camera at the water behind us. There's a school of Dall's porpoises swimming in our wake. They come along starboard, their black and white dorsal fins breaking the surface every hundred yards or so. Nicole follows with her lens. When one of the males leaps high out of the water, his thick belly creates a rooster spray as he smacks down on the surface. Nicole clicks away. I should call the others over but the Franckes seem tangled up in their own conversation and I don't see Ali.

Nicole straightens up and turns around. "They're almost too fast to photograph."

"I know what you mean." I put my hands on the rail and lean forward, as if I want to track the movement of the porpoises, too. The sleeve of my jacket touches hers lightly. "I gave up years ago trying to be any kind of wildlife photographer."

The sun is behind her, backlighting the bay, the rails, and highlighting her brown hair. She lifts a strand hanging down from under her cap and settles it behind her ear. Her skin is pale as corn silk with noticeably darker lines under her eyes. And there are patches of pink against her cheeks, windburn perhaps. She looks at me as if she wants to take my picture.

"Ali thinks you should be in the movies. The tough skipper

type." She cocks her head a bit. "She thinks you're quite good looking, like that Scottish actor whose name I can never remember, so don't ask me. Come to think of it, maybe he's Irish."

I laugh. "Can't say anyone ever mistook me for an actor before."

"Well, it's not immediately obvious." She studies my face from left to right. "You have that rugged look, but you don't quite have his sexy eyes. Oh, and your nose is crooked like his, too. Were you a boxer?"

"Hardly. I was crewing up in Bristol Bay one time and I didn't move fast enough when a boom came swinging and . . ."

"Hey, did you guys see those porpoises?" Ali bounds over, her poodle hair spilling out from under her cap. She saves me from telling the really boring tale of how young Ray Bancroft broke his nose. Her arm brushes my back as she peers over the railing. "Man, those are something." She turns to her friend. "Did you get any good shots?"

"A couple. Wanna see?"

As Nicole flips through the digital images, Ali pokes her head up from the view screen and winks at me, pointing her thumb toward her friend. Either she's encouraging me to flirt with Nicole, or praising her photography skills. These two are the kind of tourists I like spending time with, delighted by what I see every day, but we're getting close to our first stop and I need to get the gear ready.

We steer up into Frederick Sound and Felix brings the boat into one of the small coves. Once we're anchored, I reach into the bait cooler and pull out a chunk of cut-up octopus. It looks like a slab of undigested purple meat. We don't want any of the guests jabbing a hook through their thumbs. I stop a second and take a breath so my stomach can settle. The octopus starts going gray as soon as I impale it on Walt's rod, a fourteen-foot Heavy Assassin. I hold the pole out to Walt, who's placed himself right in front of me.

"Nice rod, buddy," I say, an old joke among fishermen.

Walt nods. "Buy the best to get the best."

"I'm a little concerned about this line, though," I say. "It's a bit sticky. You didn't wrap this around a block of wood and store it in a closet over the winter, did you?"

"I know how to take care of a fishing line." He yanks the rod from my hand.

"Didn't mean to imply you didn't." I point my finger just above the base of the reel. "But you've got a little kink starting there. The whole thing could snarl on you." I motion to the poles we have lined up. "You're welcome to use one of ours if you want."

"No thanks." Walt holds his rod and reel up as if it were a trophy. "This is Grade-A, vacuum-dressed, waterproof line." He turns, takes four long strides to the aft, and casts his line. So much for listening to my expert advice. Well, you can lead a horse to water, but it's up to him whether he wants to drown when you get there.

I rotate my shoulder in a vain attempt to un-kink the headache that's come back. What I really feel like doing is lying down on the cushioned bench in the pilothouse. Or even better, sack out in one of the overnight bunks for a late morning nap. But they're down in the engine room, and business is business. I bait Ali's rod while Felix finishes the poles for Cindy and Nicole. I figure I've got a few minutes of peace, so I light up a cigarette and just watch, feeling the warm sun now that it's fully broken out of the clouds.

The salmon are more abundant than I thought they would be. Every thirty seconds one jumps out of the water, slaps down, and jumps again before submerging. It doesn't take long for everyone to catch four. Felix and I start cleaning and packing them in the coolers as they come in.

I turn around to address the passengers. "Congratulations, everyone. You've all reached your legal limit of salmon."

"Four! Is that all?" Cindy moves close to her husband, putting her small hands on his chest. "I want more, Walt. I want to throw a big party when we get back."

"Cindy, I'm sure you throw the best shindigs in Chicago.

But you'll need to do it with just the salmon you've caught." I'm half-kneeling on the deck, arranging the fish I've already cleaned in a wetlock box. "You know, my wife used to make this great salmon mousse for church potlucks."

"Just a minute!" Walt demands. "I don't see why you're holding us to four measly salmon. There's a ton of them flipping around out here."

"Like I said, Walt. You've reached your annual limit."

Walt shakes his head. "Don't give me that. I watched a guy bringing in a dozen kings just yesterday."

I finish laying in the fish and close the box lid. "He was probably a resident and Alaskan residents don't have an annual limit. Tourists do. Four. That's the regulations."

Walt lumbers over and stands above me. "I'm paying good money to catch fish and there's fish as far as the eye can see." He turns to Cindy. "Put your line back in, honey."

I stand up quickly. "No!" I say this as deeply as my voice will go, even though Walt's got a good two inches and thirty pounds on me. Ali and Nicole, who have already stowed their gear and are munching on chips and fruit, look up. "You all listen up. I'm here to make sure that you have an enjoyable day. But my number one job is to ensure your safety and my number two job is to make sure you follow the regulations set out by the Alaska Department of Fish and Game. Now I don't make the rules, but I will not violate them. If that's not good enough for you, then we'll head on back in right now." To make my point, I go around Walt and head toward the pilothouse door, ready to start up the engines if necessary. "Well? What will it be?"

The big man works his fists in and out. He looks at his wife, then back at me. "Hell, what I really want is to sink my hook into some halibut."

"Then we'll move over to Thomas Bay."

Felix makes sure everything is secure while I fire up the engines, and we make it over to the bay in about forty minutes. When it's just me and Sitka fishing for halibut, I like to drift with the tide—better chance of being where the fish are going to be. But drifting can make tourists feel too unsteady on their feet, so I go ahead and drop anchor. The water here is about 200 feet deep. In the summer halibut like to hang out in the shallows; in the winter they go down farther to about 600 feet, so we're in between. We had good luck here last week, but you never know for sure if a particular place has been fished out or not.

Ali watches as Felix prepares the gear for the halibut. "Brother-in-law," he says, addressing the halibut line and hook he's holding. "We honor you. Do well for these turtles today."

He holds up Ali's hook near her face. "Spit on it," he tells her.

Ali's eyes widen. "What?"

"Spit on your hook," he insists, as if she were a five-year-old.

Ali looks at me. I nod. "Why not?" she shrugs. She tucks in her chin, makes a coughing sound in her throat, and lets loose with a pretty good-sized slab of spittle that lands directly on the hook.

"Nice shot." Felix slips on a piece of bait. "Go right to the fireplace," he says to the octopus. "Hit the rich man's daughter."

"Hit the rich man's daughter," Ali repeats as she takes the pole back. "Works for me."

Nicole studies the salty green-gray water. "I don't see any halibut, Ray."

"If they're down there, they're skimming around the bottom over the mud and sand."

We both stare down, watching the shadowy movements of small fish. The air has warmed. Being on the boat on a day like this, snuggled in a cove, somehow makes it easier for me to have what most folks would call a normal conversation. "So, you're settling up here? Seattle not rainy enough for you?"

She leans her elbows onto the deck rail. "I was ready for a change." She peers into the water as if she might find what she needs below the surface.

"A lot of folks come up here for that, though not many wind up staying after their first taste of the long, wet winter."

Nicole grips the rail and extends her arms, then faces me. "When I was a kid I used to read adventure books on Alaska, and I thought when I was all grown up and out of high school, I would just start walking north. I'd picture myself moving right across a big map. I'd travel up through Canada and into Alaska, wearing a fur-lined parka and boots. I'd crunch across the icy snow, leaving pieces of broken crystal behind me. The land all around me would be barren and white, no one around for miles and miles, maybe a puffin or polar bear off in the distance. But I wouldn't be cold or go hungry. And in no time, I'd reach the North Pole."

"And what would happen once you stood on top of the North Pole?"

Nicole stares across the inlet to the hills on Mitkof Island. "Then I'd be able to see everything."

Before I can comment, we hear a walloping shout.

"Yahoo! Yah baby!"

Walt's hooked a halibut. It's half out of the water, turning and flashing its white belly and gray dorsal fins. It's a big one all right, the biggest we've seen this season.

"This sucker will get a state trophy certificate!" Walt leans over to Felix and yells, "Should I yank her in or play her out?"

Felix looks nervous and his right hand starts to shake. "He's probably 200 pounds or more."

"So I play her out?"

"You should be okay since you're using a level wind reel and a 12/0 hook," Felix says. "Don't take her vertical is all."

"What are you talking about?" Walt roars. "I'm asking you if I should reel her in or let her go for awhile."

What the hell's the matter with me? I should be right there with Walt, helping him decide, and let Felix handle the wife. Where is Cindy? Where's Ali, for that matter? Jesus. A captain should always know what's going on with his passengers. The sound of the line whizzing out is loud, but nowhere near as loud as the halibut smacking its body as it tries to wrangle away.

"Okay, Walt." I take over and motion for Felix to check on

the others. "You got him. He's not going anywhere. Don't engage the ratchet too soon. Play him out a bit, let him tire some. We've got time."

Walt relaxes the line and the fish slips below the water line, then leaps up again.

"You're doing fine there, buddy. You're gonna take home one hell of a trophy."

Walt beams, then grimaces as he plays out the line, keeping his eye on the reel one second and the fish the next. Suddenly there's a jerk. The line starts kinking. The pole buckles and bends. Walt's hand starts shaking up and down. He flips the ratchet, trying to lock it into place. The rod shudders and Walt tries to hang onto it, but his hand slips to the faceplate just as the line starts unraveling.

"Let her go, Walt!"

He ignores me. In seconds the line begins wrapping itself over the shaft, and the overwind pulls Walt's hand into the reel.

"Drop the reel!" I reach over to knock it out of his hands.

Walt only grasps it harder. The line slices down on his middle and ring fingers. At the same time I pull my fishing knife out of my boot and cut the line free. Walt falls back. The top halves of his two fingers flop to the deck like dead minnows.

"Mother-fucking son of a bitch!" Walt pushes his injured hand under his armpit.

"Felix! The emergency kit!" I kneel down next to Walt. "You're going to be okay, buddy," I say, without knowing what the hell I'm talking about.

Cindy and Ali scramble back from starboard to find out what's going on. Cindy screams when she sees Walt. "Oh my God! Baby, what happened?"

Felix rushes over with the med kit. "What the hell?"

"Goddamn line cut," I say. "He's lost the top part of two fingers on his right hand." Christ. This is the last thing we need.

"Walt, baby!" Cindy shrieks. "You all right?"

The fingers have rolled over against the port bulkhead. "Get those in some clean ice," I tell Felix.

"You better not have goddamned lost my rod and reel!" I can't tell if Walt's screaming at me or his wife.

"You're going to be okay, honey." Cindy gasps between her words, letting sobs out. "We'll do whatever it takes to get you better, baby!"

I pull Walt's injured hand away from his armpit. "Walt, you've gotta lie still and let me take a look at your hand. C'mon, buddy. Let me take a look so we can take care of you."

Ali steps over and coaxes Cindy back to the starboard side. "Let Captain Ray take care of him. Give them some room."

Walt's still bawling his bloody oaths and I'm thinking maybe that's a good thing, but as the back of my hand brushes against his forehead, it feels clammy. Felix shows me the small cooler with the severed fingers on ice. The sight of them makes my stomach heave all over again.

"What should I do with these?" he asks.

"Cover them and put them someplace cool where they won't fall out." It's Nicole who answers. She hands me two life jackets. "Put these under his feet. He may be going into shock."

His hand is swelling up something fierce. I do as she instructs, then reach into the medicine kit and grab the bottle of Friar's balsam. I take off the cap so I can pour it over the wounds.

"Wait!" Nicole commands. "Don't put that on."

"I need to cauterize the wound," I tell her.

Nicole shakes her head. "That stuff will harm the nerve endings." She reaches into the med kit and hands me a brown bottle of Betadine. "Use this. It'll help stop infection. His best chances for reattachment and normal use are to just bandage the hand and keep the severed fingers in ice."

"You a doctor?" I ask.

"Former trauma nurse." She turns back to the kit and selects multiple packets of sterile gauze pads. She rips them open and gently applies them around the stubs of Walt's fingers. She presses just hard enough to stanch the flow of blood, then tapes the bandages into place. "Let's get him as stable as possible."

"Sure we shouldn't at least put another antiseptic on that?" I ask.

"Don't want to cause infection." Nicole takes off her jacket and settles it under Walt's head. "Get us back to town, but don't make it too bumpy. We want to keep his hand as immobile as possible until we can get him to a surgeon." Her voice is calm, her movements steady and controlled.

I take a quick look out of the cove. "Swells are building up. No good taking him back by boat. I'll call for a Medevac helicopter."

I rush into the pilothouse and radio for the Coast Guard. During the fifteen minutes that it takes for the orange bird to arrive, Nicole settles next to Walt, talking to him quietly, asking him mundane questions about where he grew up, how he met Cindy, stuff like that. Walt grunts out a few answers. But he stays focused on Nicole's face. Cindy runs back and forth between Walt and the railing, running her hands through her hair. Ali tries to comfort her, but Cindy keeps pushing her off.

Finally the helicopter is hovering over us, its blades churning up the water and drowning out every other noise. They lower two of their crew to the deck with a stretcher. They secure Walt to it and hoist him up and into the bird. Cindy insists that she go with them, so they holster her and lift her up as well. The Medevac turns and speeds off.

Felix raises the anchor, I rev up the engines, and we turn back toward St. Innocent Harbor, smacking over the swells. Nicole joins me in the pilothouse.

"Thanks for what you did back there," I say. "You really were cool, calm, and collected. I admire that."

"I did what I could." She leans against the bulkhead. "But there's a good chance they won't be able to reattach those fingers. Even if they do, they may not be really functional."

I don't have an answer except to worry my fingers against my brow. Nicole starts to reach her arm out to me, but stops short, her hand brushing along the top of the console next to the steering wheel.

"It wasn't your fault. I heard you warn Walt about his fishing line."

"That's not how Walt's insurance company is going to see it." We hit a cross wave and the boat jumps. I grab the wheel more tightly. "And they'd be right. I should have insisted he use a different rod and reel."

I could lose what's left of my savings, my boat, and my license over this.

"As the saying goes," Nicole tells me, "you can't fix stupid." She pats me on the arm before leaving the pilothouse. It's a small gesture that sustains me on the trip back.

I steer us on a direct course to Yatki Island. It's a good thing we called in the copter. The strait is choppy and going across would've only made things worse for Walt. The sun is still out, glinting on the waves. A couple of Dall's porpoises start to follow us again, but no one's taking photos.

Chapter 4

I'M DRINKING A BOTTLE of Alaskan Amber at the kitchen table and trying to complete a sudoku puzzle in the local paper. It's a level four. I've never even made it completely through a level two.

You'd be surprised at the number of fishermen who've gotten hooked on these since the *Island Sentinel* started including them on the comics page. People work on them in the diner and I know at least a dozen skippers who keep a book of these puzzles on their boats. Even Muskeg pulls one out now and then when things are slow at the Blind Dog. You're supposed to figure out where the numbers go, so that the same one doesn't appear twice in a column, a row, or a set of squares. The logic escapes me. Muskeg says to look for patterns, but that's something I've often found hard to do.

It's been two days since the Medevac took Walt Francke to St. Olga's here on the island. I've called the hospital three times, but since I'm not a family member they won't give me his status. They offered to connect me to his room, but my insurance agent Hank O'Neill recommended not doing that. I called Hank the night of the accident. He's over in Juneau. When I told him what happened, he went into damage control mode.

"Don't call him," Hank instructed. "You don't want to be doing anything that makes you look responsible."

"Hey, I didn't force the guy to use his own rod and reel. I even told him that I was concerned about his line and offered him one of ours."

"But you didn't actually stop him from using it." Hank paused and I could hear him breathing through his mouth into the phone. "I've told you before, those waivers aren't worth the paper they're printed on if someone gets himself a good lawyer. Speaking of which, you need an attorney."

"Like I can afford one."

"Your policy should handle most of the legal fees. I'm going to give you Ben Sato's cell phone number. He handles civil law cases, divorces, custody cases, all sorts of things. Used to work for one of the big insurance companies in California before he moved to Juneau. We have him on retainer to handle claims cases, and his firm usually rents an office on your island when one of the attorneys has business there. Ben's very good."

"You think he can get this to go away?"

"We'll do everything we can to settle with Mr. Francke's insurance company. But I have to be honest with you, Ray. If this guy can prove gross negligence, he might be awarded a settlement that goes beyond your coverage."

I rub my hand against my chin and take a breath. "How much beyond?"

"Impossible to say. Let's take it one step at a time."

"Easy to say when you're not the one on the hook."

"You worry too much. Just call Ben and follow his advice. And Ray?"

"What?"

"Next time take my advice and shell out a few more bucks for a higher premium so you're not stuck with a $10,000 deductible."

"Gee, thanks, Hank. Any other advice after the ship's already hit the iceberg?"

"Bye, Ray."

Very comforting talking with your insurance agent.

It's just after seven. Sitka will be home soon. She went over to Sarah's after school so they could work on their marine biology project, and she wound up staying. I didn't feel like cooking for myself, so dinner was a bowl of Rice Krispies. With a beer for dessert. At least it makes the cleanup easy.

I yank on the sliding glass kitchen door, but the aluminum runners have gotten a little bent and rusted over the years, and I have to pull inward to get it to open. Yet another item on my to-fix list. The September evening is blushed with a yellowish haze. Just to the west the sun is being pinched between a thick layer of clouds and a line of white spruce trees on top of Greenback Mountain. In a few minutes the light will spread gray.

The warmth of the afternoon has been sucked away, and the wet chill in the air means we'll get a hefty fog bank rolling in tonight. The wind gods had better scour it out by morning. We really need to go out and snag a ton of shrimp. Between the boat engine overhaul last spring and the low runs this season, my cash reserves are pretty thin. If I have to fork over a ton of money to this attorney, where does Hank expect my mortgage payment to come from? He sure as hell won't fork it over. And if this lawyer can't settle this and I wind up shelling out $10,000 or more, it's going to wipe out my savings and a good portion of Sitka's college fund. Fucking Walt Francke. Fucking insurance companies. Fucking Chinese mitten crabs. Fucking me.

What am I going to tell Sitka? Her mother's going to show up at our doorstep this week, after five years of being gone, and I haven't figured out the right words, but I'm running out of time. What could the right words be, anyway?

Sitka accepted pretty early on that she didn't have a father, or rather that I was filling in. Her grandmother died before she was born. And her mother was in the county jail for drug use before Sitka tasted her first birthday cake. Jenny swore she stopped using as soon as she found out she was pregnant. But that still left what? Six or eight weeks of meth coming into her body before she found out? I believed her when she said she was through with drugs because of the baby. After she was born, there were a few weeks when I was pretty much out on the boat constantly, which left Jenny little help at home. Sitka would cry day and night back then because of the leftover effects of the drugs. It got to be too much for Jenny or that's what she said at least. When Sitka was about five months old, Jenny got busted for meth use. As a first offender, she served a few months, but then got caught trying to sell $5,000 worth of meth while she was supposed to be in rehab. This time she was sent to the state prison up in Anchorage for four years.

Sitka has lots of photos and stories of her grandmother. I've made sure of that, since they never met. The only photo Sitka has of her mother is a school picture from Jenny's freshman year, before she started using drugs. At least I think it was before. Donna and I were clueless, it seems. The point is that there was no one to fill in the role of mother for Sitka except for me. Though from the beginning Muskeg usually watched Sitka when Felix and I were out on the boat. Even now Sitka will sometimes go down to the Blind Dog and hang out in the kitchen if I'm out crabbing overnight and she can't stay at Sarah's.

But I'm the one who read to her at night, changed her, sat up with her when she was sick—all that stuff. I told Sitka about her mom to the extent I thought she could handle. Once she was in preschool she became acutely aware that other little kids had mommies. I told her that her mother was sick and had to be away. It wasn't exactly the truth but it wasn't a lie either. Maybe I should have been straight with her back then, but she was so little. Once I started down that path, I couldn't exactly turn back. I expanded the story as Sitka got older and could understand more. Her mother had a kind of illness that made her incapable of taking care of herself. She was in a special hospital. No, Sitka could not go visit. When she was better, her mommy would come home.

Now that whole series of lies is loping back like a lost mongrel to our doorstep.

JENNY DID COME HOME the one time. When Sitka was six, her mother was released from state prison and spent some time at a rehab center, free of drugs and ready to start a new life. It was a Tuesday in mid-June, right after school let out for the summer. The weather was still cool, but with ascending clouds breaking up to reveal splotches of blue. Jenny flew into Juneau and Felix picked her up there in the boat and brought her to the island. One minute, Sitka'd be running from one side of the house to the other, or dancing in the middle of the room, twirling and singing to herself, "Mommy's coming! Mommy's coming!" The next minute she'd be clutching at my leg. I didn't know how to set any expectations. Personally, I'd just as soon Jenny had lived her own life in the Lower 48s. To me she was nothing but grief. But I knew she was still important to Sitka, so I wanted the re-union to take place at the house, where I could control things. As if I could rein in anything when Jenny was involved.

We planned a picnic homecoming. Early in the morning Sitka was in the backyard, picking wildflowers that sprouted haphazardly in the borders and on the little hillside that sloped up at the far end. She filled her willow basket with purple and pink: Alaska violets, lupine, Alpine forget-me-nots, and a large Kamchatka lily. She brought them in and laid them on the kitchen counter. She reached under the sink for a pitcher, filled it up with water, then plopped in six orange slices, "so it will look extra good." She wanted to do this by herself. She set the lily in the center of the pitcher, its eggplant-colored petals spread open to reveal bright yellow stamens. She positioned the other flowers around it, moving them back and forth until she was finally satisfied. The scent of the freshly cut wildflowers filled the room.

"There," she finally announced, more to herself than to me.

We drove to Hilda's Pharmacy, which has a party supplies section, and picked out a Happy Birthday card, since that and sympathy cards are the only kind Hilda stocks. We also picked up purple and pink streamers, a fold-out paper pineapple— Sitka's idea—and helium-filled balloons. At the Moose Market we bought hot dogs, buns, chips, iceberg lettuce, Kraft thousand island dressing, and vanilla ice cream. Then we decorated the house. With only a little help from me, Sitka made a banner from an old piece of sailcloth that proclaimed, "Welcome home, Mommy!" We made a vanilla cake from scratch, by the end of which my shirt and the top of my jeans were covered in flour. While that was baking, we strung the banner across the porch, set the pineapple on the television, and tied the balloons and streamers on the railings. I made up a pitcher of lemonade, Sitka insisting that it be strawberry lemonade for reasons that were obvious to her, if not to me.

Felix and Jenny were two hours late, and I tried to keep Sitka amused by playing Candy Land and watching a *SpongeBob, SquarePants* video. But every two minutes, she'd run over to the window, looking for the mommy she knew from Jenny's high school photo.

Finally Sitka shrieked and ran out to the porch. I followed, holding the door open for a minute before letting it squeak shut behind me. Jenny was walking up the hill to the house, Felix behind her, a blue and gray duffel bag in his hand. Although the temperature was in the low seventies, Jenny wore a black ski cap and an unzipped black parka that had its left pocket ripped down the side. Her backpack seemed unbalanced and she stopped a couple of times to readjust it. She swayed a little as she walked, moving her eyes to either side of her. It was only when she got to the bottom porch step that she turned her head upwards. The two of us eyed each other without saying any-thing. Sitka leaned into me, watching this strange woman, until Jenny smiled and held her arms open. With that, Sitka bounded down the steps and clung to her mother's leg like a bee on a hyssop flower. Jenny took off her backpack and knelt down so she was face to face with Sitka.

"Hey, Marmot. Let me take a look at you. You've been get-ting big while Mommy was away."

Sitka beamed. "I can climb up to the top of the cedar trees in back all by myself and I can gut a salmon real quick, can't I, Felix?"

Felix nodded a confirmation as he huffed up the steps and set the duffel bag on the porch. Jenny took Sitka's hand and we all went inside. Felix went into the backyard to light the grill. He knew we needed some time alone. Jenny dropped her backpack, removed her cap, and slipped off her parka, letting it fall at her feet. Sitka picked them up and toted them to her bedroom, which used to be Jenny's.

"You're sleeping in my room!"

Jenny turned her head, taking in as much of the house as she could. "Place hasn't changed much." She sauntered into the kitchen and opened the refrigerator door, just staring at what was inside. The right side of her nose was flattened, and she wheezed a bit when she talked. My daughter must have been in a fight. Probably lots of fights. I fought off the image of a gang of other women beating up on her. I didn't want to feel sorry for her. I only wanted to protect Sitka. I wanted to defend what Sitka and I had together.

"You hungry?" I asked. "You look like you lost weight."

She didn't have the body that a twenty-three-year-old woman ought to have. She was pouchy in the stomach and hips, thin in the legs. Her reedy arms looked taut, yet her skin hung in folds off the bones, like someone who had lost a lot of weight rapidly and then started working out. Dusky ridges underlined her eyes. Streaks of gray in her hair. Either it was cut in the latest style or someone whacked it with hedge clippers.

Jenny shut the refrigerator door, stepped over to me, and put her arms around my waist. She smelled like a stray cat. Embracing her was like clutching a piece of chiseled flint, fragile enough to break, but able to slice you open just the same. I barely patted her.

My prodigal daughter kept her arms around me for an uncomfortably long time. "It's so good to be home," she whispered. "I love you, Dad."

"Don't," I said, just loud enough for her to hear. "Save the 'I love yous' for your daughter. All Sitka knows is that her mom has finally returned, so don't mess this up."

Jenny stepped back from me. Her face had a yellow tinge, as if she were standing under a highway mercury lamp.

"You think that's what I want to do?" She swiped at some tears on her cheeks. Her shoulders trembled, and she pulled on her right wrist with her left hand. "I'm trying, Dad. Really trying this time."

I didn't want to debate it. I could have reminded Jenny about the hundreds of other times she promised me and Donna that she was trying, but Sitka bounded downstairs.

"We baked you a cake, Mommy!" She wedged herself between me and Jenny. "Didn't you see it on the table by the flowers? I picked them for you. Grandpa says vanilla is your favorite."

Vanilla cake was what Jenny always asked for when she was a little kid. But it's also true that she lived on vanilla ice cream while she was doing her little meth binges, because that was all her stomach and intestines could tolerate.

"We should find some candles," Jenny said.

"Yeah, like they have on the birthday card we got you!" Sitka agreed, and went off into the kitchen to rummage through the drawers.

So the day went. We grilled the hot dogs and had the cake and ice cream. Sitka wouldn't let Jenny out of her sight. She introduced her to every Barbie and stuffed animal she had, even though most of them had been Jenny's. I doubt I said another twenty words the rest of that day. Jenny slept in her old room with Sitka. After they were asleep and Felix went home, I smoked three or four cigarettes in the backyard, watching the Pleiades slide across the sky.

The next morning I went out on the porch with my coffee and the *Island Sentinel*. It was early, but Sitka was already up. She had gotten bits of rope from the shed and was tying them to sticks and then making loops and circles, setting various arrangements of these in front of the door and across the porch. I watched her as she took the longest piece of rope she had and fastened one end to a column on one side of the porch steps and then to the column at the other end. She pulled it taut and anyone would have to step over it or else take a nasty spill.

"Whatcha doing there, sweetie?"

"Making traps." She concentrated on looping another knot.

"Ah," I said. "Going to catch a bear, are you?"

She turned at me and frowned. "They're for Mommy. So she doesn't ever go away again."

It turned out that Sitka's traps were not very effective. On her fifth day home Jenny beelined down to the docks with twenty grams of meth in her backpack. She tried to sell it to a guy who turned out be an undercover cop. When he searched her bag, he found her meth pipe, two fake IDs, and two forged checks. She refused to say where she got the drugs. Who can figure out that kind of loyalty? Given the amount of meth, her past history, and her refusal to cooperate, she was cuffed and carted off. I didn't even attempt to post bail. Back she went to Juneau for trial, and then to prison.

Sitka cried for three weeks straight. She picked at her food and refused to play with friends. I tried holding and rocking her, but she wouldn't have much of that. She spent hours looking at Jenny's photo, as if she could conjure her back home. I didn't know how to mend things, only to offer her moments of distraction. Who are the gods of fractured families and what do you have to sacrifice in order to appease them?

I didn't tell Sitka that her mom had been arrested, only that she had to go away again. Gradually, as school started, Sitka settled down and asked me less about Jenny. The years went by and she hardly mentioned Jenny at all.

She used to tell her friends that her mother was a soldier, stationed overseas. I don't know why she came up with that one, the desire to save face, I guess. The thought of Sitka making these stories up burned in my stomach, but how was reality going to help her? Over time, the two of us kept the subject of her mom hidden away, like old and rotting sailcloth tucked into a corner of the tool shed.

THE NEIGHBORHOOD DOGS START yapping and I scan the hills behind the house. There have been sightings of a mom black bear and her cub scavenging in the garbage cans. People are fed up because those Forest Service boneheads couldn't catch a field mouse trapped in a glass jar. The Town Council used to pay Doug Matthews to do it. He has this way of snaring the bears so they don't get hurt, then he hauls them in his Ford Ranger back out along the logging roads and releases them. It's simple and effective, but the Forest Service didn't like someone else getting in on their action. Doug doesn't fit into their strategic forest plan. So they got an injunction to stop him from doing what they can't. Those of us who live up here don't like the government stepping in when we can solve a problem using common sense. It was the same thing when the social workers came to visit Donna and me after Jenny's first arrest. They had all kinds of programs to fix our family dynamics, when all anyone really needed to do was to get Jenny off the damn drugs.

The sky's gone dark. It's gotten chilly, but I don't get a jacket. I like the cold. I'm longing for snow, something to change the landscape. I'd like to conjure whatever force it is that rearranges rocks and ravines. The wind picks up. Maybe the fog will lift after all. The cedars creak and moan, their branches of blue-green needles flattening against the mossy shingles of the detached garage. I should prune those trees back one of these days.

"I'm home, Ray!" Sitka's voice sings out from the kitchen.

I turn to say hi, but she's already opened the refrigerator door to scrounge for an evening snack. Her sandy hair spills down to her mid-back, rogue strands splaying out, as if they were charged with static electricity. She holds her head slightly to the left as she scans the shelves. I'd swear it was Jenny when she was eleven.

"Why isn't there ever anything to eat in this house?"

"There's plenty to eat and if you don't like it, how about doing some grocery shopping? And how about we use some of your allowance money while we're at it?"

"Wow." Sitka slams the refrigerator door. "Jump on my

back just because I live here, why don't you?"

I take a breath, close my eyes, and rub my right shoulder. It feels like there's a small sack of pebbles just under the skin. "Sorry, I'm not in a very good mood."

Sitka sags against the refrigerator door. "Like that's news. You've been cranky all week."

"You're right, you're right." I have been short with her. "How about I make you a quick apple skillet tart?"

"Okay." Sitka sounds unsure, like I'm a dog that's been barking and all of a sudden quiets down, but you're not sure what's going to get it going again.

While I turn on the oven and get out some mixing bowls, Sitka slumps down at the kitchen table, hunching her shoulders as she scans her cell phone for new text messages. "Sarah just got TiVo at her house. She can watch anything she wants anytime she wants."

"Knowing Sarah's mom, I doubt that." I peel and slice three apples, put a slab of butter in a cast iron skillet, layer in the apples, and start to sauté them.

"Sarah also got a new iTouch for her birthday last month. Now everybody has one." Every single human being on this planet, and possibly Mars, except her.

I finish heating the apples and mix up some flour, cinnamon, sugar, and butter for the topping. I crumble this over the apples and put the cast iron skillet into the oven. While it bakes, I bring Sitka a glass of milk and sit down next to her.

I point to her cell phone. "Can you put that down, please? We have to talk about something."

"Uh-huh." Her thumbs still punch the buttons.

I grab the phone from her, powering it off. "Seriously. We have to talk."

"What did I supposedly do now?"

"Don't worry. It's nothing like that."

She studies my face and waits.

"Well," I start. "I got this letter Friday."

Sitka folds her arms on the table in front of her, then lays her head down, looking at me sideways, not saying anything.

"Your mom's coming this week."

"So? What am I supposed to do about it?"

Her reaction catches me off guard. And even though I know it's not right, it pleases me. "You don't have to do anything about it. But she is your mother and she's coming here to see you."

Sitka pokes her finger along the top of the kitchen table. "Well, she's *your* daughter. Why isn't she coming to see you?"

"That's true. But you're her daughter and you come first in her heart." I sound like a Hallmark card. The kind that Hilda's Pharmacy refuses to stock.

"She's not coming here for my benefit. She probably wants something from you." Sitka turns her head to look directly at me. "What if I don't want to see her?"

I should tell her that everything will be all right, that it's a good thing her mother is coming, that we can finally be a family again. I say nothing, only drum my fingers on top of the unfinished sudoku puzzle.

"So where is she coming from?"

"She's been in Montana for the past six months, apparently. Kalispell."

"It's drugs, isn't it?" Sitka grabs my sudoku puzzle and pulls it to her side of the table so she doesn't have to meet my gaze. "My mom's been away all these years because she's a drug user and she's been in jail or in a halfway house or something."

I have no idea how Sitka came to this conclusion. I shouldn't be surprised. Why else would her mother not be around? Probably she and Sarah have mulled it over. Maybe she has friends who are already toking up. Or maybe, in spite of the best efforts by grown-ups to obscure the picture, a kid is just eventually able to put together the disjointed puzzle pieces of her life.

"Prison, not jail, but I'm sorry to say that's right, kiddo."

She reaches for my pencil and adds a number into one of the puzzle boxes. "Is it possible for someone to stop using that stuff forever and be with their family?"

"Of course it is, kiddo. Of course it is." I don't have all that much conviction myself.

"Ray?" Her voice has such a plea in it that I expect her to come over for a rare crawl onto Grandpa's lap and cry session.

"Yeah?"

"Can I have an overnight for my birthday party?"

Sitka's birthday is December 6, which makes her a Sagittarian. According to the little astrology booklet at the Moose Market, she's honest and open, caring, adventurous, but can be misled when it comes to matters of the heart. There's an astrologer in Juneau who will do your entire chart, with all the ascending and descending stuff, but I'm a Gemini and we Geminis tend to be skeptical about astrology.

"Sure. You go ahead and make up a list of who you want to have over." I'm happy to drop the topic of her mother.

"Ray?" Her tone is all innocence.

"Yeah?"

"Can I get the new iTouch for my birthday?"

She's playing me, and it's working. They have a bunch of those iApple things over in Juneau, but they cost a few hundred bucks. I don't know how I can scrape that together right now.

"Sure," I tell her.

The timer buzzes and I slip on an oven mitt, open up the door, and take out the tart. The aroma of hot apples, cinnamon, and vanilla calms me.

"You want some ice cream with this?" I ask.

"Uh-huh." She scrunches her mouth the way she does when I dish up something she really likes.

Sitka takes her plate quietly when I hand it to her. We eat without saying anything. When we're done, I scrape the crumbs into the garbage pail, wash and dry the dishes, and put them away. Everything nice and neat. Jenny's visit doesn't have to be a big deal, our lives don't have to be turned upside down and shaken up just because she's coming back. As if that's something I can conjure up, like an early snowfall.

Chapter 5

It's 4 A.M. WHEN the alarm goes off, but I'm already awake. Have been since two or so. In the dark bedroom the morning air is sharp and cold. The house is close enough to the docks that I can hear the horn of an offshore freighter as it trolls past the harbor on its way to Anchorage, no doubt. The big transports bypass Yatki Island, as do the giant cruise ships. We're too small, almost off the map. You can see those sea monsters often at night, slicing their way through the water, white phantoms all lit up against the black water and sky, partying their way to the next vacation port. Can't imagine why people pay good money to float around on a giant hotel anyway. It's not like they're going to get up close and personal with the whales and polar bears from a hundred feet above sea level. And who needs them dumping their garbage or waste fuel in our harbor? Fine with me if they keep way out at sea. Keep your damn flotsam out of here.

I turn on the shower and stick my head in before the water gets warm. The sting of the cold spray helps to focus my thoughts. All night they've been whizzing around like a swarm of no-see-ums, biting at my face and neck. Jenny's visit and Sitka. Walt Francke's fingers flopping on the deck. I try to focus on Nicole coming in to help, the scent of her, how she knew what to do, but Walt's severed fingers push her away. I duck my head under again. It feels good, the frigid water and the cold air. After drying off, I rub talcum powder over my body to help my skin from chafing later. I'm hungry and in definite need of caffeine. Can't be dragging my ass just as crabbing season is really getting going.

As soon as I get dressed, I wolf down a fried egg sandwich, along with two cups of black coffee. The marine forecast is gray and drizzling, and Felix and I will venture out and see what we can haul in. I jot down one of my daily inspirational notes and slip it into Sitka's lunch sack, alongside the tuna fish and mayo sandwich and carrot sticks. "Discover something new" with a smiley face. I know she's too old for this kind of thing, and she probably throws my notes away before leaving for school, but I still like doing it.

It's a five-minute drive to the docks, close enough to walk, but I've got gear to get onboard. There are a half-dozen pick-up trucks already in the parking lot. The morning wind gusts against blue tarps stretched over the beds. John Erickson and his sons are unloading equipment and I give them a quick wave. They nod, but don't stop what they're doing. I hear the metal slam of a door. Felix walks over from his truck to mine.

"Morning," I say.

"About time this season started." Felix lowers the tailgate of my truck. "Even though they got us limited, I'm hoping it's a good one, not piss-poor like last year."

"We're gonna need it." I rub my hands on my cheeks and under my eyes. "Let's get going."

More trucks pull into the parking lot. It's another two hours until sunrise. Yellow light from the mercury lamps punches through the deep gray air. It takes four trips before Felix and I get everything unloaded and stowed onboard. By five thirty, we have the boat ready and a pot of coffee on the stove in the pilot-house. We cast off and motor out to the east end of the wharf. There's a bit of a bottleneck as five other boats are trying to depart at the same time, and it's another twenty minutes before we're free of the pier.

We head north by northeast and cut across Frederick Sound at slack tide, the boat pitching over the waves where the cross currents are their weakest. We make our way to the south end of Kupreanof Island and anchor in Kah Sheets Bay. There are no other boats within sight, so we picked either a really good spot or a loser. By the time we set the pots in, charcoal-colored clouds sweep in from the northwest. Another thirty minutes and black rain funnels down. We put on our heavy-duty rain jackets, but it still feels like someone's throwing buckets of ice water on us.

The rain morphs into white pellets that pummel our exposed hands and faces. The wind beats the cold into my bones. When I try to secure the hoist line, my feet slide on the hailstones and I go sprawling onto the deck. The pot swings out and comes back wide, nearly taking my head off. Felix isn't faring much better. As he's closing one of the latches, his right leg twists sideways. He stumbles and lets go of the latch, which slams down, just missing his hand.

"You okay?" I yell through the hail that's stinging my cheeks and nose.

Felix scrambles to his feet and takes a moment to catch his balance. "Hang on a second!" He climbs up to the pilothouse, opens the port, and disappears from view.

When he gets back on deck, I ask him how many times he rubbed the belly of the Billiken.

"Seven."

"You ready to get on with making a living now?"

"Don't give me that." Felix pushes his face right up to my chin. "You know as well as me, we could be running around like spider crabs being chased by a seagull out here, or I can take a minute of our precious time and try to make things right. You want to tackle this kind of weather without so much as a by-your-leave to the powers that be, you go right ahead."

He's right. No sense ignoring the gods on a day like today. "Jesus, don't be so sensitive. Help me get this pot cinched up."

"I should have brought me some incense this morning," Felix says as he returns to the pot. Standing on each side, we latch the door and secure the lines. "I told Muskeg that. I told her."

So the day goes.

By three o'clock, the hail turns to sleet. We've sunk our pots, emptied them, and re-sunk them five times over. What do we have to show for it? Twelve hundred pounds of crab. Half a load. With another dozen Chinese mitten crabs mixed in the bunch. We should try our luck at another spot, but the storm's bearing down pretty hard. There's not much choice but to head back to port, and see if things are any better tomorrow. Felix and I empty and secure the pots, neither of us saying more than a couple of words at a time.

Turning out of Kah Sheets, we head south, then southwest. I watch the early evening sky get stitched together with thick patches of midnight gray. Not a sliver of yellow or red to be seen. Even in the pilothouse I'm still shivering, like I'm never going to feel warm again. By the time we unload our catch and dock, I can barely move my lower back. In spite of my rubber boots, my feet swell. Every other part of me is frozen, but it feels like someone's holding a hot metal rod against the tips of my toes. Felix hunches his back and walks with a slight limp to his truck. He pulls himself into the cab with barely a wave good night.

It's completely dark now. The muscles in my arms and legs feel like they've been chiseled down. When I finally pull into my driveway, it feels like I've run a marathon. I peel off my wet clothes and change into dry ones. In spite of the talcum powder, sea water has made my skin chafed and raw. I'm too tired to run a shower. The skin on the bottom of my left foot has cracked so much that it split open near the big toe, like someone had slit it with a boning knife. I rub Norwegian Fisherman's cream into it. Stings like hell, but I know it's good for it. Sitka is over at Sarah's but should be home soon. I should get something together for dinner but I'm drained. I need to rest, just for a minute.

The slam of the front door wakes me up, or partly so. I'm sprawled in the frayed lounge chair in the living room, and my legs and feet are still half asleep. I try to move them and get a jolt of nerves shooting up into my knees. Dressed in a pair of sweatpants and a flannel shirt that Donna had asked me to throw out fifteen years ago, I still reek of crab and winch grease. Sitka throws her backpack onto the sofa cushions, gives me a once over, and scrunches her nose.

"God, it stinks worse in here than the boys' locker room. What if I had one of my friends with me?"

I yawn before answering her. "Then the two of you could fix dinner together while I finish my nap."

"You mean there isn't any dinner? I'm starving and I have a ton of algebra homework and I have to finish a stupid paper on the stupid French Revolution."

I've wiggled my feet enough that I can stand up. "I'll make a deal. You cook dinner and I'll clean up while you do your homework. There's some scallops in the fridge that we should eat today or tomorrow. Throw them over some noodles with some butter. Heat up a box of frozen spinach and we'll call it good."

"Aagh," she says, but steps into the kitchen anyway.

"And how do you know what the boys' locker room smells like anyway?"

No answer on that one. This wouldn't be the first time Sitka's made dinner. She's actually a pretty decent cook. I move back and forth on the balls of my feet, trying to get some more circulation going. Donna used to have one of those plug-in foot bath things, but God knows where it is. As I rotate my shoulder, trying to work out the kinks, I hear Sitka rummaging around, banging out pots and pans.

There's a sudden loud crash, and when I limp into the kitchen, my ceramic statue of Ganesh is on the floor. Or rather, a hundred charcoal-colored ceramic pieces of the Indian elephant god are scattered across the linoleum. Sitka stands over a good portion of the trunk and one eye.

"That's the only Ganesh I have!"

Sitka kicks at a couple of the broken pieces. "Well, why do we have to have all this junk everywhere?"

She's referring no doubt to the small Tibetan Buddha and the larger Japanese Buddha, both made out of monkey wood, the resin-made-to-look-like-amber statues of Shiva, Matsu, and Lei-Zi, and the plaster-made-to-look-like-marble figurines of Demeter, Poseidon, and Horus, and about two dozen others made from varied materials. St. Anthony, the only fully-painted figure, stands out in the crowd, which only makes sense since he is the saint of lost articles. Ganesh was the largest god in my collection and he's left quite a gap at the edge of the kitchen countertop.

"You can't even move in this house, it's so crowded with this junk! Why can't we live like normal people?"

Did I mention that Ganesh is the god of domestic harmony?

"We are normal people." I swipe the broom next to the kitchen door and shove it at Sitka. "Sweep up the mess you made, and I mean all of it, but save the pieces."

"Like I'm the only one making messes around here." But she takes the broom anyway. "I don't have any space in this house!" Like her bedroom suddenly disappeared into a black hole. "And now your stupid daughter's coming here and probably bringing all her junk and I won't have enough space to even breathe!"

As she sweeps, I get the dustpan and bend down, holding it in place for her. My legs and shoulders feel like cast iron.

"Why are you jumping down my throat because your mom is coming? I thought you were okay with this."

Sitka sweeps up the final bits of gray and white ceramic into the dustpan and stands up. "Like it matters what I think. She's coming. Nobody asked me."

"Yeah, well, nobody asked me about it either."

Sitka slides the broom back into its usual spot. "She's not going to start living here, is she?"

"She's coming just for a short visit. This is our house." I smile to reassure her, but Sitka's mouth looks like a salmon that just got hooked and barbed. "I'm not expecting you to do anything differently or behave differently. I'm sure your mom just wants to see how you're doing. We'll have to see how it goes. That's all anyone can do, right?"

Sitka thrusts out her right hip and rolls her eyes. "Everyone's trying to make my life miserable."

I don't have a good comeback and I really am too tired to take any more of this on tonight. "Go on upstairs. I'll fix dinner. Just do your homework."

Sitka turns and leaves, not happy, but not stomping mad either. I realize I've now volunteered to do the cooking and the dishes. But I'll take that over another run-in. I still have the full dustpan in my hand. I pour the broken Ganesh into a sack. I'll take him out on the boat and throw the broken pieces overboard into whatever reincarnation awaits him.

AFTER DINNER SITKA RETREATS straight back up to her room. Maybe she's right. The kitchen table is full of unopened bills and old newspapers I keep meaning to recycle. Sitka and I push those things aside when we're eating dinner. On top of a three-shelf bookcase stuffed with cookbooks I never use, there's a reel of fishing line, some wire snips, a bottle of wood glue, half a dozen nuts and bolts, and a few more bills. Jesus. This place was never like this when Donna was alive. I pick up the fishing line and consider taking it out to the truck, but I'm not done trying to untangle it. While I'm mulling this over, the phone rings.

"Hello."

"Is this Captain Bancroft?"

It's a woman's voice, brassy and somewhat familiar. People around here don't usually call me captain unless I'm actually on the boat. "Yeah. Who's this?"

"Don't pretend you don't know me, Captain." This time she spits out the title like undercooked crab meat. "You think you can walk away from what you did."

The burning sensation in my upper chest flares the way it does when I've eaten too many jalapeño peppers at the local Mexican restaurant. Walt Francke's wife.

"Listen, Cindy? Nobody's walking away from anything. I've already talked to my insurance guy. He'll talk with yours. Let's let them handle this."

"You think you can hide behind your insurance people? My husband's maimed for life! We are going to sue you for everything you've got. We'll file a complaint with the Alaska Tourism Board and the Fish and Game bureau, and anyone else we can think of."

She's making about as much sense as a bag of rusty grommets. Walt was hurt, but he seemed like a guy who can take his punches. I bet he's bragging to his buddies right now about the big seafaring adventure he had. Cindy's just being hysterical.

"Does your insurance agent know you're calling me?" I ask her. "Because mine said that we—"

"We won't be satisfied with a measly insurance settlement. Walt and I are going to make your life miserable."

"You're obviously upset, Cindy. Let me talk with Walt."

"He's still in the hospital, you bastard!" She's sniffling now. "I'm here all alone in Chicago and my poor Walt's still in your crummy little hospital!"

"I'm sorry all this had to happen," I say, even though Hank O'Neill told me not to apologize to the Franckes, or it might look like admitting the accident was my fault.

"You think you're sorry now." The next thing I hear is a click, and then the dial tone.

After a bit of searching, I find the notepad with the phone number of the attorney that Hank recommended mixed into the pile of unpaid bills on the kitchen table. I punch in the numbers, planning to leave a message, since it's late. Surprisingly Ben Sato not only answers, but he already knows much of what has happened.

"Hank filled me in. He was worried because you hadn't called me yet."

"I'm not exactly flush with cash. How much do you need for a retainer, Mr. Sato?"

"Call me Ben. We can work something out." His voice is

steady and calm. Very practiced. "Besides, I'm going to do everything I can to get the opposing side to pick up all of your costs. We just have to show how frivolous this is."

"Pick up my costs?" My shoulders loosen. "Is that possible? If you ask me—"

"Hank said there was a reliable witness onboard. A nurse."

"Nicole Harris."

"Do you know how I can get in touch with her?"

It's on the waiver form, which is filed, temporarily, under the passenger seat of my truck. "I'll call you with her number tomorrow. You think we can settle this out of court?"

"Depends on the degree of negligence they're trying to prove." I can hear a pen scratching on paper on the other side of the line. "Just keep your head down. And don't take out any more tourists for the rest of the season."

"You can't be serious." My shoulders tense right back up. "I'm counting on that until crabbing season gets going full-bore."

Ben's voice drops, gets quiet. "You take tourists out again and one of them gets a hangnail, Francke's lawyers will have a field day with it. No more tourists, got it?"

"Yeah. I got it."

"You're doing the right thing, Ray. Lawsuits can get messy. Let me handle this and you'll come out on top."

"There's nothing I should be doing?"

"Just hang tight. I'll get back to you in a few days."

When the hell did everyone in this country start believing they had to sue everyone else? If this goes to court, besides dealing with the cost, I could lose my charter license, maybe even my boat. How would I get Sitka through high school and into college without my boat? And losing the tourist gigs is a sucker punch I didn't see coming. They can be a pain in the ass, but they pay the bills when the shrimping and crabbing are slow. It'll free up some of my time, I guess. I've got boat maintenance to keep me busy, and Sitka, and Jenny's visit to worry about. I could start working on the house foundation. Lift it up and see if I can level it off. There are a couple of screw jacks around here somewhere. I might get away with just using those, shifting them around and cribbing under the other areas, but that's really slow and tedious. Probably need closer to ten or fifteen. Maybe Phil Poulson has some I can borrow. And I'd still have to get more wood for cribbing.

I go back into the kitchen and pick up the palm-sized statue of Matsu. The plastic figurine feels cool in my hand. Matsu is the Chinese goddess of the sea, known to help calm stormy waters and rescue sailors who are in danger. She's also the goddess of reconciliation.

"You'd better come with me tomorrow."

I take her out to the coat rack in the living room and slip her into my jacket pocket.

A HIGH-PRESSURE FRONT PUSHES up and over from British Columbia, calming the channel winds and smoothing out the currents. It takes almost no time for Felix and me to gear up in the dark. I set the statue of Matsu on the dashboard of the pilothouse. Felix glances at her and nods his approval. I'm not sure he knows who she is, but I don't feel like explaining. We cast away from the pier, this time ahead of the other boats. Felix doesn't like to say anything when the weather turns for the better, for fear he'll jinx it up. But as we pass Murder Cove and Surprise Harbor, he sits next to me, singing an old Canadian ditty, something he doesn't do unless he's in a really good mood.

> Farewell young lasses and ladies
> It's up through the channel I steer
> I'm off from the Deadman I reckon
> So give us a bottle of cheer, way-hey
> So give us a bottle of cheer!

Picking up on his mood, and grateful for Matsu's company this morning, I join in.

Don't blubber like lubbers, my girls
Our captain's well-seasoned and bold
And when the topmast disappears
Don't wail like lovers and misses, my dears
For I'll bring you whalebone and gold.

"That is so politically incorrect," I kid him. "We don't go after whales anymore, don't you know that?"

"Speak for yourself. Last I heard, the courts gave us natives back one ritual whale hunt a year." He pours himself a cup of coffee. "Not that I'd ever do it. You ever taste whale blubber? My grandmother used to try to get us kids to chew on it. It was like gnawing on a rubber ball. I'd drown it in A-1 Steak Sauce just to get a little flavor."

He looks out at the port as our headlights bounce off the waves. He closes his eyes and starts singing in Tlingit.

Akwshéi weidu k'éex'aakw eeyaa aha,
Anáx x'awataana eeyaa aha,
Akwshéi ax'a s'éetk'ee eeyaa aha,
Aha aha aya!

I turn the wheel to steer us due north out of Frederick Sound to Chatham Strait, and when Felix finishes singing, I ask him if it was a song about blubber.

"It's about a boy putting his hook and cedar twine into the water to catch halibut. It's one of the few songs I remember from my grandmother." Felix looks starboard for a minute, then back at me. "She sang all the time. I wish I had paid more attention. It's a sacred duty for one generation to hand down what it knows to the next."

I take a cigarette out of the pack that's lying on the console. "Mickey Dobbs wants to buy new sonar. Maybe we can take his old equipment off his hands for dirt cheap. Hell, it's five years newer than what we have." Of course if Walt and Cindy do sue my ass off, I'll be the one selling off old equipment.

"Hmm," Felix stands up and stretches. "I'm going to grab me another slice of Muskeg's crowberry bread. Want any?"

I hold up my cigarette. "No, I'm good."

It's still pretty dark out, but I check our bearings and see we're coming up to Catherine Island, so I cut west into Peril Strait, motor over the north end of Baranof, and anchor off the west end of Chichagof Island. Preparations go smoothly. No tangled lines. No broken latches or misbehaving winches. We're quick and efficient with the baiting. As we drop our pots overboard the sun yawns up over the island hillside, revealing various shades of green: silver-green, blue-spruce green, pea-green, the mossy-lime green of low-lying ferns. We drop fourteen pots on the south end of Salisbury Sound, then move two miles north to set the others. It's almost 9 a.m. by the time we sink the last pot, and the sea lightens from murky gray to clear.

"That should do it." I wipe sweat from my brow. "Let's go see what we got from the first batch."

Felix hauls up anchor and we double-back to the first round of pots. When we winch up the first pot, it's teeming with crabs. They're stacked end to end. You can barely see daylight through the holes in the pot.

"All right," Felix says. "This is more like it."

We tilt and unlatch the pot, and the crabs spill into the hold, clacketing over each other.

"There's gotta be 600 pounds of crab right there." Felix grins at me. "The sea gods are looking at a couple of working stiffs, and they say, 'Why don't we throw a couple of extra crab their way?' At least today they're saying that."

We settle the pot onto the deck. "That's just the first one. We got another twenty-seven to go."

"Nah, it's gonna be a good outing today." Felix slaps his chest twice. "I can feel it!"

I feel it as well, the mid-morning air brushed with warmth, the long chill of the last two days finally being pulled away from my shoulders and back. The dull gray stink of constant rain and wet wood that filled us yesterday has dissipated. The aroma of fresh crab spills out of the hold. The world smells possible again.

"You gonna help me with the next pot?" Felix asks. "Or you just gonna stand there admiring your handiwork?"

"I'll swing the winch around. You grab the line."

The second pot is nearly as full as the first, hundreds of tan and orange claws tilted every which way, flexing in and out, trying to pinch their way to some kind of stable position. The crabs that got turned on their backsides wave frantically, having exposed their soft underbellies to whatever predator might come along.

"I told you it's a good day!" Felix shouts. "I told you, didn't I?"

It takes all of the morning and into early afternoon to retrieve all of the pots. Only three of the twenty-eight are less than full, and even those are more than half-filled. By the time we leave for home, the bow of the ship dips slightly forward from all the crab we have in the hold. When we get them unloaded and weighed, it's the best catch we've had in the past two years.

"Think I'll pick up some beer and flowers to celebrate with Muskeg," Felix tells me as we tie up the boat. "It's her night off from the Blind Dog."

I grin and slap him on the back. "You were right, Felix. A damn good day. I forget sometimes what a couple of guys can accomplish when things go their way."

"That's what I'm saying. The gods were with us today. I'm just glad we could take advantage of it."

I rub my fingers over the statue of Matsu, which I remembered to return to my pocket. "Let's hope it stays with us."

"Why wouldn't it?"

WHEN I GET INTO my truck, I think about what Felix said about the gods being on our side today. I still feel like anything is possible. Guys understand accidents. Hell, we wear our scars like badges of honor, right? Walt and I should be laughing about this over a bottle of booze. There's nothing a couple of guys can't work out on a day like today, especially with a little help from Matsu.

On the way to St. Olga's Hospital I stop at the Moose Market and pick up a bottle of Jack Daniel's and have Helen the cashier put a dark blue bow on it. What says let bygones be bygones better than a bottle of JD?

I park the pickup at the hospital. The cream and brown three-story structure sits up on the bluff that overlooks the harbor on the south end of town. It was originally constructed by the Feds during World War II to house wounded veterans fighting off the Japanese takeover of Attu and Kiska islands up in the Bering Sea.

We're a small enough island that I know the woman at the information desk. Margaret Schultz retired from the Coast Guard about seven years ago. She keeps herself busy volunteering. We exchange pleasantries, and when I ask her for Walt Francke's room, she doesn't hesitate to tell me. Room 241. The hospital is small enough that I could wander around and find it myself, but it would be rude not to ask Margaret. I follow the signs upstairs and to the end of the hallway. At least Walt scored a nice view of the harbor.

I take a deep breath and knock, then enter when I hear a grunted "Yeah?" Smells like isopropyl alcohol and body odor. Walt's partially propped up in his bed, watching TV, his right arm held at a ninety-degree angle by some type of plastic cast. His hand is heavily bandaged. Wires extend out of the bandages, from the ends of his two cut fingers, and are held taut by an arcing band of metal.

"How you doing there, Walt?" I hold out the whiskey.

"Bancroft." Walt has a pasty look after a few days in the hospital, or maybe because he misses his wife. He fumbles for a control dangling at the side of the bed from a short white wire, and the TV snaps off.

He probably hasn't had any visitors since Cindy left. This might go okay.

"I thought I'd bring you a little pick-me-up." I put the bottle on the nightstand, not wanting to draw attention to the fact that opening it might be difficult with only one functional hand. "You want some, you just tell me, and I'll find a cup."

"Bancroft. You had the guts to show up here." He shifts in the bed, spilling the beige blanket onto the floor. "Cindy told me she called you. I told her she was an idiot."

I pick up the blanket, shake it out, and tuck it back over his legs, careful not to touch his body, then I pull over the orange plastic visitor's chair so I can sit at the end of his bed. "I had this gut feeling that if we talked things out, you know, man to man, we wouldn't need to get all these lawyers involved. Hell, let the insurance companies fight it out."

Walt uses his good hand to adjust his cast, pushing the elbow part close to his body, and pointing those protruding wires straight at me. "My football days are over."

"You play football?" Given Walt's size, it would be a fairly good guess, but surely his playing days were over twenty years ago.

"Northeastern. Defensive MVP junior and senior years. Nine sacks in one season. I could have gone pro, but tore up my knee the last game of the season. Now I just throw the ball around with my nephews." He pauses. "How about you, Bancroft? Play any?"

"In high school. Mostly offensive line. You and I would have been on opposite ends, I guess."

"When you take somebody down, charge them from the side, full-force." Walt looks me square on. "No warning."

"I guess so," I say. "I had my hands full just trying to keep up with the bigger guys."

"That's the sweetest way to do it." Walt uses his good hand to fiddle with the control dangling off the bed. "Don't let the son of a bitch know you're coming. And when you hit him, hit him with everything you got." The hospital bed hums. He adjusts the angle until he's propped up as straight as possible.

"Let me get some ice." My hands are sweating now but I'm

trying to sound normal, like I didn't notice him threatening me. "And a cup—how about two cups—for the Jack Daniel's."

Walt leans forward as far as he can, still pointing those accusing finger wires toward me, his face red, but his words come out slow and controlled. "What I'm saying, you moron, is that you made me a cripple!"

"C'mon, Walt. It was an accident." I stand up and hold my palms out, like what can do I besides offer some whiskey, but that makes his face even redder.

"I've got to learn to do everything with my left hand."

"They can do wonders now with rehab. I know this guy who was working up in Bristol Bay last year and he just about got his whole hand sliced off. Why, he's completely back to normal."

Walt leans back a little in the bed and stares at his bandaged hand. "My wife went back home without me. Orderlies wipe my ass and prattle on about encouraging my own healing. I haven't had a good steak in a week. Why the hell shouldn't I sue you for every penny you're worth?"

He swings his eyes back to me, and I step behind the chair, as if it'll protect me, but also because my knees feel like they're ready to buckle. My hands press against the orange plastic but I need to say what I came to say. "Let's be honest here, Walt. You didn't take care of your line, and you didn't keep your hand out of the way when it was unraveling. This was your fault, not mine. "

Walt twists his body, reaching his left hand over his torso to grab the bottle of Jack Daniel's off the nightstand. "Get the hell out of here and take your cheap whiskey with you!" He throws the bottle at me. It's a strong throw, but it misses me by a good two feet, hits the wall, breaks, and drops to the linoleum floor.

I step back before the brown liquid runs onto my boots. "Guess we can see why you didn't play quarterback."

I leave the door open so someone can come in and clean up his mess. Walt hurls threats at me as I head down the hall, my knees still wobbly from the confrontation. Outside, the sky is a deepening blue. There doesn't seem to be any wind. Gorgeous fall evening. I run my finger over the figurine of Matsu still in my pocket. The goddess is smiling on somebody, even if it isn't me.

Chapter 6

THERE ARE FOUR SEPARATE "No Smoking" signs posted around the front entrance of the hospital, but I free a cigarette from the package, settle it into my mouth, and light up. Too rattled to drive home right away. An acne-faced security guard points me to a designated area about twenty feet from where I'm standing. It's on this side of a three-foot high rock and cement wall that serves as a barrier to the steep hillside overlooking the bay. I station myself next to a standing ashtray.

The fatigue of the day begins to catch up with me. Or maybe it's just the exhaustion of dealing with someone who's pissed off. What did I think was going to happen? I try to construct a better way I could have handled the conversation, but all I wind up with is me pouring the Jack Daniel's over Walt's head and telling him to shove the bottle where the sun don't shine. Which would have made things worse. Not that they could get much worse.

"Ray!"

It's Nicole Harris, wearing gray slacks and an unzipped parka, heading toward the smoking area, waving at me. Her walk is confident on land, fluid and limber, hips jutting out just the right amount, her back and shoulders straight, that sweet flash of a smile. I stub out my cigarette in case smoke bothers her, even though I haven't finished it.

"What brings you to St. Olga's?" she asks. "Nothing wrong with Felix or your granddaughter, I hope."

It's starting to get dark now, but it's plenty light enough for me to notice the outline of her breasts against her maroon turtleneck sweater. "You know I have a granddaughter? Yikes. There goes my young bachelor image."

"Uh oh," Nicole says. "I shouldn't have let that slip. One of the nurses, Karen—her son goes to school with your granddaughter—mentioned that when she told me you're a widower." She pauses, looks at me, and chuckles. "I confess. I was trying to find out more about you." She winks, cocking her head slightly. "Ali wasn't the only one who thought you were good looking."

There's a warm tingle across my cheekbones. I'm more than a little jazzed about Nicole asking about me. On the other hand, if Karen told her I was raising Sitka, then she's probably told her about Jenny. It's a small island, so it's not easy to hide the bilge that seeps into your life.

"Felix and Sitka—that's my granddaughter—they're fine." I finish the last of my cigarette and crush it under my boot. "Actually, I just got done visiting Walt Francke."

"I see. How is our injured friend?"

"He'll live. Although I wouldn't use the term friend. As a matter of fact, have you got a minute?"

"You're in luck. I've just started my break." She sits down on one of the benches. A gust of wind blows some strands of hair across her face and she tucks them behind her ear. "I've got fifteen minutes or so."

I sit down next to her, straddling the bench. "I may need a favor."

"Your attorney called and asked if I'd give a statement or be a witness, if necessary."

"That's the favor. Would you be okay with that?"

"Well, Captain," she says in a stiff voice, "I can only swear as to what I actually witnessed, nothing more, nothing less."

She must see my mouth turn down. She slaps me on the arm and laughs. "I'm joking. Of course I'll help you in whatever way I can. That guy was such a jerk. His wife, too."

"Thanks."

Nicole reaches her hand across the bench and puts it over-top my hand, sending a little wave of warmth up my arm. "Don't worry, my brave captain. It was an accident. And you did everything you were supposed to do."

"So did you." I shift a bit, moving closer to her. My right knee touches her left, and she doesn't pull back. "You were tremendous out there, Nicole. I could have done some damage if you hadn't been there. I owe you."

The air is cooling down. Nicole takes her hand away to zip up her parka, and that disconnects our knees. She keeps her hood down and her brown hair blows around her face whenever there's a gust. The concrete wall protects us somewhat.

"You don't owe me anything. Well, maybe a dinner at the local five-star restaurant, which I have yet to find on this island, mind you." When I don't answer, she widens her smile. "Relax. Just let your attorney and insurance company take care of this. They know how to handle these things."

"So I've been told." I stare at the wall, as if instructions for not screwing things up any more will appear in easy-to-read runes. Nothing there. At least I have a sea goddess in my pocket—not that Matsu helped with Walt. "How's Ali?"

"Back in Seattle with her boyfriend. "She told me to say hey if I saw you."

"Boyfriend, huh?"

Nicole laughs. "Having a boyfriend never stopped Ali from enjoying a little flirting. You don't want to see her in Vegas."

"I've never been there. Never want to go."

"No reason you should. We went for a friend's wedding. Crowds and lights and noise and glitter, it gets tiresome pretty quickly."

We can see trees, pavement, sparse grass, and the hospital doors from our perch on the bench, and if we stood up, we'd have a view of the harbor. Nothing glamorous, but it is beautiful.

Nicole asks to bum a smoke. "I'm fresh out."

I hand her the pack. "Need a light?"

"Got it." She takes out a cherry-red disposable lighter from her pocket, flicks it open, and settles the flame under the tip of the cigarette.

"I'm surprised to see a nurse smoke."

"We all have our vices." When Nicole exhales, the blue-gray smoke blows back toward the hospital. "And besides, I'm not a nurse any more."

"But you work here, right?"

She rubs her index finger across her teeth before answering. They're remarkably white. She must use those whitening strips. "At the Counseling Center."

"You mean helping people with emotional problems. Like in those antidepressant ads on TV."

"Addiction counseling, actually." Nicole crosses her legs, and I lean toward her in the hopes that our knees will touch again, but now she has them crossed away from me. "I work with alcoholics and drug addicts."

"I didn't know they had any drug specialists here."

"Apparently the hospital's been working to fund this position for years." She taps her ashes to the ground. "Someone comes in for treatment, I try to help them change their behavior."

I slide my hands between my thighs to keep them warm. "I sure could have used you a dozen years ago."

She looks at me the way Sitka does when we're playing toss in the backyard, and she's wondering if I'll lob the baseball high or chuck it across the grass as a bouncing ground ball.

"It wasn't me, don't worry." I rub my forehead, then spread my fingers through my hair. "It's a long story."

Nicole reaches out her hand and places it on top of mine again. "I'm here if you ever want to talk about it."

I want to turn my hand over so I can squeeze hers, but I don't. We don't even know each other. "Here as a counselor or here as a friend?"

"Whichever one you need. But not both at once." She lets go of my hand and stands up to study the darkening bay. "So striking and spacious up here. There's room to breathe. Room to start over."

I can't see her face from the bench, so I get up and join her. "You don't seem like the kind of person who needs to get away from her old life."

Nicole moves her shoulders up and back, squeezing her shoulder blades together, then letting them drop, like she's trying to work a kink out of the middle of her back. "Let's just say that I did some things I'm not so proud of back in Seattle. People deserve a new start, you know? It took a while to decide that was true for me, not just my patients."

"A second chance? Sure. Maybe even a third." Donna and I gave Jenny a third and fourth and fifth and sixth chance. Even more chances than that. "But if someone keeps digging down into the same hole time after time, keeps breaking the hearts of everyone who loves them, at some point you have to let them go."

The wind shivers up the hillside and tumbles over the cement wall. The half-moon makes its late afternoon ascent above the top ridge of Sawtooth Mountain. I move closer to Nicole so the sleeves of our jackets touch.

"Think I'll get my second chance up here?" she asks.

My hands are sweaty. But here she is, so close to me, talking about second chances, and I haven't been on a date since Donna died. "You want to go out some time?"

Nicole looks me up and down and grins. "Smooth tacking, sailor. Didn't see that one coming."

"Granted, there's not much to do, but we really do have a couple of good restaurants and the movie theater. And a movie rental place. Or we could go hiking or kayaking."

"Sure, I'd love to." She runs her hand up and down my sleeve. "I saw some posters up around the nurses' station for a fall festival that starts tomorrow night."

"The Feast of St. Nicolai. They have all kinds of food and

Russian folk music, and there's a raffle, and the proceeds go to the island's food bank. Nothing big like you have in Seattle."

Nicole says that sounds perfect, and we decide to meet at St. Innocent's, the Russian Orthodox church, around six. She takes a small notebook and pen out of her parka and jots down her number just in case. "By the way, who is this St. Nicolai? The Russian Santa Claus?"

"A bishop who came over with the early Russian settlers. He's the patron saint of our island and fishermen. We call him St. Nicolai the Wet."

She snickers. "You call me 'Nicole the Wet' and I'll slap you silly."

I put my hands up in mock defense. "Hey, I don't come up with these things. I just respect the religious traditions."

"Ah, like that Billiken thing on your boat."

"Among others," I say. "You can't have too many spirits looking out for you."

"And yet you don't strike me as a religious person."

"I'm not, if you mean attending church. There's the whole thing with sailors and superstition, but for me it started after my wife died." I tell Nicole how Donna was a big churchgoer. She even read the Bible at home. But it didn't do her any good, not when she needed someone or some *thing* to reach out and save her. And while she was dying I prayed to God to spare her. "He was either too busy or too vindictive or just not up to the task. And then I was given this little baby to bring up and I knew I couldn't protect her by myself. I needed all the help I could get."

Nicole slips her arm through mine. It feels electric and soothing at the same time.

"And you seriously believe in more than one god?"

"Why not? One god doesn't seem to cut it, at least for me. I count on this god for the weather, that one for illness, others for a good catch. Quite a few for protection out at sea."

"And just how many gods are we talking about here?"

Her question is nearly impossible to answer. "You know

how many gods the Hindus believe in? Ten thousand."

"I saw something about that on public television once." She leans in closer to me. "You think they're right, Ray? Ten thousand gods?"

There's a flush of dusky rose fanning across the lower half of the sky. The gray water line has turned a deep purple. The harbor lights cast a soft yellow haze over the wharf. Most of the boats are in, and it's quiet, like the entire island knows it's time to settle down. I answer Nicole's question without looking at her.

"I think they've underestimated."

Chapter 7

I CATCH THE HEEL of my left shoe on the threadbare hallway runner.

"Set it down, set it down!" Felix says. "You're losing it."

His face is so red that I begin to worry all this furniture moving is too much for him. My shirt is soaked with sweat. The knuckles on both hands are scraped. My left shoulder's a sore puzzle of knots. And it feels like someone's poking the inside of my right knee with a knitting needle. I let my side of the chest of drawers slide down between my palms, getting a splinter in the process, until the bottom corner thuds against the floor. We both take a moment to steady our breathing, and I yank the splinter out with my teeth.

Felix winces as he twists his back from side to side. "Even with the drawers out, this thing's heavy as a moose carcass. About as much fun to move as one, too."

"Don't be insulting my furnishings. My grandfather made this, back when furniture and everything else was built to last."

Felix shakes his head from side to side. "Let me give you some Tlingit wisdom, pal. Nothing we build is meant to last forever. It's the nature of the universe to let things fall apart."

I slump my back against the wall. "That explains why you

guys let that old totem pole village over on Little Sukoi Island keep rotting away. It's a damn shame. Your great-grandfathers spent who knows how long carving and erecting those totems and now they're just toppling over and sliding right into Frederick Sound. Every time I sail by there, it's oops, there goes bear-man, oops, there goes wolf cub, there goes killer whale. All under the water."

Felix shrugs. "Where else should a whale go? There's no use fighting the whole death, decay, and regeneration thing."

"I'll be sure to quote you the next time I see Muskeg in Dottie's House of Beauty getting her hair colored."

"Don't you have a hand cart we can use?"

I stand up straight again and brace my hands against the sides of the dresser. "We're ten feet from the bedroom door. Put some of that eagle clan strength into it."

"How many times I gotta tell you, Ray? Eagles use brain over brawn."

We lift the chest up again and wrestle it into the room, setting it into the corner. Felix has to take off to refuel his propane tanks, but I can handle the rest myself. The small room used to be my office, but I'm converting it into a temporary guest room for Jenny. It was one thing when Sitka was six to share a room with her mom, but now that she's almost a teen, she'll want her privacy. The purple magic marker sign taped to her door that screams *Sitka's Room, Keep Out! This Means You!,* which I routinely ignore, is one clue.

As I'm wrangling the drawers back into the warped slides, I notice something wedged on the underside of the top drawer. It's a bent photo of Jenny and me when she was seven. Summertime along the waterfront pier in Seattle. We were visiting Donna's parents and took Jenny to the shops along Pike Street Market. I remember how angry Jenny was when she saw the fishmongers throwing the king salmon to each other. She flinched as the silver and pink bodies of the kings smacked into the arms of the young men in stained aprons, who urged shoppers to buy in their loud, waterfront voices.

One of them missed the catch, and the whole-bodied king skidded along the concrete floor of the market and under the fruit stand counter. The tourists shrieked, but Jenny went right up to the young man who had bobbled the catch and slapped him on the side of his leg.

"That's no way to treat someone just because they're dead!" she yelled. "Animals have feelings too!"

The people gathered around us laughed, which made Jenny even angrier. Donna was outside with her parents. I quickly bought a pint of Rainier strawberries at the fruit stand. The intense sweetness of the red berries mollified Jenny a bit, but she still glared back at the fishmongers as we exited through the north door of the market. I'd forgotten how sensitive a child she was, how small injustices could move her.

In the photo, Jenny and I are standing at the railing, our backs to the camera, looking out into Puget Sound. Faded blue sky and ocean. Ferry boats, headed to Victoria or the San Juans, making white V-shaped wakes in the distance. A pair of seagulls following the boats. Jenny's hair is tied into pigtails that are almost, but not quite, matching. You can see the zigzag line of the part. I must have been the one who brushed her hair that morning. I could run a comb down her scalp five times, and the part would never come out straight. She's wearing yellow shorts and a blue and white striped shirt, although the photo is so old that the colors are mostly washed out. Jenny's no taller than my waist. Her right arm is curved around my hip, and she's leaning into me. My hand is on her shoulder. We look like a father and daughter who love each other.

I flip the photo on top of the dresser and it lands face down. I move an old milk-chocolate-colored metal bed frame that was packed away in the attic into the room. The paint's flecked off and it squeaks, but I can always spray some WD-40 and Rustoleum on it later. Felix and I picked up a used gray-and-white-striped full-size mattress from Jake's Outlet this morning. Getting it into the room by myself takes some doing, because it keeps folding in on itself, like a jelly sandwich on soft white bread. The frame is missing a support bar and the mattress sags enough that I'll have to cut a piece of plywood to fit within the bed frame and support it. I should have been better prepared, but it only occurred to me last night that Jenny would need a place to sleep.

I head out to the garage for tools. The mid-morning air is thick with fog droplets and pretty soon my hair is matted down like a mongrel dog. Everything is gray and brown, except for the citron-yellow moss that's replaced any hope of a lawn. It's one of the few things you can count on around here. Moss. You can fight it with pressure washes and iron pellets, but it's as ever–present as the ocean itself.

The cold seeps right through my sweatshirt, but I stand there and smoke a cigarette. When I'm done I crush the butt into the gravel under my boot. Then I smoke another, watching the blue and gray swirls of smoke rise up. I want to watch them circle all the way up to the darker clouds, but they disappear into the tufts of moss that outline the roof shingles.

JENNY FIRST GOT INTO serious trouble in the middle of tenth grade. She hooked up with a group of kids whose leader was a little twerp by the name of Diesel Kurtz. Diesel was the second-oldest child of Becky and Jack Kurtz. Well, it was just Becky, really. Jack had been a fitter working on the big pipelines running out of Prudhoe Bay. You can make some pretty big bucks doing that. So it surprised us when he got busted for stealing expensive tools and laptop computers, and fencing them to a resale shop in Yakima, Washington. That must have been when Diesel was about nine or ten. Jack went off to prison and their oldest son, Robby, had to drop out of high school to work in the cannery. It wasn't long before Diesel gained a reputation for having run-ins with the sheriff's department. Nothing big, mind you. Juvenile pranks, like shoplifting and busting into a gas station late at night, which was stupid because the owner never kept any money there overnight. Diesel was the first kid on the island to try the neo-punk rock look, dyeing his hair green, wearing torn jeans and chains, sporting a what-the-hell-are-you-staring-at expression.

Of course I warned Jenny about getting mixed up with him. But then Donna would say something about how sad it was that he didn't have a father around, and I'd say that was no excuse for being a petty criminal, and Jenny would roll her eyes and walk out of the room, leaving Donna and me to argue. We didn't think that Jenny would stick around with a kid like that, though. And like most parents, we were dead wrong.

One night when Jenny was fifteen, she sneaked out of the house and met up with Diesel and his gang down in the town square. They broke into the First Baptist Church and spray-paint-ed the walls with big, squarish letters. None of us adults even thought our kids knew how to do graffiti. We couldn't even tell for sure what it said, although FUCK and JESUS were in there somewhere. We made them apologize to the minister and to the congregation, and we all pitched in to undo the damage, over the course of several weeks, all except for Diesel's mom, who couldn't afford to take time off from her job on the slime line or help pay for the new paint. Diesel always had an excuse to not show up for the mandatory cleaning sessions, while I shelled out my part of the money and took off three Saturdays to help repaint the sanctuary.

Six weeks after the graffiti business, a bang on the door woke us up around two in the morning. I checked Jenny's bed-room on the way downstairs, but she wasn't there. Maybe she had sneaked out and then lost her keys. I bounded down the stairs ready to read her the riot act. At the bottom landing, I saw the lights of the patrol car flashing. My hand was wet and shaky as I opened the door. A deputy sheriff stood there, backlit by the street light out front. The blood seemed to drain away so quickly inside me, my stomach felt like a seized engine. Donna came down the stairs, already choking out sobs.

I flipped the porch light on and invited Rusty Baines inside, but he stayed put on the porch. He and I had worked some salmon boats together when we were younger. He tipped the brim of his hat, but didn't take it off. I didn't know if that was a good sign or a bad one.

"Ray. Donna," he said, and Donna's sobs got worse. I just nodded, because my jaw was already trembling, and I was afraid of breaking apart in front of my wife.

"Your Jenny's gone and got herself into an accident with a bunch of other kids up on Heart Lake Road, near the turnoff for Greenback Mountain."

Donna clutched my arm, leaving half-moon indentations in my skin that lasted a few days. I pulled her to my side, her tears soaking through my T-shirt.

"She's all right," Rusty said, the words even and clipped. "We've taken her over to St. Olga's. Banged up a bit, but she's going to be fine."

"And the others?" I asked.

"Not so lucky, except for Diesel Kurtz."

"Diesel Kurtz!" I slammed my palm against the door frame. "She knows she's not to have anything to do with that punk!"

"This isn't the time for that," Donna said, her voice steadier. "She's all right you say? You sure, Rusty?"

"Yes, Ma'am." Rusty tipped his hat one more time, maybe to reassure us. "Go ahead and bring her home tonight. I cited her for drunkenness and disorderly conduct. The DA may have additional charges. Either way, she's going to have to appear in Juvenile Court in the next couple of weeks, based on the DA and Judge Lindstrom's calendar."

Before I could ask any more questions, Rusty turned and headed down the porch steps. At the bottom he looked back up. "You just be thankful I didn't have to tell you the news I gave to the Beckers and McLoughlins tonight."

Donna wanted to drive but I insisted on doing it. I was wrong. Donna stared straight ahead, calm, while I shouted and banged my left hand against the dashboard until the fleshy underside swelled red and purple.

Once we got to the ER, a nurse took us to the exam room where Jenny was. The glare of bright white lights ricocheted off the tiled walls and metal surfaces. It was disorienting, with everyone running around and shouting. Jenny was sitting on a stretcher, watching a young doctor pour some brownish liquid onto a gash in her left arm.

"I think a butterfly will do." The doctor moved his fingers down the rest of her arm, checking for any signs of breakage. Her right arm was resting on top of a pan of ice.

Jenny flinched when she saw us. "Mom, Dad," she started, then began sobbing.

Donna went right to her and put her arms around her, and they cried and cuddled like a mother bear and her cub. While I stood there, arms folded, half-relieved and half-exploding with anger, breathing in the smell of rubbing alcohol mixed with vomit and blood.

"I'm Dr. Ames. You're Jenny's parents?"

He stayed on his examining stool and did not offer a handshake. He couldn't have been more than thirty, but he had a sizable bald spot, which seemed pronounced under those bright white lights.

"Yes, we're Jenny's parents," I said. "How bad is she?"

Donna pulled back from hugging Jenny to hear the diagnosis.

"She's a lucky girl," Dr. Ames said. "We're waiting for the X-rays to confirm, but I think her right wrist has a simple fracture. Her laceration isn't too deep. There's no internal bleeding and no concussion. She'll feel pretty banged up for a few weeks. She's got contusions pretty much up and down her body."

"Contusions?" Donna grabbed Jenny's hands, squeezing her fingers.

"Bruises, Mom," Jenny answered, pulling away from her mother's grip.

"Is that it?" I asked.

"Pretty much," Dr. Ames said.

I nodded, like Jenny was a boat in the repair shop.

I didn't ask.

I didn't ask.

I did not ask, "Is she high?"

As we waited for Jenny to finish being treated, we managed to get bits and pieces from a nurse in the hall, and one of the on-call EMTs, but very little from Jenny. She claimed she couldn't remember much. We eventually pieced it together from the police report and from talking with the other parents.

The kids had broken into the Moose Market and stolen a case of beer and the delivery truck. Anyone who ever worked part-time at the market knew that Dan Parsons kept a spare set of keys behind a loose brick at the edge of the building. And just about every kid in town worked there at some time, or knew someone who had. Diesel Kurtz sure did, because he swiped the keys, and he and Jenny and the others took the truck for a joy ride out along Route 22. Jenny sat up front with Diesel, while the other two kids stood in the cargo section, holding on to straps with one hand, drinking beers with the other.

Diesel raced the truck up the forest road to Greenback Mountain. When they came to the sharp bend in the road at milepost four, he lost control. From the skid marks, the Highway Patrol investigators said that Diesel must have been going around sixty when he slammed on the brakes, which is about the dumbest-ass thing you can do when you're well into a curve. Fool idiot should have eased on the brakes and then accelerated a bit to give the truck some forward motion, but he was too drunk stupid.

The truck skidded down the hillside and flipped a few times. Tony Becker was thrown from the back, smashing into the trunk of a Douglas fir, his body nearly cut in half. Mary Ann McLoughlin held on for one or two flips, but when the truck landed upside down, it crushed her into the ground, snapping her spinal column. Diesel was the only one who escaped without any injuries. The doctors said he was the only one wearing a seatbelt. Probably he was so high his body relaxed against the jolts, like a salmon moving with the tidewater.

A physician's assistant finished casting Jenny's arm and placed a soft collar brace around her neck. As she got up off the stretcher Donna hugged her again. Jenny looked ashamed for once in her life. Maybe seeing her two friends being covered over with white cloths, watching the blood soak through, had gotten through to her. Dr. Ames opened the curtain, stepped in, and scribbled on a prescription pad.

"Fill this first thing tomorrow. She shouldn't need any more pain meds tonight." As he handed me the prescription, he patted Jenny on the shoulder. "I'll say it again. You are one lucky girl. I don't want to see you in here again for something like this. Will you promise me that?" He smiled, as if that was all it would take to keep Jenny in check.

"I will, Dr. Ames." Jenny watched me put the prescription in my pocket. "I promise."

In the car, Donna turned around to talk to her. "You have me so worried, hanging out with these kids, doing foolish things. This isn't like you."

"How do you know what's like me and what isn't?"

"You could have been killed tonight, Jenny!" I cut in. "And you're probably going to get arrested and go to court. Didn't you learn anything from your last idiotic episode? Do you know how upsetting this is to your mother?"

If Jenny had wanted to answer me, I didn't give her any room to do so. I gave her the standard parental spiel, how much she had disappointed us, that she was grounded until she was thirty-five, and that from now on I'd be on her like a tick on a dog. "And if I ever see that Diesel Kurtz with you again, I'll chain his butt to an anchor and drop him in the middle of Glacier Bay." As I went on and on, Jenny shrunk down into the back seat until I lost sight of her in the rearview mirror.

After the accident, Donna and I fought over how to deal with our delinquent daughter. She wanted to turn Jenny around by appealing to her better nature. But in my mind, Jenny was a runaway fish that needed to be reeled back in. The biggest mistake you can make when trying to bring in a fish is to let the line go slack. You get the hook set, then let the fish run away from you and take out line. At the same time you keep the line taut. The whole point is to let the fish tire itself out.

That meant setting down tough and clear rules. The hook was basic. If Jenny wanted to keep living at home, eating our food, and getting money for clothes and other things, then she had to go by our rules. Plain and simple. None of this pampering and ego-building stuff. Keep the line tight. If Jenny broke the rules, we would come down hard. Reel her in.

Donna said that was all good and well for me, since she'd be the one left holding the reel every day. She also reminded me that most fish will literally fight to the death if you let them. She showed me articles from parenting magazines. The social workers who showed up pushed for the same approach as Donna. Studies from this university and that university show that blah, blah, blah. We tried my way for a week or so, then I gave up and let my wife handle it. Donna constantly reminded Jenny that she was a smart girl, a decent and loving soul with a bright future ahead of her.

"You have so much going for you, Jenny. Father Albers always said you were the most promising child in Youth Group. You have it in you to be anything you want. Don't you know that, sweetie?"

Jenny never answered her, just looked down or rolled her eyes. This became the dance they did.

The entire island turned out for Tony and Mary Ann's funerals. Closed casket, each one. Jenny didn't want to go, but we made her. At the gravesites no one would come within ten feet of us. Jenny and Diesel went back to court three weeks later. Given prior arrests, and the fact that he was the ringleader, Diesel got ten months in state prison. Jenny got off a lot easier: house arrest for six months. The judge left it up to us whether or not Jenny wore a monitoring bracelet on her ankle. I put my foot down on this one. She wore that damn bracelet. Donna homeschooled her so that she wouldn't have to be held back.

During those six months, Donna never let up on her campaign to guilt Jenny into being a good kid.

"You're so much kinder than the other teenagers on this island, Jenny. I remember when you were nine and we nursed that puffin back to health. That's the kind of girl you are."

My mother pulled the same crap with me. I'd swipe a box of crayons from the kid who sat next to me in school and she would be all over me. Oh, Raymond, I would expect this from other boys, but not from you. All I wanted was to have the right to covet that shiny box of new crayons. I'd take punishment over always being expected to be good. I'm betting Cain was originally the always-obedient son before he got fed up, and knocked Abel dead in his tracks.

We didn't know exactly how or when the addiction started, but for sure Jenny was on meth when she got pregnant just after her seventeenth birthday. Donna blamed me for ignoring Jenny. I said it was because we weren't strict enough. We didn't reel her in. Maybe I could have reached out to Jenny more, or taken her to a drug counselor in Juneau. Maybe Donna could have laid down the law. Either way, it was no excuse for Jenny getting pregnant and running off to live with Diesel Kurtz. No excuse for Donna dying the way she did.

If Jenny's coming home for understanding and forgiveness, she can forget it.

I FIND AN OLD frame in the garage. Donna used to buy them cheap at yard sales. She loved having a lot of family photos around, but when she died, I ripped most of the pictures out of their frames and stashed them in a shoebox in our bedroom closet. I threw most of the frames into the garbage. The only one I can find is a white ceramic oval with the Norwegian rose-maling pattern. It's attached to a white cup that can hold pens and paperclips.

Back upstairs, I insert the photo of me and Jenny at Puget Sound and set it on top of the dresser. The photo is a little small for the frame, so that empty space shows to one side. I tilt the picture to the right, then to the left, then back to the right, trying to fill in as much of the gap as I can.

Chapter 8

BEING ON A FIRST date is more fun than I remembered. And it's a good distraction from the fact that Jenny is arriving late afternoon tomorrow. It's easy to be with Nicole. She laughs easily, even when I tell her that lame old joke about how many fishermen it takes to change a lightbulb—five, because it was this big. She keeps herself in shape, although she has no problem sampling the halupki stuffed with salmon and cream cheese, the chicken piroshki, and even the borscht.

As we stroll past the festival booths, Kathy Finnegan waves her arms at me, trying to get me to sign one of her idiotic ballot initiatives. Six years ago Kathy's husband, Mike, hooked up with a Canadian wildlife photographer and the two of them took off for Alberta. Since then Kathy has been a self-proclaimed do-gooder. She devotes herself to taking up causes and writing up petitions and initiatives. Ban smoking. Build a new arts center. You can't go to a public event without seeing Kathy and her fold-up card table and kitchen chair with the chipped green paint. The Feast of St. Nicolai is no exception. This particular initiative would make it mandatory for hunters to wear bright orange hats and vests. I put my hand up and start to walk by.

"How can you not support this?" Nicole asks, neatly writing

her own name on one of the signature lines. "If you ever had to treat even one gunshot victim like I did down in Seattle—especially teenagers . . ."

I never did see the connection between kids shooting each other in the city and hunting. "They did a study," I point out, "about how wearing an orange vest makes absolutely no difference in the number of accidental hunting shootings."

"That study was probably conducted by the NRA." Nicole taps her finger on top of the petition. "They should at least make it so kids have to wear them. Wouldn't you want to make sure your granddaughter was safe?"

"Sitka doesn't go hunting. But if she did, I'd make sure she knew how to handle a rifle."

Nicole folds her arms. "And how would wearing an orange vest not help her handle herself?"

"False sense of security. I'd rather she pay attention to what's going on around her than rely on some artificial means of protection."

I wonder if refusing to sign will throw a kink into our date. But as we walk away, Nicole slips her hand into mine and steers us straight over to the open church door.

"Let's go see the icons." She pulls me up the steps of St. Innocent's. Muted light from the candles and incense waft over the gold-haloed saints. Nicole slides her hand around my waist, leaning slightly into me. When someone behind us coughs, I turn around, thinking it might be Muskeg or Felix trying to get my attention.

"Evening, Ray," Sarah's mom says.

"Hi, Julie."

Even in the dim light I can see Julie's eyes moving up and down Nicole, with the same serious expression as the icons. Nicole drops her arm from around my waist and extends her hand. "Nicole Harris," she says warmly. "Nice to meet you."

The two of them exchange pleasantries, Julie's expression softening. Nicole tells Julie about her job and moving up here, and Julie fills Nicole in on Saturday yoga classes and which days fresh produce comes in from Juneau. I take another look at the icons around us, until Julie pulls back the sleeve of her sweater to check her watch.

"I promised Phil I wouldn't be gone for more than a few minutes. We're chaperoning the dance. Oh, and thanks for bringing the girls down here tonight, Ray. We'll drive them home."

Sitka knew I was meeting Nicole here tonight, but we didn't talk about it like it was a date, and I didn't offer to introduce them. I don't want Sitka caught up in my dating life unless something serious starts to happen. More importantly, I don't want to throw another wrench into her life right now.

Julie gives Nicole a pat on the shoulder. "Nice to meet you. I hope I get to see you again."

Nicole slips her hand around my waist again. "Same here, Julie."

"Tell Phil hey," I say.

Julie shoots me a wink of approval as she turns to leave.

Nicole and I spend another half hour or so at the festival. When I walk her back to her car, we do some serious kissing before she gets in. It feels warm and smoky, full of possibility.

I'M UP AND READY to go early the next morning. Jenny may be coming home today, but I still have to go out on the boat. Before leaving the house, I check in on Sitka. She's sound asleep. When I went to bed last night, she was at her desk, updating her blog on My Private Place, one of those social networking sites. It's supposed to be safe for kids, with a lot of firewall stuff and parental controls built in. I was tempted to look over her shoulder and see if she was writing anything about her mom. The rule is I have full access to anything she does on the computer. But I didn't think it was the best time to exercise that prerogative.

"Be off that in fifteen minutes," I told her. "You have school tomorrow."

"I know," she answered, without taking her eyes off her laptop.

"You have a good time at the dance?"

"Uh-huh."

"Sitka, look at me."

She took her hands off the keypad, slapping them on the desktop. "What?"

"You okay? I mean, you doing all right with your mom coming home tomorrow?"

"Fine," she said in that tone that means just leave me alone.

I decided not to push it. Not sure what I would have told her anyway.

I STOP BY THE Moose Market on the way to the boat to pick up breakfast fare for me and Felix. Some smokes, two bananas, a couple of bear claws, and two cups of coffee. Helen Blanchet strokes the top of my hand when she gives me my change. It's barely a touch, a mere brushing of her two fingers. I've been coming here every other morning for the past fifteen years, and the only other time Helen's done anything like that was a couple of days after Donna's funeral. Either she heard about Jenny coming home or she saw me with Nicole last night. Either way, I'm going to be a hot topic of conversation at Dottie's House of Beauty this week. When you live on an island as small as Yatki, it doesn't take long for folks to hear about the latest chapter in your life. Part of that is natural gossip and part is because we look out for each other. We have this natural contradiction of believing that people should mind their own business, but as soon as the winds shift, it seems like everyone is giving you the fish eye.

"You hanging in there, Ray?" Helen's wearing a pink angora sweater that looks like tufts of cotton candy stitched together. Her platinum blond hair is freshly dyed and lacquered, piled on top of her head, so it's like staring at a double-cone of strawberry and vanilla cotton candy.

"Doing fine," I answer, securing the cellophane pack of Camels in the front pocket of my jacket. "You got some matches?"

Helen points to the dusty bowl that's been encrusted on the counter since 1962. "It must be so hard having a daughter who's been nothing but a boatload of worries."

I don't want to get into this. "Well, Jenny's been through a lot."

This time when Helen pats my hand, she lets it rest on mine. "And there you've been, raising Sitka all by yourself." She leans forward. "By the way, I just happened to run into Becky Kurtz the other day."

Diesel's mother. My jaw tightens like the ratchets on a pipe wrench. I pull my hand away from Helen. "So?"

"Diesel's getting out on parole in a couple of weeks. Becky was practically bragging about it. He used to hang around with your Jenny, didn't he?"

Helen, and everyone else on Yatki, knows exactly what happened between Jenny and Diesel. "I better get on down to the boat."

"You must be pretty busy these days." She gives me the doughnuts and coffee, and then holds out two white packets, shaking them in front of me. "Don't forget your sugar, Sugar."

So she did see me with Nicole at the festival, or at least she heard about it. There's a heavy frost on the October ground and my boots crackle on top of the blacktop pavement as I walk over to my truck. It's just after six, still a couple of hours before sunrise, and the air is clear and cold. The tail of the Big Dipper rests on top of Bear Tooth Ridge, casting a silver sheen on the high Douglas firs. Even in the dark you can see the termination dust, that light dusting of snow at the edge of the tree line that marks the change of season.

Endings and beginnings. So Diesel Kurtz is getting out of prison too. I wonder if Jenny knows. If that's why she's really coming home.

The Draconid meteor showers are in full force, bits of light shimmering across the front of Orion's belt. Orion has his bow tilted downward, just waiting to rip an arrow through the black and windless sky into the Icy Straits. I get in the cab of my truck and munch on one of the doughnuts, wishing I had as clear of a line of sight as the night archer.

Helen means well, but I also know from Muskeg that she's always had a little crush on me. She thinks I might be a good catch because I didn't abandon Sitka to the child welfare society. Like if a guy is good and true in one area of his life, he's good and true everywhere else. And if he's got a few burrs and rough edges, all he needs is a good woman to buff them out. I don't know. Maybe that's true. Donna had a way of smoothing out my jagged spots. Had a way, as in past tense. As in, get with the program, Ray. Helen may not be my type, but maybe having a woman around would help me and Sitka. Sarah's mom said as much. I guess Sitka could use the guidance of an adult woman. And it's not like Jenny's going to be any kind of role model.

It's almost six thirty when I get to the dock. I meet up with Felix in the pilothouse. He's restocking our emergency medical supplies.

"'Bout time you got here." He lays in a stack of gauze pads and places a pair of bandage scissors on top of them. "I hate starting the day out of rhythm. We've already missed the best tide."

"Sorry, sorry. Let's just get going." I start running down our checklist, flitting from port side to starboard and back again. Mid-stride I trip over my own feet, falling against the table and knocking the tide charts onto the deck.

"Hang on, sailor," Felix says. "You're more agitated than a salmon smacking up a waterfall. Your hurrying up is gonna make us go slower. What's going on?"

"Nothing." I scramble the charts up in my arms. "Jenny. But other than that, I'm hunky-dory, okay?" I settle the charts back into place. "Let's just get our work done. We've got crab to catch."

"Of course. She's coming today." Felix holds up his hand. "We ain't going to catch squat until we cleanse the jumpity air around here. So just give me a minute here. Let's see . . ." He peers out through the port to the sky. "Old woman moon is still out." He takes out a bit of brightly-colored cloth from his back pocket, and cuts off a thin strip with his pocketknife. He sets the cloth into a cracked blue saucer we use as an ashtray. "You got anything on you that's ancestral in nature?"

"Like what?"

"That was a patch from one of my father's shirts." Felix points to the cloth in the ashtray. "I always carry a bit of it around with me. Keeps me connected with my heritage. You got anything from your dad or grandfather or uncle?"

I shake my head. "Maybe we could poke our fingertips and put our fingers together and become blood brothers. Then your dad's shirt could work for both of us."

"What do you think this is? Some old Hollywood movie?" Felix sighs. "Well, I'll just have to ask old woman moon to disinfect the atmosphere in general."

Taking a book of matches from the table, he intones some Tlingit words and holds the flame against the strip of material. But instead of burning, it melts like plastic.

"Hey, you charlatan," I say. "That's polyester."

Felix lifts his right eyebrow. "Hmm. Must have been from one of my old disco shirts. Oh, well. It's the thought that counts."

"You done? Can we go now?"

"It's up to you. You're the captain." He turns his gaze to port side. He's not going to decide if we should disembark, not with his stroke-damaged brain.

With the cleansing ceremony out of the way, we move quickly to get the boat ready and head out to Kah Sheets Bay to check the crab pots that we submerged last night. I motor up to the buoys that have our markers tied to them. Pulling alongside, I put the engine into neutral while Felix moves to the stern. He grabs hold of the crab pot buoy as it comes alongside. It's no more than twenty feet to the bottom. Dungeness crabs prefer shallow water. I anchor and help Felix pull the pots up, listening to them clank against the side of the boat. Lifting the lids, we remove the dusky purple and reddish brown crabs, avoiding the two main claws that could crush our fingers. My first year on a crab boat, this guy got to talking about his girlfriend and how sweet and ripe her pretty little thing was, and it wasn't more than a few seconds before he started screaming and his right index finger was mashed to a pulp of blood and splintered bone. It's a series of quick and powerful lessons out here.

We scan each crab for legal size and gender, and wind up tossing about a dozen female and undersized crabs overboard, and they plunk back into the bay. We don't find any mitten crabs and I take it as a sign that in spite of the polyester shirt, Felix's little ritual is paying off. Once we empty the pot, Felix re-baits it with large chunks of octopus, halibut, and salmon. He coils the rope and buoy and we return the pot to the water. We finish the pots on this buoy, then move to the next, and then the next one after that, in the steady, silent rhythm of familiar work.

When we finish emptying and re-baiting the last one, I stop and light up. Felix lifts up his Greek fisherman's cap and looks down at the slate-green water.

"We got about another day or two at best before this spot's all crabbed out."

I swipe away some cigarette ashes that have blown against my coat. "The other side of the bay is done too. Everyone's saying this could be a damn short season. And we can't even take tourists out. Any suggestions?"

Felix scratches his scalp. "Better off without the turtles anyway. Maybe try up north to Kake and if nothing's going on there, over to the north end of Admiralty Island?"

"I sure as hell hope we don't have to go over to Juneau. Too many drunks piloting boats."

"It's an armpit, all right," Felix agrees. "Speaking of Juneau, which ferry did you say Jenny will be on?"

"The four thirty. About an hour after Sitka gets home from school."

"Maybe we'd better start in, then. By the time we get these crabs unloaded, and the boat tied up and cleaned, it'll be after two. You picking her up?"

I flick my cigarette butt into the water. "She didn't ask and I didn't offer."

Felix needs confirmation before he can steer us someplace. "You wanna go in, then?"

"I want to go to My Private Place."

"Huh?"

"Yeah. Let's go in."

IN SPITE OF MY intention to make Jenny's homecoming as normal a day as possible, I give in to the impulse to cook a special dinner. If you didn't live up here, you'd think that every meal would center around crab or salmon. But believe me, we get sick and tired of those.

I've picked up a couple of fresh elk steaks from Muskeg's brother-in-law Earl. I'll grill them with some onions on the back deck. For a salad, I'll throw together iceberg lettuce and vegetables with some ranch dressing. That and a few baked potatoes should make a balanced meal. I've got a frozen apple and blackberry pie heating in the oven so it can cool off in time for dessert. I'll top the potatoes with bacon from a shaker and green onions. Even the real kind of sour cream. Who says I'm not making an effort? And the chopping and mixing keep me from going stir-crazy. I like the thwack of the knife against the wood board. I use it to steel my nerves, to get clear about what I'll say to Jenny; the truth is, I don't know what I'll say because I don't have a clue as to who she is.

I open up the kitchen junk drawer. Jenny's letter is half-hidden under two screwdrivers and a buy-one-large-and-get-one-small free pizza coupon. I lift it out, unfold it for the umpteenth time, and read the part about how she's clean and sober. But who's going to walk through the door—a mature, grown-up daughter, who I haven't yet met, or the junkie I know? I push the letter to the back of the drawer and close it. Picking up a bottle of Alaskan Amber, I twist off the cap and take a good swig. Okay, bad idea with a recovering drug addict about to show up, but I'll finish this second bottle and chew some breath mints before she gets here.

Sitka should be home any minute. If I can just get these carrots chopped and throw the potatoes in the oven, everything should be set. Maybe I should have gotten some sourdough bread. Jenny liked sourdough when she was little. When the front door opens, I shout out that I'm in the kitchen.

"When you put your books away, do me a favor and set the table so that it's ready when your mom gets here." I wait for the requisite groan, but nothing's forthcoming.

"Sitka? Did you hear me?" I gulp the rest of the beer and throw the bottle in the recycling bucket. I pick up a dish towel and turn around. There's a woman standing in the kitchen doorway with a large blue and beige duffel bag. Donna's gray hair, though cut shorter. And Donna's eyes, dark and clear.

"Hi, Dad."

"Well, I'll be."

Jenny's in jeans, a simple buttoned-down blouse, and an all-weather coat. Her clothes are clean and pressed, her hair combed, her face washed. Not at all like the rumpled scarecrow that came home last time. She's gained back some of her healthy weight.

"I thought you knew I was coming."

"I did." I cross my arms, pushing my shoulder blades back so I look a little more in charge of the situation. "Bring your stuff in and get settled. Dinner will be ready soon."

Jenny doesn't move. "You look surprised to see me."

"I thought you'd be later is all. Ferry get in early?"

"Yeah." She pulls the duffel strap over her head and sets the bag on the kitchen floor. "It didn't take long to dock and I got a cab here. Didn't mean to startle you."

"You're looking better than the last time I saw you. That's what startled me."

I should hug her, because that's what family does, but my hands are sticky from cooking. I take the towel and rub them dry, but when I'm finished I don't know how to approach her, or if I even want to. I toss the towel on the back of a kitchen chair.

She smiles and does a little pirouette. "A new me, Dad. That's what it's all about."

Is she joking? She seems serious, and a bit of the sheer hunger look has dissipated. The lines in her face look less craggy. "Are you off the drugs or not? Because I don't want you around Sitka if you're not clean."

"Three years, eight months, Dad. No drugs, no alcohol." Jenny closes her eyes. She stretches out her arms and extends her fingers. She takes a deep breath, lifting her arms higher. "Peace be upon this house," she intones. "And upon all who dwell within, through the grace of Our Lord Jesus Christ."

Chapter 9

JENNY'S INVOCATION HANGS BETWEEN us, the particulates of each word suspended in the air. I stand at one end of the kitchen table, my mouth open.

"Praise you, Jesus!" she adds for good measure.

The religious fervor is a surprise. Jenny hasn't stepped inside a church since she was a kid, when Donna used to take her to St. Innocent's. The only other choices were the Pentecostal church in the alley behind the Blind Dog—and Donna would have no part in that—or the First Baptist Church.

I'd tag along once in awhile because Donna would nag me about spending time together as a family. Most Sundays Jenny sang in the choir. Often off-key, but she belted out the hymns and she looked like a little Hallmark cherub in her maroon and white choir robe. Later, when we found out that Jenny was hooked on cocaine and meth, I went to St. Innocent's seven times and lit two candles each time to St. Maximilian Kolbe, the patron saint of drug addicts. And not just the little votive candles, but the huge, cream-colored beeswax ones. Either Max wasn't listening, or else because he was Polish and Roman Catholic, his heavenly influence withered in a Russian Orthodox stronghold.

Jenny lowers her arms and opens her eyes. "I've wanted to do that for the longest time."

As if this house needed to be exorcised. As if my countertop gods and goddesses weren't doing their jobs. As if she were descending from some higher ground. After all my debating about hugging her, Jenny rushes over and puts her arms around me and squeezes. I lightly pat her, the edge of the shoulder blade as thin and sharp as it was five years ago, but her body seems softer, better nourished. Instead of cigarettes and rotting mushrooms, her skin smells fresh, like bergamot or chokecherry.

She lets go of me and swivels her head to take in the entire kitchen. "It's such a blessing to be home." She opens her mouth more widely and shouts out, "I praise the Lord for this day!"

"How about we tone down the hallelujahs? There's no need for this kind of dramatics."

"I'm not being dramatic." Jenny puts her hands on her hips. "Gratitude and attention need to be paid. Isn't my coming home something miraculous? Isn't it something to celebrate?"

I head over to the counter and slice into a red onion, even though I have enough for the salad already. "I'm fixing you a homemade dinner. I should be out setting crab pots, but I'm not. I'm here." I whack at the other half of the onion, but it's soft under the knife, and the edge slips. I pull my finger back just before the knife can slice off the tip. What's left of the onion has a large brown spot under the skin that goes all the way to its heart. I flat-blade it into the garbage pail.

"I thought you'd support my recovery, Dad," Jenny says. "I thought you'd really want to welcome me home."

I slam the knife onto the counter, and turn around to face my daughter. "That's rich. We treated your last homecoming like it was a national holiday. We rolled out the red carpet and you pissed on it. You broke Sitka's heart, Jenny. So if you're looking for a ticker-tape parade this time around, you're going to be disappointed."

This isn't the way I meant for this to go. Two minutes into her visit and Jenny already has my hackles raised. What the hell did I expect? I wait for her to hurl a comeback, anticipating the usual excuses, the deflections and denials.

But she drops her shoulders and says, "You're right, Dad. I have no right to expect anything special from you or Sitka. That's the first thing we learn in recovery, to take responsibility. And, with the help of God, I want to do just that."

She raises her left hand up to her eye as if there were tears to be dabbed away. Is she really crying? I can't tell for sure. Maybe it's only the fumes from the onion.

"I have to put my faith in the Lord, to get me through this, and to open your hearts, yours and Sitka's." Jenny stands on tiptoe and looks over my shoulder. "Is she here? Is Sitka here?"

"On her way home." I grab a carrot and guillotine it, scooping up the pieces and pitching them into the stainless steel salad bowl, the largest chunk pinging against the edge and falling onto the floor. I let it lie there. "So, what are you now? Some kind of born-again Christian?"

Jenny rolls her eyes upward. "It's been five years since you've seen me, Dad. There's nothing sudden about my sobriety or my beliefs." She pauses, her lips curling up into a smile. "I've accepted Jesus as my personal savior. He's the reason I've finally made it to real recovery. It's been a long road for me to come to where I am. It's God who's gotten me here and I praise Him."

She opens her mouth into a wider smile. Her teeth are caramel-colored, the edges a bit ragged. Some effects of meth use never wear off.

"That all the baggage you have with you?" I point to her duffel. "You didn't say how long you were planning to stay."

Jenny folds her right arm, thrusting her hand under her left armpit. "Right, Dad. Pay no attention to what's important to me. That's what you've always been good at. I've got another pair of suitcases in the living room."

I rip the cellophane off the head of iceberg lettuce. "I've converted that little office space into a bedroom for you. But you're right. I haven't seen you in ages and here you come out of the blue, showing up on our doorstep and singing the praises of the

Lord. Given your past history, you'll forgive me if I'm a little bit suspicious." Now is not a good time to mention Diesel.

Tears well up in Jenny's eyes. This time they look real enough. "Why all of these questions? Why won't you just give me a chance?"

"All right," I say. "I'm sorry. Sit down. You must be tired, coming all the way from . . . Where did you come from?"

Jenny wipes at her eyes, pulls out one of the kitchen chairs, turns it around, and straddles it. "This last month in Kalispell. I was thinking of going back to school, but the Lord told me that I had to see Sitka instead. I've mainly been in Billings the last six months. Casper before that."

I leave the lettuce on the counter, scoot out a chair, and sit across from my prodigal daughter. Neither of us seems to know what to say. Undertones of gray discolor the skin around her ears and cheeks, and across her forehead. There are crusted patches bordered by inflamed stretches of pink and red. It's as though her face was a salt marsh invaded by red kelp.

"So, did you like Montana?"

"It's where I met Big Bob." She's smiling, as if she were telling me about a wonderful vacation spot where she saw her favorite movie star.

"Big Bob?"

"Pastor Barley. He's the one who brought me to the Lord. Everyone calls him Big Bob."

"They call the Lord Big Bob?" I'm trying a little humor here to keep things light, but Jenny scowls.

"Do not make fun of my faith, Dad. I wouldn't be here without it. I started praying in prison, because I wanted to heal my body, but my soul was healed in Montana."

"Sorry. No offense." I put up my hands, as if I had no intention of casting aspersions on her beliefs. "You met this Big Bob character and found Jesus."

"Then I knew I had to come back home," Jenny says.

I lean forward, studying the lines around her eyes. "Just why are you here, anyway?"

"Forgiveness." She runs a finger over the surface of the Formica table. Her fingers are thin, the ridges deep. The knuckles of her right hand are ringed with red welts. "I want to make it right with Sitka."

"Don't expect her to come around right away. You're going to have to work at getting her trust back."

"Is she excited at least?" she asks, her voice suddenly softer. "I mean about me coming home." Jenny looks eager, like a Malamute sniffing at the edges of the campfire.

"I'm not sure I'd say excited. Maybe. Also a little apprehensive. You can't expect to be out of her life for so many years and have her run into your arms the moment she sees you."

Jenny presses the tips of her fingers against the tabletop. "I'm trying my best with you, Dad. Big Bob said it's really important that I do so, but I'm not sure, in my heart of hearts, that I'm ready to forgive you."

"You forgive me?" I get up. My left hip is sore and unyielding in sideways movement—it's not hard to overdo it on the boat these days—and I stagger and knock my chair over. "You've got to be kidding me. Jesus H. Christ!"

Jenny narrows her eyes. "Do not take the Lord's name in vain!"

I pick up the chair and bring it down into place harder than I intend to. "This is my house, goddammit. And in my house and on my boat, I make the rules. And if I want to swear, that's my business. You don't like it, go check in at the Thunderbird Hotel."

"Is this the environment you've been raising my daughter in?" Jenny picks up my ceramic Tibetan Buddha from the end of the kitchen table. I moved a few of the gods and goddesses there so I could wipe down part of the countertop. "A house full of idols and blasphemy?"

"Put that down!"

The voice startles both me and Jenny. Sitka stomps in from the living room through the kitchen door, dropping her backpack near where her mother's duffel rests. She runs over and snatches the Buddha from Jenny's hands, clutching it to her chest. "This is ours! You leave Grandpa Ray alone! You leave us alone!" Her coat is half-on, half-off her shoulders. Her bangs are flying out in all directions. Her face and ears are red. "No one asked you to come here!"

Jenny bends down toward her, as if Sitka were no taller than a toddler. "Sitka, sweetie. Let me look at you, Marmot. Your eyes are just as blue as ever." She steps back. "But you're so big. I didn't think you'd be so tall. Almost a young lady."

Sitka wrinkles her forehead. She takes a step back, away from her mom, and folds her arms. "My eyes are hazel. Sometimes they look green, sometimes they look blue. But they're hazel."

Jenny bends down and opens the zipper on her duffel. "Here, I brought some gifts for you." She pulls out a magazine with a blond-haired, blue-eyed family on the front cover. *Today's Young Christian.* She holds it out to Sitka, who tightens her hold on the Buddha. Jenny lays the magazine on the kitchen table.

"Well, maybe you're not ready for that just yet, but here's something all of the girls at my church loved, so I hope you'll like it too."

She lifts out something wrapped in dark yellow tissue paper, maybe a foot and a half tall. Sitka hesitates. Finally she settles the Buddha onto a kitchen chair and accepts the package. As Sitka peels away some of the scotch tape, Jenny straightens up.

"You're all I've thought about, Sitka. Night and day I've prayed about you. You're all that matters to me now."

Sitka removes the tissue a bit at a time, revealing a doll with light brown hair curled in ringlets, like Shirley Temple as a little kid. The doll looks like she's just stepped off a Civil War era plantation. Big white ribbons in her hair. A frock with a pale yellow bodice trimmed with lace and some kind of fancy purple embroidery. Then it has these white ruffle things sticking out from the bottom. Petticoats, maybe? And a pair of white patent leather shoes. Donna used to call them Mary Janes. Believe me, no one around here wears Mary Janes.

"Her name is Elsie Dinsmore," Jenny announces, as if we were all sitting down to tea together. "She's a Life of Faith doll. There's a whole book about her, written by a wonderful Christian woman. Oh, and she has several friends. There's Kathleen McKenzie and Millie Keith, and Violet. I don't remember Violet's last name just now. Oh, and Laylie Colbert. Can't forget Laylie Colbert."

Jenny grins, as if we were all talking about the antics that crazy Laylie pulled on us just yesterday. Sitka rotates the doll around in her hands. A black ribbon with roses is tied into a big bow in the back. The bow is so large it covers the doll from her neck to her ankles. You'd think Elsie would fall over from it. Maybe as a counterweight, she clutches a Bible with a black cover and gold-leafed pages between her right arm and waist. Sitka turns the doll once more, looking at Elsie's blue eyes, long eyelashes and syrupy smile. The doll radiates so much southern belle sweetness and charm, you'd think the inside of her was filled with warm pecan pie.

Sitka, with the pre-teen look of disgust she has mastered, throws the delightful doll to the linoleum floor. Perhaps in order to break her fall, Elsie lands on her miniature Bible, bending the pages.

"This is stupid. What do you think I am? A baby?"

Jenny gathers up the doll lovingly. "Look, Sitka." She bends the doll's arms and legs. "See? You can move all of her parts." Jenny forces Elsie's palms together. "You can even have her pray to our Lord if you want."

"That is the lamest thing I've ever seen," Sitka says. "You think I want some idiotic doll? You're so pathetic. You can take your stupid doll and go to hell!"

"Hey, language in the house," I say, but Sitka is already disappearing through the living room, up the stairs, and into her room, the door slamming behind her.

"Stay here," I tell Jenny.

I pick up Sitka's backpack, go upstairs, and knock.

"Go away. Can't you read the sign on the door? Go away."

"We have to talk about this, Sitka."

"No we don't!"

"Open the door, young lady. I have your backpack. You'll need it for your homework."

The door cracks a bit and Sitka's left hand sticks out. "Give it here."

I hand the backpack to her, holding onto the straps for an extra second. "You can't stay in there forever, sweetie."

"Please, Ray," her voice soft and muffled, like cotton. "Let me be by myself for a bit. Then I'll come out."

"Dinner in an hour. I want you out here by then."

"Fine," she says, like she's accepting a life sentence. "Only don't expect me to say anything to you-know-who."

"Honey?" Jenny's voice is suddenly right behind my ear and Sitka wastes no time slamming the door shut.

"Way to go," I tell Jenny. And to Sitka's door, "This doesn't change things, young lady. You're out here in one hour, with an appetite."

Jenny follows me downstairs into the living room, flopping herself onto the couch the way she used to when she was a teenager. "She hates me. My own daughter hates me."

I should probably say something about how she doesn't, or how she'll come around. It'll just take a little time, something along those lines. "What did you expect?"

Jenny swipes at her tears. "I feel like such an idiot. I should have known she wouldn't like a doll. But I didn't know what else to get her, what kinds of things she likes. I wanted to give her something nice."

I sit down in the chair across from her. "Look, don't bust a gasket over that doll. Sitka's eleven years old. I can't figure her out half the time. Why don't you go ahead and unpack? I'll call you when dinner's ready. Don't worry. You'll have your chance with her."

It's the best bone I can offer, and Jenny seems to take it. She sniffs up the last of her tears, then looks around at the walls and corners, as if assessing a construction site. "I'm going to have to find a good Christian community around here. I see I'm going to need help outside of this house."

She lifts herself off the couch, picks up her two suitcases, grabs the duffel from the kitchen, and clomps up the stairs. At least she doesn't bang her door closed.

While Sitka stews, and Jenny unpacks and prays, and the potatoes bake in the oven, I go out to the porch and slap a cigarette out of the pack. It's only four thirty, but the twilight darkness has already swept over the ocean and landscape. It's cold as a baby berg's butt, the wind rushing down from Bear Tooth Ridge and whipping around the south end of the house. The alder pine tree next to the garage bends and moans, dropping its brown cones, an offering perhaps to Boreas. I put the cigarette in my mouth, light a match, and cup my hand around the flame. It takes three tries to get it lit.

It's a mess, between me and Jenny, between Jenny and Sitka. Even I can see that. I have some satisfaction that Sitka took my side, that she was loyal to me. Yet Jenny is my daughter. Shouldn't I be loyal to her? And help her reconcile with Sitka? Has she really turned a corner? She seems different. Maybe this born-again stuff is going to work for her. Or maybe not. I've been down this road before too many times. How long before she's back down by the pier, looking to score?

I look up to the sky, looking for some stellar signs of how to fix things. I search above the trees for Orion, to see which way the night archer might be pointing. I crush out the cigarette. May as well go back inside. It's a night without stars.

Chapter 10

OVER THE NEXT FEW days the three of us settle into an un-spoken truce of sorts. I wish I could say that this was because of some great game plan I put into play, but the truth is I'm like a tanner crab yanked out of the ocean, clacking my claws around the underside rim of a pot. I don't have much idea where I'm headed and the space around me suddenly seems a lot more crowded. Jenny and I are quietly polite to each other. I try not to mention her drug use and she leaves my idols alone. Sitka spends a lot of time in her room or on the phone with her friends. But gradually, her open hostility has dissipated, until now it's hard to distinguish between the antagonism she has for her mother and her usual, pre-teen moodiness.

Elsie Dinsmore, the southern Christian doll, spends her time on the kitchen windowsill, huddled between a four-inch potted spider plant and a replacement of the Ganesh statue that Sitka broke. I placed Elsie there, not knowing what else to do with her. Sitka refused to have the doll in her room, saying it would give her creepy nightmares. Because of her damaged Bible, Elsie tilts into Ganesh's right ear, and you can't quite tell if she and the elephant god are jockeying for position or are secret lovers.

Sunday morning I wake up to the smell of freshly brewed coffee. I got damn little sleep last night. I kept dreaming that my wife was still alive and that she was downstairs talking with Jenny. I couldn't understand the words, like they were speaking Lithuanian or something. They were drinking bergamot tea and Donna reached out and patted Jenny on the forearm. I could only see Donna from the back. Jenny looked like she did when she was in high school, her hair lighter, her face clear of lines, her skin fresh instead of like waxy fruit. It was one of those dreams where you wake up and then when you fall back to sleep, the same scenes continue and you think, no, this is really happening after all, and the idea that I was dreaming is wrong. Then you wake up again, so that throughout the night you're continually confused as to what's real and what's not. If that wasn't enough, I kept getting a charley horse in my right leg, and it felt like someone had attached a pair of vise grips to my calf muscle and clamped down.

The aroma of bacon frying finally gets me out of bed, although at first I thought that must have been a dream as well, because Sitka doesn't usually fix her own breakfast unless it's a bowl of cereal or a granola bar. Besides, she spent the night at Sarah's, and won't be home until the afternoon. I half-expect to see Felix in the kitchen, because sometimes he'll come over and meet me to go down to the boat. But it's Jenny standing at the stovetop, moving slabs of bacon around in the frying pan. She's wearing a jean skirt and a turtleneck top and her hair is half-pulled back, exactly the way Donna used to wear hers.

"You're up early." Jenny had never been a morning person. It used to take Donna three or four attempts at cajoling, bribing, and threatening before Jenny would emerge from under her blankets, usually with a look of disdain that someone had dared to declare it morning. Sitka's like that, too.

Jenny lifts the bacon out of the skillet and sets the pieces on some paper towels, the dark yellow grease spreading to the edges. "I thought I'd make you breakfast."

"You don't have to do that."

She cracks a few eggs in one of the mixing bowls, adding some milk and dried herbs. "I'm not going to sit around and do nothing. I need to be useful."

"Glad to hear it." I walk over to the counter and pour myself a cup of coffee. "That part of your recovery program?"

As Jenny whips the eggs, a mound of bubbles builds into a frothy volcano. "Big Bob says we have to earn our way in this world if we are to get right with the Lord." She takes down two plates from the door-less cupboard and sets them on the table. "I didn't know where the napkins were."

"We just use paper towels, unless it's Thanksgiving."

"But Mom always . . ." Jenny starts. I feel myself stiffen and she must feel it as well, because she rips off a few paper towel sections and places them on the table with two sets of forks, knives, and spoons.

While she finishes cooking, I scoot out a chair and sit down. In a minute, Jenny sets down a plate of eggs, bacon, and toast in front of me. As I pick up a fork and hack off a small bit of bacon, Jenny stands behind me.

"Lord, we thank you for yet another day. Let us make it a day for your glory. We thank you for this bountiful food. Amen."

I don't repeat the amen, but I take that bit of bacon and place it into a small dish that's sitting in the middle of the table.

Jenny wipes her hand on a dish towel. "Something wrong with it?"

"Nope. I just make it a habit to put a token amount of my morning meal aside as a thank you to the powers that be. It's a Buddhist tradition."

My born-again daughter slaps the dish towel so hard against the table that some of my papers slide off. "You're doing this to get under my skin, aren't you, Dad? You're deliberately making fun of my religion."

"This is something I've been doing for years. It has nothing to do with you. I let you say grace without taking offense, didn't I?"

She shakes her head back and forth, then retreats to the stove to serve herself. I take a bite of the scrambled eggs. They're light and fluffy, just wet enough, and whatever herbs she's put in—oregano? thyme?—give it an added kick. The bacon is cooked perfectly as well, crisp but still pliable.

"This is pretty good," I tell her.

She sits down across from me at the table, laying a pack of Camels and a lighter beside her plate. "Glad you like them."

"No, seriously, these are good," I insist. "Where'd you learn to cook?"

Jenny nibbles on a piece of bacon, her eyes focused on the kitchen clock on the wall in front of her. "The basics when I was housed up in Anchorage. They assigned me to the kitchen. Then when I was in recovery, the church program arranged for me to take some real classes."

"So you worked in the prison kitchen. That sounds like it wasn't so bad."

She shakes her head. "Unbelievable. Yeah, Dad. It was a real picnic. Lucky me."

I don't understand what the big deal is. I'm just trying to make conversation, to encourage her. "It's good you've learned a trade, that you got something out of your time there. Doesn't that fit with your faith? Doesn't it mean that God put you there?"

"You want to see what I got out of working in the prison kitchen?" She rolls up her right sleeve. A ragged ridge of pink skin rages from her biceps down across her forearm. Jenny rolls down her sleeve. "I've got others on my left leg, if you're interested. But I almost bled to death from this one. A little disagreement over who was going to scrub the big pots."

My mouth goes dry with a sour, metallic taste. "Oh, Jenny."

"Don't talk to me about what God has intended for me. You don't know the first thing about what my life's been like over the last ten years."

She's right about that. I visited Jenny a grand total of four times when she was in prison the first time, and not at all during her second stint. I wrote her every few months, but she didn't answer. Maybe I should have gone more often, but it's hard to sit and look at your child through scratched Plexiglas while she's wearing an orange DOC jumpsuit. To talk to her through a monitored phone, with her not wanting to look you in the eye. Jenny was mostly silent anyway. I hated having to get on that ratty bus with the plastic, cigarette-burned seats, crowded in with all of the other visitors. And I hated standing in line at the prison, hated being scanned and poked and prodded, like I was the criminal. And the waiting room stank of God knows what. Besides, I had the baby to take care of, and Donna was gone, Donna who would have known what to say to our daughter during a prison visit, and it was a whole day and almost the night to go up there and back, and I had to be out on the water, making a living, and paying the bills, so I could take care of Sitka.

"I'm sorry as hell you had to go through that. But it's not like your mother or I ever wanted you to end up in prison. We gave you a good home. No one abused you."

Jenny moves the tines of her fork around her plate in concentric circles, pushing bits of eggs and bacon to the edges. She lifts the fork up and makes little stabbing gestures at the linoleum floor. "I see everything is still off kilter here. I had to tilt the pan to keep the eggs from pooling at one end."

The kitchen floor slopes toward the living room. It's been that way since we bought the house twenty-six years ago, when Jenny was two, only it's a little worse now. "It's a big job to put in a new foundation. I'll get around to it one of these days." I tear off a piece of toast, scoop a forkful of eggs against it, and pop them into my mouth.

"That's what you always told Mom." Jenny scans the linoleum. "I remember taking my marbles and setting them down in the corner and watching them roll all the way across from the refrigerator to the doorway."

I wash the eggs and toast down with more coffee. "Sitka used to do that, too."

Jenny turns back to me. "Really? She did that?"

Her voice is high and almost giggly. She seems desperate

to make some connection, to show that they have some special bond. But I'm determined not to let her swoop in and steal mine. I let her question fall to the uneven floor and roll away. The sliding glass doors that lead to the backyard are streaked with water droplets. The morning air is heavy, like vapor spat out from a generator with a bad valve. Everything is murky. You can tell the whole damn day's going to be like this.

"Don't you have church or something?"

Jenny looks up at the clock. "I've got about twenty minutes yet." She takes the pack of Camels and pinches out a cigarette. "There's a photo of you and Sitka on the boat out in the living room. You're standing in front of a hundred-pound halibut."

"Felix took it last summer. We caught it up near Mitkof Island."

"She goes out with you, then? She works on the boat?"

"Over summer, when she's not in school, or until the weather turns. She helps bait and empty and clean the shrimp pots. Nothing dangerous. No crabbing."

"It's always dangerous, that's what Mom used to tell me." Jenny fishes a pack of matches from her skirt pocket and lights up. As she exhales, she looks at me like I'm a picture to be studied. "I always wanted you to take me out with you. I wanted to catch kings with you."

"I wanted to take you, but your mom wouldn't let me. Said I'd be putting your life at risk."

"But you think it's okay for Sitka." She takes a saucer and flicks her ashes over it. I don't object.

"Your mom was a bit over-worrisome. Sitka knows her way around. She's smart and she's careful. She's fine."

Jenny exhales the cigarette smoke. "Yeah, Dad. She's fine."

"What the hell is this all about?"

Outside a gray squirrel bounds to the edge of a lower limb of the pine tree, then recoils to a loose board on the fence, sending a reverberating thud across the backyard.

"Nothing," Jenny says to her plate. "Forget it." Her eyes flit over to Elsie Dinsmore, then to me. "I don't want to fight with you all the time. I want to be of help around here. I can do the laundry and fix dinner if you want."

"You don't have to," and then I see her mouth turn down. "That would be great. Thanks."

She fetches a slip of paper out from the pocket of her jean skirt. "I've already made up a menu and a grocery list. For the whole week. "

I scan what she's written: eggs, cheddar cheese, pastry flour, cabbage, carrots, onions, stewed tomatoes, potatoes, celery seed, garlic, ground beef, a whole chicken, turkey cutlets, canned artichoke hearts, ground beef, sourdough bread, butter, and on it goes to the other side of the paper.

I place the paper on the table and slide it toward her. "Quite a list."

"Proper ingredients make a proper meal," she quotes from God knows where. "I can go by the market after church." She opens her palm above her plate. "A hundred and fifty dollars should do it."

Seeing my mouth open, Jenny quickly responds. "Don't give me that look. It's not like you're poor. You own this house. You make money from the crabbing."

"Uh-huh. Regular life of Riley I got going here. Hundred dollar bills just spilling out of the drawers. But if you think I'm going to give you that much cash, you're pissing off the wrong side of the boat."

Jenny grimaces. "So vulgar, Dad."

"No, Jenny." I give her a cool, even look. "Taking my money to go out and buy drugs is vulgar."

She lowers her head, and when she raises it, her cheeks are wet with tears. "I don't know how you can say that, Dad. I don't know how you can undermine me like that."

"Excuse me—"

"No," she demands, her voice quivering now. "There is no excuse for a father like you. No wonder Sitka doesn't trust me. If you cared about her at all, you'd try to help me be her mom and not tear me down all the time. I've worked so hard these past three years, and I haven't asked you for anything, and all I want to do is to be of service, but you can't believe that can you? How about having a little trust in me, huh?"

I scan the kitchen walls and cabinets, as if the faith Jenny is asking for is hidden behind the dish soap or the saltine crackers. Maybe it's a packaged toy inside the box of Cocoa Puffs.

"Let's take it a step at a time." I take out my checkbook and write the check, payable to the Moose Market. Of course Jenny could buy one item and, since they know me and know that Jenny's back, they'd go ahead and cash the check and give her the change. But I decide the risk is small enough. Besides, if she's going to screw up or rip me off, better to know right off the bat. I tear out the check and hand it to her.

When she sees how I've made it out, her mouth tightens. But it doesn't stop her from thrusting it into her purse. She pushes back her chair, stands, and grabs her coat and Bible. I expect another insult or plea to heaven to come flying back at me, but all I hear is the door slamming shut. In the wooden echo, I can hear Donna telling me to be patient with Jenny. That she'll straighten herself out. Come back to us.

I clear the dishes from the table. The plates, forks, and knives clatter in the sink. I run water and dish soap, swirling my hand in the hot water. My fingers turn pink as salmon parrs. As the water suds up, I see Ganesh. He seems to be grinning at the porcelain face of Elsie Dinsmore, and I could swear she's laughing, as if the two of them have been playing an awfully funny joke on someone.

Chapter 11

ON WEDNESDAY EVENING I drive over to Nicole's apartment. I had planned to take her to see some George Clooney movie, but the projector at the island's only movie house broke down the other day and they have to wait for parts to be sent down from Anchorage. So we decided to have dinner at her place.

It's not a great night to be out. Bands of rain cascade down, as if a sky goddess and her daughters were rehearsing a ribbon dance. The downpour streams across my windshield. Even with the wipers and defroster turned on high, I have to crack open the window and swipe away the fog that builds up on the inside. It's a noisy shower, a mid-October tinnitus, slapping and bouncing off the roofs, streets, and sidewalks. It will turn winter cold in another week or so, and the driving rain will fly down like tiny ice picks, silver-tipped, prickling eyebrows and hands.

Nicole's apartment is a few blocks from the hospital, just up Fireweed Hill. This morning Jenny was excited to have a night alone with Sitka, saying that they could paint their nails and have some girl talk time. By the time I left, they were arguing whether or not Sitka could watch a DVD about teenage mermaids and vampires in Baja, Mexico. It was something Sitka and I had picked up earlier. As I left, Jenny was shouting about what kind of parent would let a child watch a movie that glorified the undead.

I park my pickup in front of Nicole's apartment. I turn off the engine and sit in the cab, letting the windows fog up, obscuring my vision. This whole situation with Jenny is crazy-making. And here I am escaping all that, on my second real date in years. I jerk on the door handle and get out, rain soaking my jacket in seconds. I jog up a short flight of cement steps and punch the call button. It makes a quick zzpp-zzpp sound, like a mosquito hitting a bug zapper. Nicole buzzes me in.

The apartment is warm, much warmer than my house, probably thanks to the fancy fireplace with tempered glass on three sides, so you can see the fire from anywhere in the living room. Nicole is barefoot, which I find strangely erotic on such a cold, rainy night. I hand her a cellophane-wrapped bunch of oxeye daisies that I picked up at the Moose Market.

"Thank you. They're lovely." As she sniffs the bouquet, the cellophane crinkles and one of the stems swoons over just where the blossom starts. She sets them down on the hallway table.

She's wearing jeans and a sage-green hooded pullover. I catch her scent, not perfume or body lotion or fruity shampoo, but the natural smell of her skin. It's almost palpable, a tingling I feel along my neck and arms. Welcoming and sensual. I'm tempted to sniff my sleeve to see if I reek of crab.

"I'm really glad you're here," she says.

"Me, too."

I lean in to give her a small kiss somewhere in the vicinity of her mouth, just as she inclines her face as well, and I wind up pressing my lips against the corner of her mouth and half of her left cheek. I'm off my game, like trying to run a split line through a small chock when you've been hauling crabs for fifteen hours straight. Still, when I press my hand against the small of her back, she bends just a little, and it feels natural and right. And those lips, those lips the color of salmonberries in late August.

"You look a little worn." She holds out her hands to take my wet jacket. "Putting in long hours out on the boat?"

"Not as much as I would like. Fish and Game has been tightening up the catch allowance. They've cut us back to three days a week. We're hoping the numbers pick up later in the winter."

"You crab in the winter?"

"January is usually the height of the season."

"Terrific. Remind me not to sign on as a crew member."

My laugh is loud and choppy. My palms itch and I twitch my fingers against my jeans. Nicole hangs up my jacket on a coat rack, next to her navy blue parka. I slip off my boots before stepping on the beige carpet and following her into the living room.

"Make yourself at home." Nicole points to a green sofa as she picks up the daisies and heads into the kitchen. "I'll take care of these."

The sofa looks new, so I check the backside of my jeans as best I can before squelching the firm cushions. The apartment is at the southwest corner of her building, so it takes full advantage of the little daylight there is in October. It still has that new apartment scent; it hasn't had time yet to absorb that permanent wet smell of southeast Alaska. The wood floors and carpets in my house are saturated with the mixed odor of damp cedar and sea kelp.

The apartment walls are painted a pale yellow. I read somewhere that it's supposed to have a calming effect, but I can see Nicole's partial silhouette in the kitchen, and I feel anything but calm. There's not much in the way of paintings or art, just a couple of framed black and white photographs, one of Mt. McKinley, the other one of Glacier Bay. No family pictures. Behind the couch there's a music stand and a clarinet leaning against its own metal stand.

"Would you like something to drink?" Nicole brings in a tray of fruit, cheese and crackers, and two water glasses, and sets it on the coffee table.

"An Alaskan Amber would hit the spot."

She scrunches up her face, closing one eye. "That's a beer,

right?" She turns and looks back to the kitchen, then back at me. "I've got some O'Doul's."

"Non-alcoholic beer? What's the point?" When she winces, I say, "But, hey, whatever you got is fine. No big deal."

She taps her finger against her cheek. "Wine?"

"Sure."

Nicole heads back into the kitchen. I hear her open the refrigerator door and then the ting of glass jars and bottles knocking against each other. She returns with two opened bottles, the white wine and some kind of fizzy water. She sets the water on an open area of the tray.

"I have no idea if this is any good," she tells me, tilting the label of the wine bottle toward me, as if I were any kind of expert. "It's a Chardonnay from British Columbia. My neighbor across the hall brought it over when I moved in." She pours the wine into one of the water glasses and hands it to me. "He's in his seventies and I think he was trying to flirt with me."

"That's how it is with the virile men of the North," I joke. "There's so many more of us than women up here that if your neighbor came back again right now, the two of us would have to butt heads for you like bull elk."

Nicole sits at the edge of an overstuffed chair across from me. "And once you've knocked your rival senseless, then what?"

She raises her eyebrows in expectation, but nothing witty comes to my mind. My dating compass isn't providing me any kind of accurate reading. I take a long drink of the wine, which tastes all right, and then point to the musical instrument behind the sofa. "You play the clarinet?"

Nicole tilts her head. "The oboe, you mean. Just for fun. I should switch to a different instrument, though."

"Why's that?"

She takes a drink of her water before answering. "The oboe takes a lot out of you. It's a real demand on your lungs. Professional oboe players take years off their lives."

"Like smoking."

Nicole considers this for a moment. "Like a lot of things."

I'm not sure how to respond to this, whether she's making some philosophical statement or talking about something personal. I play it safe by staring at the black and silver instrument and sipping on the wine.

"How about you?" Nicole asks. "You play anything?"

"Nah. I'm completely non-musical. My wife played the piano. She had long fingers like yours. They could stretch really far." I hold up my hands and spread my fingers that are thick as bratwurst. "These guys are made for ordinary stuff, like hammering or digging up potatoes."

"I don't know," she says, picking up a slice of apple from the tray. "I think people make too big a distinction between what's art and what's ordinary."

"Well, if hauling crab is art, I'm a regular Pablo Picasso."

"How about Sitka? Did she inherit any musical talent from your wife or your daughter?"

A home video flashes in my head: Jenny sitting next to Donna on the piano bench, playing together, singing Joni Mitchell songs. "Big Yellow Taxi." "The Circle Game." "Both Sides Now." But the video is grainy, all the color washed out. The sound is muted and full of gaps.

"Sitka fools around on the guitar a little." I look past Nicole, to shadows of flames wavering on the wall behind her. "I haven't heard her mother play anything in a very long time."

She reaches over and places her hand on my forearm. "I hit a sore spot again, didn't I?"

My long exhale disturbs the air. I don't want thoughts of Jenny to ruin this evening. The wood in the fireplace crackles. Nicole slides out of her chair and sits next to me on the couch.

"I'm not trying to pry, Ray. How about we change the conversation back to the virile men of Alaska?" She slides her arm over my shoulders and puts her face so close to mine I can almost feel the brush of her eyelashes. "Because I don't think you're going to have to do any head butting around here tonight."

"That's good." I comb my fingers through the hair above her left ear, lightly massaging her temple. "Though just to be clear, I could have taken down that seventy-year-old neighbor of yours."

"No doubt," she answers, leaning her forehead against mine.

I close my eyes and draw in the scent of her. Slipping my arm around her waist, I pull her closer. She kisses me with those marvelous salmonberry lips. I don't know if it's art or not, but I lift up her hoodie with my rough fingers. It takes two attempts to unfasten her bra and she slides it off. I run my fingertips over her breasts, hoping my rough hands aren't scratching her. She responds with a sigh and opens my mouth further with the tip of her tongue. She tugs on my sweater and helps me lift it up and over my head. Before it's all the way off she stands up and pulls me down the hall, and by the time we reach her bedroom, the rest of our clothes are spilled in random piles on the hallway carpet.

The bedroom walls are a rich honey gold with red trim. Not calming at all, and for that I'm grateful. The furniture is modern, the lines clean and simple. Nicole turns on the iPod slotted in a speaker base on the night table. She lifts the paisley coverlet from the bed and slides under it. She holds it up, pulls on my hand, tucking me in with her. She kisses my neck, nips a bit at the base of my left ear. The cool white sheets begin to warm.

Music tumbles out of the speakers: Django Reinhardt, Alicia Keys, Diana Krall, a playlist of heat and romance. I silently chant the name Backlum-Chaam, the Mayan god of male horniness, to stop my thoughts from spinning out of control. Nicole strokes me on the arm. My fingers trace the outline of her spine. It curves ever so slightly to the left and then back to center. I've almost forgotten how a woman's skin can feel, how it can be its own island of smoothness.

Her scent is richer now, musky and damp. I move my hand to her inner thigh, exploring the path between the inner crease and her knee, back and forth. I lean in and lightly kiss the underside of her chin, her neck, the top of her left shoulder. It's only when I look at her face again and see her smiling that I explore the black ringlets of hair between her thighs. She turns on her right side and lifts her left leg into the air in a way that makes me think of her in a yoga class, and then my breath quickens and I am not thinking, there's no need to think, there's no need to chant Backlum-Chaam. With more skill on her part than mine, we make love looking at each other until she arches her back and neck. I think that I could kiss the underside of that neck for a very long time.

She falls asleep, and I relax into her gentle, feminine breathing against my shoulder. I close my eyes, my mind a ship of balsam wood adrift on a gentle stream. We nap for over an hour. Or I do at least. I wake up to the stir of pots and pans, the smell of roasted chicken and buttery potatoes. I retrace my path back through the hallway, putting on my clothes in the haphazard manner in which I find them.

When I go into the kitchen, Nicole is turning the handle of a salad spinner, drying the wet lettuce leaves. I can still taste her kisses, the edge of summer in a perfectly ripe pear. She's put her jeans and top back on, as well as a pair of simple, slip-on shoes. I step up behind her and wrap my arms around her. She presses her buttocks against me, letting out a small laugh. She points to the faucet. I wash my hands, pour myself another glass of wine, and finish making a salad of the lettuce, carrots, and green onions. In the fridge I find a bottle of diet Italian dressing and another of blue cheese. I go with the blue cheese. Nicole dishes up the chicken and potatoes on a large white platter. We move to the dining room table that's already been set. Simple white plates, wine-red napkins, flatware with slender handles, tall water glasses. Two thick vanilla-colored candles are in the center, a box of matches in front of them. Nicole asks me to light them.

We sit down and for the first time in a while, no one thanks Jesus for the food. In deference, I forego any tidbit sacrifice to Buddha. A few bites into the meal, I stop and sip some wine. "This is really delicious. I love how you got the flavor of the chicken into the roasted potatoes."

Nicole smiles. "And you, sir, make a mean salad."

"That's about the extent of my culinary skills. My daughter Jenny, though, is a really fine cook. She learned how when she was in . . ."

Damn it. I wanted to keep the conversation light and easy, having arrived at this exact moment, a delicate opening of what could be a long-term relationship. I don't want to screw this up. But my thoughts keep spinning back to Jenny. They're like a net I keep getting caught up in, no matter which way I try to swim. Has she really gone straight, or is she just playing me? Is she going to turn her back on Sitka again, trading her family for some meth?

Cold liquid runs off the table and onto my lap. I've tipped over my wine glass. "Damn."

Nicole rises from her chair. "Let me get a towel."

"No, I've got it." I stand up and dab my pants with the napkin. At least it's Chardonnay. "Can't take me anywhere." I pick up the now-empty glass, relieved that I didn't actually break it. "Be right back."

In the kitchen I set the wine glass on the countertop and turn on the faucet, placing my hands under the warm stream of water. I squirt some purple liquid from a plastic dispenser. Little eddies form in the stainless steel sink.

Nicole comes in and stands next to me, her back against the counter. "Everything okay, Ray? Food's getting cold."

I shut off the faucet and rinse my hands and dry them on a dishtowel. "I don't know if it's something I can even talk with you about."

"You mentioned your daughter. Sitka's mom?" Nicole folds her hands, both index fingers pointing up to just below her lower lip. I bet that's her professional pose. Encouraging, but a bit guarded.

"Yeah." My fingers smell like lavender instead of roast chicken. "Jenny is back in town and, if you haven't heard the island scuttlebutt yet, my daughter is a drug addict. Has been since she was a teenager. Well, supposedly she's not anymore.

But who the hell can tell for sure? That's where all this gets messy. On one hand I want Sitka to get to know her mom, but I'm worried to death that Jenny will go back to her old ways. Maybe you could give me some guidance. Or even talk to her."

"There are rules about this, Ray." She drops her hands and pushes herself away from the counter. "We just slept together. I can't be your family counselor and your lover."

My stomach tightens and my mouth goes dry. "I know. I'm sorry. I know I'm completely out of bounds here, but I'm so worried about Sitka, what this is going to do to her. Can we talk about it just for a minute, then I promise not to bring it up again?"

"Here's the deal. I'm the only certified drug counselor on Yatki. I can point you to some resources in Juneau. But if you want me to counsel you or your daughter, even informally, then I have to keep boundaries." She jabs her hands into the pockets of her jeans. "Girlfriend or counselor. I can do either, but I was hoping that we would stick to the romantic route."

I don't want this to be the end of our evening. Of what we've started. "Me too," I tell her. "I'd like us to be a couple. I would want that. But do you have any idea what it's like to live with a drug addict? I know you're a counselor and all, but have you actually had to deal with this craziness personally?"

Nicole scuffs the toe of her shoe against the linoleum. "Yes, I have had to deal with someone who's an addict."

"Then you get how—"

"Ray, that someone was me. I was the addict. I am the addict."

I feel like a jib swung around and smacked me on the side of the head. "A meth addict?"

"An addict, yes. Not meth. Prescription drugs. Mainly pain meds. Vicodin, oxycodone, hydromorphone." She counts them out on her fingers like they were merit badges. "Percodan. Others."

I'm stunned. I don't know what to say. I look past Nicole into the dining room, pretending to study the trembling candlelight. The whole apartment smells like the meal that's going cold out there, half-eaten chicken and potatoes, now clammy on the white plates, the salad lifeless.

"I haven't taken a drug or a drink in six years. Before that, my parents, my family, and my friends had to go through hell. So, yeah, I've been through the tornado."

"You mean you created the tornado." I should have known when she offered me an O'Doul's.

Nicole meets my eyes and nods. "Yes, I stole money from my parents and I lied to my friends. I whipped up my own little path of destruction. And I've been cleaning it up ever since, getting my life back in order. It's part of what makes me a good counselor. I've been there."

I rub the heel of my hand in small circles over my forehead. "Jesus H. Christ."

"Yeah, Ray, Jesus H. Christ, Allah, and Buddha, and any of those other gods."

"I don't get it. How did you even get involved with that stuff?"

"You remember those teenagers I told you about? How these kids kept coming in for gunshot wounds?"

"When you were working in Seattle."

She sticks her hands in her pockets, takes a long breath. "One night I was trying to put some EKG leads on one, so we could monitor his heart. He was a big kid, but only fourteen years old, in a lot of pain. He didn't like the idea of anyone touching him. Screaming something fierce. I should have waited for help, but we were backed up. As I was bending over his chest he swung around and punched me in the face. Broke my left cheek bone. As I tried to reel away he kicked me in the stomach, sending me crashing into the wall railing. Separated my elbow and bruised a disc in my lower back."

"Oh my God, that's awful." I take a step toward her, wanting to comfort her, but she shakes her head no.

"Just let me get through this," she says. "I had two surgeries and was laid up in the medical unit for two weeks. In rehab for three months, mainly for my back and elbow. They put me on

OxyContin. It was the only thing that seemed to get me through the day. It was worse when I went back to work. I'd take the OxyContin when I got up and follow it up with a Vicodin chaser by my first coffee break."

"And your doctor kept giving you them?"

"My doctor? No. In spite of the precautions and regulations, I knew how to find extra sample pills at the hospital. And I got pretty good at convincing everyone I knew to either write me a scrip or get me some pills on the side."

My jaw aches from holding it tight. "So even though you were a nurse, someone in the medical profession, you abused those drugs, and your colleagues helped you along." It's more an accusation than a question, even though I want to understand. Even though understanding Nicole might help me connect to my daughter and the choices she made, it's hard to get there.

"Who do you think abuses prescription drugs more than anyone else?"

This beautiful woman, the neck I kissed, that soft brown hair, this body I pulled close to me, how normal she looks, how in control of her life. Her long, delicate fingers are clasping each other, the thumbs relaxed now, and her arms begin to shake. I should move over to hug her, let her lovely hair fall against my neck, but I don't. The recessed kitchen lights in the ceiling feel bright and hot, like we're on a stage. Like this isn't really happening.

"So is that it, Ray? Is that the deal breaker for us? Is that what you meant when you talked about second chances? Second chances are okay except for addicts?"

"Donna and I gave Jenny plenty of chances." This sounds harsher than I mean it to. But she surprised me.

"All I'm aiming for is to cope up here. I could use a friend to help me do that."

"Cope? Is that enough? Just to cope?"

"Believe me, that's a lot."

She's probably right. Why can't I see this with Jenny? "What made you stop using?"

"There was no one thing." She bites her lip. They're pale

now, not the color of salmonberries at all. "I got tired of living in that tornado, I guess. But if you're looking for a silver bullet, then sorry, I don't have one." She looks me directly in the eye. "I can see your daughter if you can convince her to come into the clinic. But, and I want you to hear me on this, at the moment she becomes my patient, you and I can no longer be a couple. And whatever she tells me is in strictest confidence, even if it's about you and Sitka. So are you sure this is what you want?"

The truth is I don't know. Why would I throw away a chance to have a relationship with a woman like Nicole on the slim chance that Jenny will turn her life around? There's only one reason, and she's eleven years old, and she deserves that chance, no matter how small the odds are.

"Yeah, I want you to see her."

"Which means you don't want to see me any more. Because of my past?"

"Because of your past," I tell her, "you understand what Jenny's been through. You've been sober twice as long as her. If anyone can help her stay clean, it's you."

Nicole's mouth sags, and she looks away.

"If this were just about me, it would be so different," I add. "You're the most fascinating woman I've—"

"Tell Jenny to make an appointment to see me at the clinic." Nicole hugs her waist and keeps avoiding my gaze. "Of course it's up to her if she follows through. And if she doesn't . . ."

She lets the possibility hang in the air, but I walk right by her, through the dining room, into the living room, and to the front door. We stumble through a good night. I give Nicole a quick peck on the cheek, like she's my aunt or something. She doesn't return the peck but wishes me a safe outing tomorrow.

"One more thing, Ray. If there's one piece of friendly advice I can give you, reach out to your daughter. I suspect Jenny came back to reconnect with you almost as much as with Sitka. Involve her in your life."

I jam my fist and arm into the sleeve of my jacket. "My life is fishing and Sitka."

She helps me on with the other side of my jacket. It suddenly feels tight in the shoulders. "Then take her out on the boat with you. Have her help you with the books. Something that welcomes Jenny back as your daughter."

"We'll see." I open the door, then stop and turn, wanting to say something that lets Nicole know that I have real feelings for her. "Thank you. I trust you."

"Goodnight, Ray," she says, closing the door.

It's still raining, but there's a faint pink cast behind the clouds to the southwest. I'm betting the swells will go down. I'll listen to the marine report later on tonight, once I fix myself cereal, but it looks promising. By the time I reach the harbor drive, the rain has tempered down, almost to a mist. It's still there, but no longer pounding, a mere murmur behind the heart of the sky.

Chapter 12

SITKA LOWERS HER HEAD deeper into her biology textbook. I can't tell if she's actually studying even though I'm sitting right next to her on the couch.

"What's the matter with you, Miss Grumpy Face?"

She reaches down, lifts the leg of her pants, and scratches her ankle. She hasn't said two words since getting home from school. I nudge my toes against her hips to encourage an answer. When she doesn't say anything, I pick up the television remote and turn the volume down on the evening news.

"Something going on at school?" I point to the textbook. "You having trouble with biology?"

"Everything's fine," she says, as if the new definition of the word meant that you were tied up in a canvas bag and suspended over a snake pit.

I lift up my sweatshirt and rub my bare stomach. Jenny's been cooking a lot lately and if I'm not careful, I'm going to get a paunch. "Some dinner, wasn't it? Your mom makes a fine chicken pie. I can't remember the last time I had a homemade pie crust."

"She's my mother. She's supposed to feed me." Sitka gets up and retreats to the tattered, over-stuffed chair on the opposite side of the room. On the way, she looks upstairs towards her mom's closed bedroom door. Jenny's out at her church for some type of evening Bible discussion. "She's not so special, you know."

"Sitka, enough. What's eating you? Did you have a fight with one of your friends? Did that Connor boy you like say something to you or not say something to you?"

Her face reddens, but she doesn't answer. She arches her back and neck, leaning into the back of the chair.

"This can't be about me taking your mom out on the boat."

Sitka rolls her eyes up to her bangs, grabs an entire handful of hair, and starts twirling. "I don't care what you and her do together."

I hoist myself off the sofa and go over and squat down to her level. "Yeah, I can see that." What I also see are tears in Sitka's eyes. "Honey, why is this upsetting you?"

"It's not. I just don't see why she gets to go." She juts her hand under her chin and looks past me to Jenny's rubber boots next to the door. "She's not going to be any good out there. You think because she went out with you for a whole four hours today, that makes her Starbuck material." Sitka's Advanced English class is reading *Moby Dick* this year.

"I need the help," I tell Sitka, "and it may as well be your mother. You're still too young for crabbing, it's too dangerous for you to go out with me this time of year, and besides, I don't want you missing any school."

This morning, Jenny and I made a small run up to the north end of Admiralty Island, just enough to see if she had sea legs. I showed her the basics of how we bait, how we hook up and drop the pots, and how we empty the pots into the holding tank. To my surprise, she paid attention. I guess Nicole was right about Jenny wanting to be involved. She baited the pots without being squeamish. And despite a steady wind blowing from the bow, she worked without bitching about the cold. I even showed her how to operate the winch. She had trouble with it, especially with stacking one empty pot on top of another, but by the time we finished, she was no worse than any of the newbie deckhands who come up from Portland and Seattle each year. I told her that she had done all right. Jenny proudly told Sitka how the day went, over dinner, but it's clear now that Sitka is having none of it.

"She doesn't know anything about crabbing. If she's your crew, good luck. "

My right calf begins to cramp from squatting, but I keep balancing there anyway. "She's not going to be my only crew. Felix will be there. And I'm bringing aboard four other deckhands besides your mom. I need a good catch this time around."

I don't tell Sitka that when we tied up the boat this afternoon, there was this guy waiting for us on the pier. He was in his mid-twenties, dressed in jeans and a hooded jacket, so I thought he might be looking for work. When he asked if I was Captain Bancroft and I said yeah, I discovered he already had a job. He was one of those legal guys who go around delivering you court papers you don't want to get, like divorce papers and jury summons. His little gift for me was an official lawsuit from Walt Francke for grievous harm due to gross negligence.

When Jenny peered over my shoulder, I tried to hide the document.

"You in trouble?"

"Nah." But then I figured if she wanted to be part of the family again, she may as well know. "It's a lawsuit from a guy we took fishing a few weeks ago. He got injured. If he gets as much as he wants, it could wipe out my savings, Sitka's college fund, maybe even the boat."

Jenny tugged hard on my sleeve, turning me around. "You can't lose the boat, Dad. You just can't!"

I'd forgotten that Jenny always felt a connection with the boat. Back when she was six, I named it after her. The *Jenny-Sais-Pas*. Roughly translated as "Jenny Doesn't Know," a nod to her childhood innocence. She used to sing-song the words when I'd bring her down to the docks. "Jenny says Pa. Jenny says Pa."

I stuffed the papers back into the envelope and told her not to worry. "I'll settle this. It'll be fine."

But the truth is that I am damned worried. Chinese mitten crabs have overtaken four of our usual crabbing spots. With the restrictions F&G have already placed this year, money's tighter than ever. I need a fantastic catch over the next few days. That's why I'm anxious to get out early tomorrow. Word's gotten around that tons of tanner crabs have suddenly gone on the bite up at the north end of Lynn Canal, and I want us to get our fair share. It's the biggest sighting all season.

Usually, when it's just Felix and me, we use the 450-pound six-bys, the smallest and lightest of the pots. We can work maybe fifteen pots a day. For a potential haul like this, I've rented thirty large ones, the 750 pounders, and hired a crew to work them. We'll be gone a few days, working day and night until we fill the hold with crab, and Sitka will stay with Sarah and Julie.

I try to downplay Jenny's role. "Your mom will be just another deckhand. She'll help bait the pots. She'll bunk in the engine room with everyone else, and get the same four hours of sleep everyone else hopes to get."

Sitka shakes her head. "The way I remember it you had me cleaning the galley and scrubbing the decks for a year before I went anywhere near the shrimp pots."

"Honey, you were just a kid. You still are." The cramp in my leg flares, so I ease myself up from squatting with a grunt. "Your mom's an adult."

"An adult, uh-huh. Like the rest of the crew is going to be thrilled about having a greenhorn woman onboard."

"They'll deal with it. Everyone has their first time out. Besides, it's not like she's going to get the same cut as the rest of them."

Typically, each deckhand is given seven percent of the gross haul. With any luck, the outing could be worth $6,000 or $7,000 for each of them. As a greenhorn, Jenny will get four percent. That would leave about $35,000 each for me and Felix. It's not a hell of a lot, especially after we subtract the expenses of the extra pots, the equipment, keeping up the boat, bait, gear, dock fees, and so on. On the plus side, nothing's ever deducted. The government treats all fishermen, boat captain or deckhand, as independent contractors. No social security, no federal income tax, no state tax. Bottom line is that Jenny's no financial threat to the other deckhands.

Sitka folds her arms. "Do they know she's a meth addict?"

"That's enough, Sitka. Your mom's not using meth. Not any more." I rub my hand against my calf muscle. "And a good way for her to stay clean is to do something useful. And you and I are going to help her do that."

"To do my job. That's what you mean. Well, she can't. She's a scammer. She'll gundeck the whole day. You'll see. You'll think she's coiling line or cleaning the head, but she'll be hiding in there, shooting up, just pretending that she's doing what she's supposed to do."

I lean over the chair and put my arm around her shoulder. Bending down makes my cramp get worse again, but I don't care. "No one's replacing you, Sitka. You're still my number one crewman. Come this summer, when the weather's better, I expect you to be teaching your greenhorn mom a thing or two. Okay?"

Sitka pushes my arm away, gets up, and stalks off toward her bedroom. "I've got three chapters of *Moby Dick* to read."

IT'S STILL DARK WHEN we idle out from the dock. The boat coughs out diesel fumes as we head out to the channel. It's raining steadily, but the current isn't too bad. The air has the slushy smell of winter slipping in. The morning's cold, even for October, the thermometer reading just thirty-four degrees. Up to the north there's a band of gray light under the dark clouds. That's about where we should hit Lynn Canal.

As we pilot up past Chichagof Island, Jenny helps Felix chop up the squid and halibut. Two of the deckhands, Darryl Hoyt and Tony Green, prepare the pot lines by looping them into neat, three-foot-high coils. Carl and Charlie Bailey, twin brothers from Chehalis, inspect the pot webbing for any last-minute tears. The four of them are under twenty-five, strong and quick. They've all worked small boats before, so they know what they're doing. Each of them is waiting for a chance to be hired on one of the large vessels that carry a couple hundred pots or more. If they're lucky, they'll sign on to work up near Kodiak or on the Bering Sea.

We cross over the edge of Chatham Strait and into Lynn Canal just as the sun comes up, opaque as a pearl above the charcoal sea. We anchor near Vanderbilt Reef. While Hoyt and Green finish checking the webbing, Felix stands behind Jenny as she places bait into the first pot. Carl ties on the line that secures three buoys to the lid. As he does so, Jenny takes a few steps back and stares out at the water. Then she lifts her right foot off the deck to scratch her ankle. Felix kicks her left leg out from under her. In an instant she's on her back.

Carl opens his mouth wide with laughter and though I try my best, I can't help but grin. Jenny scrambles to her feet, waving her arms in front of Felix.

"What the hell did you do that for?" She spins around at me and Carl. "Do you think that's funny? Is this some kind of macho bullshit?"

Before I can answer, Felix grabs her arm. "Settle down, missy. I don't know what your dad taught you yesterday, but you'd better learn right now that *that* is one of the stupidest things you can do. You never, ever, lift a foot and just stand there." He jabs his finger at her and then at the railing. "All it takes is a second for a wave to move one of the lines and before you can think, it snags around your foot and BAM! Over the side you go, right with the pot. And those suckers are going down hundreds of feet. Plenty of deckhands get killed that way, and I don't aim to see it happen on this boat."

"Don't be mad at Felix." I step between the two of them. "He'd do the same to anybody else. And if he didn't, I would. Better a sore rump and a little embarrassment than to be dragged under with the weight of those pots. Now finish baiting the others. And be sure to secure the door ties when you're done. We don't need the crab spilling out when we raise them up."

Her jaw trembles, but, to her credit, Jenny walks to the aft cooler and retrieves another bucketful of bait. I secure the launch cable to the first pot while Green and Hoyt help position it onto the hydraulic platform. Felix works the controls to tilt the rack up and the pot slides over the side into the water. We repeat this process of baiting, tying lines with buoys attached, positioning pots on the rack, and dumping them into water. It's like we're doing mass burials at sea.

Once we've sunk half the pots, it's time to motor over to the opposite side of the canal. I head into the pilothouse. As we pull up anchor, Felix comes in and pours himself a cup of coffee.

"How's she doing?"

He lifts up his cap and scratches his forehead. "Not bad. She's getting her sea legs if that's what you mean. At least she didn't get up and punch me after I knocked her down. I've had cheechakos who've reacted worse."

"But will she make a deckhand?"

"Guess so."

"There's a 'but' in there, Felix. What is it?"

Felix squints his eyes. "She won't rub Billiken, Ray. She refuses, calls it idolatry. I don't like it. Everybody's supposed to rub Billiken."

"Well, don't push it. She has her convictions and we still have freedom of religion in this country, or so I hear."

Felix eyes the horizon. "Makes me nervous is all."

Jenny steps in and stops our conversation. Water slides off her slicker. Her face looks red and she rubs her arms up and down her sleeves. "I don't think I've ever been this cold."

Wait until nightfall, I want to say, but I don't. She wants to be here and didn't complain when I told her we'd be taking turns sleeping in the bunks.

"I better go check on Frick and Frack." Felix means the

twins. "Make sure they know how to tell a male crab from a female when they pull up the pots."

"There's coffee," I tell Jenny.

"No, thanks." She takes out a pack of cigarettes from the pocket of her raincoat, removes a cigarette, and lights up. "Where are we headed to now?"

"About eight miles up or so, opposite Comet." I turn the wheel and pull out into the middle of the canal. There's about a half dozen other boats in the neighborhood, some setting pots, others still choosing a place to lay anchor.

"How will we know which pots are ours when we come back?" Jenny pushes her hood off. Her bangs are slicked down from sweat, or rain, or both.

I point to the buoys on deck. "Every boat has a unique set. Ours are red with an orange tip and blue dolphins. When we see them floating, we know we're at our pots. And the other boats know theirs."

"What about someone coming along and stealing yours when you're out of sight?"

It's a natural question, I guess, maybe more so if you've spent time in prison. "We have a pretty good honor system around here. No one wants to be known as a crab thief. It's been known to happen once in a while, mainly up in the Bering Sea and usually in the middle of the night."

Jenny sits in the captain's chair and fiddles with her cigarette. "We should get one of those commercial bait cutters like they use on the big boats. It would be safer and a lot less work."

"When we have the extra money for that, I'll be willing to discuss it."

Jenny runs her hand lightly over the control console, not actually touching anything. "Felix should treat me with more respect."

"You've got a lot to learn. Like Felix said, a cheechako. You get respect around here when you do your job well. You want a gold star or employee-of-the-month award, go work for some corporation."

"Technically this boat is in my name, remember? Mom left it to me in her will."

I ball up my fists, alternately rubbing my thumbs over my fingers, fingers over thumbs. It gives me time to take a breath.

"Yeah, well possession is nine-tenths of the law." I swivel in my chair to face her. "You really want to own this boat someday, then you have to earn your way. You're a deckhand, a new one at that."

Jenny smashes out her cigarette, crushing it into the cracked blue ashtray saucer. "I'm not a cheechako. I may have been born in Seattle, but I grew up here, remember? You think I'm so green I don't know how to survive around here?" She pulls on her gloves and zips up her jacket. "You try spending a decade of your life in an Anchorage prison. Then talk to me about survival."

"I'm captain of this boat and I don't want you or anyone else getting hurt. Do your job. Mind what Felix tells you. Then we'll talk about who owns what."

Jenny gets up and strides to the door. She opens it and she turns back to me. "The *Jenny-Sais-Pas*," she snorts. "I used to think you named this boat after me because you loved me." She steps out to the deck, letting the door slam behind her.

My neck and shoulders tighten, but I focus on the controls and piloting us up to Comet. When we get there, it takes an extra hour to drop the pots. The hydraulic launcher jams, causing the chain to back up on itself. I have to move the gears back and forth, while Green and Hoyt help untangle the links. It's almost eleven o'clock when we're finished. I hate to lose that much time. And I don't like the looks of the weather either. When we started out, the temperature was just above freezing, but it's worsening. Instead of getting warmer, the air has thickened with cold. Clouds have erased the light from the northwest sky. If those suckers move down here, we'll get ice. I push the engines to get back to our first set of pots. We anchor quickly once I spot our dolphin buoys. I move down onto the foredeck and prepare the winch.

Hoyt and Green secure the 5/8-inch lines. Charlie and Carl straddle each side of the first pot as we hoist it up. It's teeming with tanner crabs. Probably three quarters of a ton. If we do as well with the others, we'll all be getting a nice sum of money. Hoyt and Green help Charlie and Carl maneuver the pot onto the deck. When it's settled, Jenny unlatches the gate and helps Felix guide the tanner crabs into the hold. The smacking and tumbling is the sound of cold, hard cash.

Hoyt fixes the line to the next pot and puts his thumbs up. But when I pull back on the levers, the cable goes taut and the winch vibrates so hard, I can feel it through the soles of my boots. I turn the motor off, and it shudders into quiet.

I slap my hand uselessly against the side of the housing. "Goddamn it to hell!"

Felix comes over and we both examine the winch, but can't see any fouled cables or anything else obviously wrong.

"I'd better take off the back plate. Maybe something's off track behind there." I look around. "Where in the hell is my wrench set?"

Felix points to the aft hatch. "Down below. You left it there after lubricating the engine."

"Damn. All right." You see if you can spot anything else. I'll be back in a minute."

I start sliding on the now-icy deck. It's not so much a fall as a career into the bulkhead. I let out a good "mother-fuck!" as I regain my balance and make my way to the hold below. The engine room smells like burnt motor oil and hot metal. There are piles of boxes, leftover engine parts, and five or six old boat fenders. It's probably time to clean it out one of these days, but moving junk is the last thing I want to do after being out at sea.

When I pick up the toolbox, my back spasms. Must be from being on the wrong end of all that vibration, not to mention the cold. I drop the toolbox and twist from side to side. Jesus, I'm getting too old for this shit.

Back on the aft deck, a vibration runs through the boards under my feet. By some miracle, the winch is back in operation.

Hoyt and Green look up as the next crab pot is coming up and over the starboard railing. If possible, it's even fuller than the first one. Hundreds and hundreds of tanner crabs crawl over each other, as they rise up out of the ocean. The twins are halfway between Hoyt and Green, getting ready to guide the pot to the hold, where Felix is waiting.

On the forward deck Jenny's working the winch controls. Her tongue's halfway out of her mouth as she moves her hand back and forth, back and forth on the control knobs. As she slams the drive gear backwards, the winch lifts the 750-pound pot higher into the air. But it arcs too far forward and starts to swing out of Hoyt's reach. Green tries to grab a line, but can't manage it. Jenny looks panicked and starts moving the gear levers in one direction, then another. The heavy pot swings around. Carl and Charlie have to jump out of its path. The sheer weight of it carries it to the port side. As it swerves in front of Felix and the holding tank, the cable snaps. The groan of the pot scraping and banging against the side of the boat is near deafening, a metal ghost plunging off the deck, plummeting more than 250 feet to the sea floor.

I think it's about as bad as it can get. But then my nostrils flare at the stench of burnt rubber and oil. "Shut that winch down!" I run toward the pilothouse, lose my balance, and smack my hip against the bulkhead. I scramble inside and pop the fire extinguisher from its quick-release bracket.

I can't tell if Jenny heard me or not. Hoyt shuts off the motor. Black vapors rise out of the casing. I release the valve on the extinguisher and spray the motor and surrounding area. The white, aqueous foam suffocates the smoke. Everyone, except Jenny, comes over to where I am.

"You've got her, Captain." Green kicks at the foam-splattered metal.

Felix takes off his cap and wrings it in his hands. "Ray, I don't know what happened. You were getting the tools and Jenny got behind the controls. She asked me if it was okay for her to try, and I didn't know what to say, and next thing you know she's got the motor going, so I thought, okay, we're back in business, and then . . ." He looks around for someone, anyone, to confirm his story. "You know I don't make decisions."

"Not your fault, Felix." I squat down to assess the damage.

Charlie takes a rag and wipes away some of the foam. "This winch is toast, Captain. Not only is the motor shot, but look here." He points to a large fissure in the arm. "I'm not even sure welding can fix this."

Hoyt jams his hands inside his jacket. "You've got your rookie daughter running equipment she's got no business being around. What the fuck do we do now? This is our livelihood."

"You're not helping things, Hoyt!" I snap back. "Let's focus on solving this. We're just under two hours from Juneau. We'll have to go there and get a replacement. Let's get moving."

The crew stands along the flaking deck railing, Charlie and Carl with their thumbs in their pockets, Green rocking on his boots, like they were waiting for the dinner bell, Hoyt with his back turned.

"Well, c'mon, then! Carl and Hoyt, get everything secured so we can get the hell outta here. Green, you and Charlie get some boards from below and put in a makeshift rail." They straighten up and go about preparing the boat so we can anchor up. "Felix, you come below with me. Let's make sure there's no damage on the underside of the deck."

The two of us walk aft, go down the ladder, and make our way to where the winch is anchored. We carefully inspect the deck above us with our flashlights. Fortunately, it looks as though the damage was pretty well contained to the winch.

Felix switches off his flashlight. "That's a blessing."

"We still have to replace the winch and repair the railing," I tell him. "With paying off the engine repair, I'm tapped out on cash right now. And I'm guessing you don't have a spare few thousand. Do you think Muskeg could loan us the money?"

"I don't know, Ray. Muskeg's pretty frugal."

"Once we've got a good haul, we can pay her back."

He grins and pats me on the shoulder. "On the other hand,

she's got a soft spot in heart for you and Sitka. Don't you worry, Ray. I'll turn on the old charm and sweet talk her into it. When we get close to Juneau, I'll call her on her cell."

"Good enough. Let's get going."

The currents work against us and it takes close to three hours to reach Juneau. The crew hunkers down in the bunkhouse, playing poker, as we motor south. Jenny keeps out of sight, too, which is just as well. I should probably find her and tell her the winch has been on its last legs for a while now, accidents happen, or some other fatherly stuff. But she had no business trying to operate it on her own. What the hell was she trying to prove?

I don't have a lot of faith in Felix's ability to sweet talk Muskeg into anything, but sure enough, she comes through and agrees to loan us the money. I radio ahead to Betty's Boat Repair. They agree to meet us at the Seadrome Marina with a new winch, for an additional service fee. Then there's the labor cost to remove the old one and install the new one. And there's the extra charge to move us to the head of the list. And of course the hourly moorage fees. We call Muskeg back with an estimate of $7,000. I give her my bank account number and she does an online transfer into my account.

"I owe you big time, Muskeg," I tell her.

"You and Felix can start by fixing the oil heater at the Blind Dog as soon as you get back here. It's burning rough again."

Felix, who's been listening in on the conversation with me, grabs the phone out of my hands. "You got it, Sweet Buns. You know I'm the man who can heat you up all winter long."

I just roll my eyes.

It's already two o'clock when we dock, but at least the boat repair crew is waiting for us. After looking things over, they say it'll take three hours of work. I offer them a tip of $300 if they make it in two. No problem. I gather my crew on the fore-deck, including Jenny, and tell them they've got a two-hour shore leave.

"Everyone back here by fourteen hundred hours. Don't be late or we take off without you and you can find your own way back home. And no drinking and no fighting. You come back drunk or high, then I've got no use for you here." I make a point not to look directly at Jenny. "We've got pots out there waiting for us and I need everyone ready to work well into tonight. Is that clear?"

There's murmurs of "yeah, yeah" and Hoyt lifts his hand to his eyebrow with a mock "Aye, aye, sir." The men slide down the ladder one after another onto the pier and head off into town. Jenny lingers on the deck.

"Do you want me to stay behind and help?"

I wave my hand toward the dock. "Do whatever you want, but there's nothing here right now for you to help with."

"Fine." She heads to the bow ladder and hoists her right leg over the side. Her hand slips and she almost loses her balance. She shoots me a look like it's my fault, but I turn to the foreman of the repair crew from Betty's.

"What are we waiting for?"

The workmen begin dismantling the engine mount and replacing the winch. They also tear out the makeshift railing that Green and Charlie put in, and reconstruct a pretty good replica of the original. I help them slap a couple coats of high-grade varnish onto it. It doesn't look pretty, but it'll do the job. We test the winch with one of the large pots. It hums and lifts smoothly. At last a positive sign. Getting the winch to lift a pot without a rumbling protest.

By four o'clock, the repair team has packed up and disembarked. All in all, today's disaster cost $6,684.72. My crew is back and ready to sail—all except Jenny.

"You guys see where she went?" I ask the men. "Anybody?"

They shake their heads. "We thought she stayed onboard," Carl says.

"Yeah, it's not exactly like we wanted her hanging out with us," Hoyt adds, spitting over the new railing.

I look over the starboard side, peering down the wharf. On the dock are scattered scraps of plastic bags, remnants of beige condoms, torn Styrofoam cups, crumpled beer cans, and sea gulls pecking at abandoned french fries. "Felix, seen her?"

"Not me." He holds up a shopping bag with the outline of a young woman in lingerie. "I was up at the shops on Whittier Street. Getting Muskeg a little thank you gift."

"Damn it." I pull back my sleeve and check my watch. "We'll give her another half hour, then we disembark."

Green spits over the side. "She's AWOL, Captain. You'd give any of us that kind of slack if we were this late?"

"My prerogative. Everyone go settle in."

Thirty minutes come and go. Another twenty come and go. Finally I give the order to pull up anchor. As we pull out of the marina, I scan the dock and surrounding streets. Not a hint of Jenny. Tourists from the big ships are winding their way between the shops on Franklin Street and the pier near Marine Way. Above the town, the afternoon light shimmers briefly against Mount Roberts before being swallowed up by a bank of clouds, flat iron gray and moving fast.

Chapter 13

TWENTY MILES NORTH OF Juneau, a strong west wind drives the rain sideways. Clouds straggle down like old gray suits strung across a clothesline. The darkening sky dulls the light from the headlamps. At the edge of the Lynn Canal, the confluence of the Icy and Chatham straits creates a series of crosscurrents. I cut back on the motor, slowing our progress, but speeding would put us in too much danger. As we stutter along, Hoyt and Carl inspect the pots, mending any tears in the mesh. Green lubricates the new winch, making sure the cable runs free, while Charlie hacks the halibut and squid bait. Jenny should be out there helping him.

When we reach the Vanderbilt Reef, a tide-spawned chop runs against our path and I'm barely doing eight knots. We seem to buck against every wave. It's like trying to maneuver over an expanse of fallen tree logs. Swells keep spraying across the bow.

Felix distributes a simple dinner of pre-wrapped sandwiches. He has to steady himself in the doorway of the pilothouse as the boat skews. Water pours from his slicker onto the deck as he holds out a small package wrapped in aluminum foil. "You going to take this or do you want me to spoon-feed you?"

"Thanks." I grab the sandwich, keeping one hand on the wheel. I unwrap the upper half of the foil and take a bite. Ham. It needs mustard. "How's it going with the crew?"

Felix lifts his right shoulder. "Nobody's out there dancing a jig, if that's what you mean. But they're buckling down. They're ready to work through the night. Everyone wants this haul to be a good one, Ray."

"Like I don't?"

Felix unfolds the foil over his sandwich, lifts up the bread and sniffs it before taking a good bite out of it. I shouldn't be taking my personal problems out on him. He's right. Everyone needs the earnings from a successful run.

"Thanks for getting Muskeg to loan us the money," I say.

"You know, it ain't exactly hard to find drugs in Juneau if you want to." He wipes his mouth with the sleeve of his jacket. "You must be worried sick about Jenny."

I wolf down the rest of my sandwich, crumple up the aluminum foil, and throw it toward the waste basket. It bounces off the rim. Picking up a mug of coffee, I take a gulp, and point the rim of the cup toward the window panel. "I sure hope the weather doesn't get any worse."

"We should improve the odds. Hold on a minute." Felix unlocks the portside storage locker and takes out his ditty bag. Untying the thief knot, he reaches into the canvas and pulls out a small bone.

"What the devil is that?"

"Toe bone of a sea otter. Found it on the beach near my cabin." He holds the tobacco-colored bone up above his forehead. "The otter always knows how to return from the sea to the land." He rotates his hand in small circles, bringing the bone to his belly button. "Brother otter," he intones, "watch out for us today. Bring us all back safely from the rough seas and from the rough streets of the city." He slips the bone back into the ditty bag.

"So you're including Jenny in that incantation?"

Felix reties the thief knot. "She has her own kind of returning to do. I don't see any reason to be exclusive on the wish list."

"And now we'll get a decent haul, make it back safely, and Jenny won't be shooting up in some Juneau back alley? That's a heck of a lot of luck for a small bone to guarantee."

Felix regards me like a third grader who can't understand the simplest math problem. He dangles the ditty bag in front of me. "You'll note that there's no guarantee written on the package." He puts it back into the storage locker. "But you and me have both been around long enough to know that you spend most of this life being thrown between luck and misfortune."

I rev the engines to keep the boat aligned with the currents. In another hour, the sun has fully set, Felix has turned all our navigation and deck lights on, and we've crossed the channel. We spend the next few hours dropping pots and buoys along the west side. Then we circle back to the second set of pots we sank this morning. Charlie and Felix snag the buoy line on the first pot, and as I raise it with our new winch, everyone leans over the railing. It surfaces, packed full of wriggling tanners. Charlie and Felix steady the pot on the deck railing. The crabs look big. We won't have to throw many back. Green turns around and gives me a thumbs up. I give a loud whoop and angle the pot onto the deck. When Carl and Green snatch the second one, it's as full as the first.

I clap Felix on the shoulder. "Looks like your otter charm worked, buddy. At least for the crabbing."

Three hours later, we've got fifteen pots of tanner crab in stowage. We set anchor a mile into the canal and about a half mile off shore. I switch on the anchor light, then turn on the weather station to check the marine forecast. The report is for clearing skies and calmer seas. That means we can stay a few days up here at least. By the end of the run, we should have the hold and the decks packed with crab.

"Good work, guys!" I yell to the crew. "Charlie, you have the first watch. Felix has second. Everybody else get your four hours of sleep. We're going to have a busy day tomorrow."

I go below to the engine room, quickly take off my heavy coat and pants, and fall into my bunk. I'm already so tired, I pull my sleeping bag over the top of me and do some quick calculations in my head. If our catch holds to predictions, I'll have more than enough to pay Muskeg, the insurance deductible, Ben Sato's retainer, and replace the money I've borrowed from Sitka's college fund. It doesn't take me long to fall asleep.

At two in the morning, Felix shakes me. "Trouble, Ray."

The boat is rocking harder than it should be, even with the heavy rains. A loud groan vibrates throughout the hull as if a band of ghosts were haunting the bulkheads. I recognize the sound instantly.

"We're icing up!" Felix tells me what I already know.

Squamish, those arctic outflow winds that funnel down from the north, turn the already cold air freezing.

I jump out of the bunk and yank on my orange rain gear over my long johns and two wool sweaters. My calves are stiff and my toes cramp as I scramble into my boots. I pull on my vinyl gloves and follow Felix onto the deck. The cold slaps me. Pellets of ice riddle my face and hood. With the wind chill, it's gotta be minus five Celsius and dropping fast.

"How bad is it?" I have to yell over the wind.

Felix points to the bow. "It came on fast. We've got inches of ice on the hull and it's getting thicker."

Spray washes up and immediately makes a covering of frost on the deck. "Get every hand up!" I shout. "We've got to knock this ice off fast!"

While Felix rouses the crew, I grab a rubber mallet from the aft deck and begin banging ice from the railings and bulkheads. With the first couple of poundings, whole sheets of ice break into the water. The mallet hits some dense areas and ice chips fly back, stinging my face even worse than the hail. When I grunt and swing again, the edge of the mallet slides along the slick surface, the momentum almost taking it over the railing. I pull back and barely regain my balance. Already breathing hard. Tightening my grip on the mallet, I attack the coating again, knocking blocks of ice over the side. There's sweat inside my clothes. I strike again, and once more the hammer slips and thwacks my left arm instead. Green and Carl are moving along the port side, batting away. But everywhere I look, ice is coating cables, railings, rigging. I look over the side. The boat is heavier in the water than she should be.

Felix inches his way back to me. His eyebrows are covered over in white crystals. "It's building up faster than we can knock it off!" There's a shake to his voice that I haven't heard in a long time, not since right after the stroke.

Ice building on the hull is bad enough. But if it encases the upper structures we're in real danger. The boat will roll right over on her side. She rolls far enough and she'll start sliding into the water. The *Jenny-Sais-Pas* is becoming an ice bucket. And if she keeps it up, she'll turn into an ice coffin. It's happened to plenty of boats out here in conditions like these, to seasoned fishermen like us. And we're short a crew member.

"Forget about the sides," I yell to Felix. "You and Green focus on the pilothouse. Have the twins do what they can with the upper bulkheads. I'll take up anchor and start the engines. We've gotta get her moving."

I switch on the small anchor winch. It stutters in the cold air, once, twice, then coughs out. I switch it on again, and it takes several minutes for it to warm up enough to pull the anchor free. Finally, I jump into the pilothouse, kick the engine, and move the boat into gear, turning her into the strait. The radio crackles when I flip it on to listen for reports. The antenna must be bent over with the white weight. Through the static I hear enough to understand that the storm is sweeping the entire area. We're going to have to head all the way back down to Yatki Island to get out of its grip.

We buffet through the water like a tank through a muddy field. The deck is inches thick with ice. When the spray washes up, it explodes with hardened seawater. The boat rolls and groans under us. Triangles of ice jut out from her sides at forty-five degree angles. But the pilothouse is heating up and I have to take off my coat and one of my sweaters. The Squamish winds have revved up to sixty-five knots. As I turn southeast, the bow takes a deeper descent as it slaps into the crosscurrents.

Felix sticks his head in, water streaming off his slicker. "It's the pots stacked on the bow, Ray." His voice has gone quiet, despite the raging of the storm. "We can't knock enough of the ice off them."

All that crab we planned to catch. Those pots aren't even all ours. The bow keeps dipping, and it takes all my strength to keep us on course. I steer a bit leeward, hoping conditions will change, praying for them to change. Felix opens the door further, the arctic blast blowing in from behind him. He grips the hatchway, watching me, waiting for me to make a decision.

"All right. Damn it! Go ahead!"

He tugs his fisherman's cap forward in acknowledgment. He, Green, and Carl work their way to the bow. Green clambers onto the stack of pots. It's a dangerous place to be. He has to get the cable free that's holding the top row of pots without getting blown off the bow and into the sea. I try to hold the boat steady. Green slips once, twice, but finally I see the cable snap and five of our pots roll starboard into the water. He unsnaps the second cable and another five pots fall away to the port side. Immediately the bow balances her dip. We won't sink, at least not at this moment. But we've sacrificed ten empty pots, half of them rented, to the ice gods. Eight thousand dollars in less than ten minutes.

For four hours we fight against the storm, trying to head south in the dark. Two hours to daylight. My shoulders and arms feel like they're being pulled out of their sockets. The crew keeps batting away at the white coating. The boat buckles and heaves, but slowly we make progress. When we finally cross out of Lynn Canal and enter Chatham Strait, the downpour changes back to rain. I thank the gods and increase our speed, heading home. When we are within view of Yatki Island and St. Innocent Harbor, the weather finally begins to break. Barely visible under the black clouds, the sun rises, flattening on the horizon like a bruised apricot.

But the reprieve is only temporary. Now that our radio's working again, the marine reports say the storm will press down on us for at least another three days. We'll have to wait it out and try again. There's no telling what the conditions will do to the crabbing by then. We've got the tanners from the first pots to unload, but the rest of our traps are up in the canal. They might hold, or they might be scattered throughout the sound, or a rogue ship might swing by and pick up our haul before we can get back to them. At least everyone onboard is safe. It's not difficult to lose someone at sea in an ice storm.

It takes two hours to unload. The take is about a third of what we had set out to get. I tell the crew to go on home and that I'll call them when we're ready to venture back out. Felix and I inspect the boat to see how badly hurt she is from the storm. She's been thrashed, but there's no major damage to the hull or the engines. It takes another hour for Felix and me to wash and tie down the boat. It's grueling work after what we've been through. My body feels beaten, raw, though it's so cold that the numbness helps me ignore my swollen fingers and aching feet. The only way I get through these chores is because I've done them so many times before, and because Felix is doing them right alongside me, quiet and methodical.

It's almost noon when I finally get home from the docks. The temperature has turned again, the air chilled. Outside on the porch, it takes me five minutes to undo the knots, remove my boots, and throw them in the boot bench. My toes are stinging. I've got bruises up and down my legs from slipping around on the ice and being banged against the bulkheads. My left hand is swollen and my shoulders feel like they've been pummelled with a bag of rocks. I open the front door. Sitka is lying in the overstuffed chair, her hair splayed across the armrest. She's wearing her jeans and an Alaska Raptor Center sweatshirt.

She jumps up as soon as she sees me. "Grandpa! Thank God you're back!" She wraps her arms around my waist as I shut the door behind me. "All anyone's been talking about is the huge ice storm. They canceled school for the day."

"It really battered us out there. Lost ten pots." I feel like I could slide down the wall, right onto the floor. "Jesus, I'm beat."

Sitka steers me over to the couch and tells me to sit down. "Let's see."

I dutifully show her my hands. It's all I can do to hold them up. Sitka examines both sides.

"They're red and swollen. But I'm not seeing any signs of frostbite." She removes my socks. "I don't know how you even got your boots off. Your feet don't look any better than your hands. Your toes are all bruised up. I thought you were going to get new boots."

She retrieves an electric blanket from the closet, unfolds it, and lays it across my lap. She tucks my hands under it before switching it on. "Do you want me to run you a hot bath?"

"No, kiddo. But I need to talk to you about your mom."

"You need a glass of whiskey." This isn't the first time she's nursed me after I've returned from a stormy sea. Before I can answer her, she dashes into the kitchen, returning with a bottle of Jack Daniel's and a glass.

"Two fingers should do it," she advises.

She pours the whiskey neatly into the glass and hands it to me. My fingers start cramping and I have to take the glass with both hands. My arms feel wobbly and the glass shakes as I raise it to my mouth. The smell of the alcohol thaws my nostrils even before I take a sip. Warms my tongue and throat. I close my eyes and hold the glass against my forehead, as if it could work its therapeutic magic on my throbbing head.

I open my eyes. "Your mom."

Sitka's face scrunches like an otter's just before it slides into water. "I told you she wouldn't make it out there. I'm not surprised you kicked her off at Juneau."

"What do you mean kicked her off?"

"Oh, come on, Dad. At least be honest with your grand-daughter." Jenny throws her words from the stairs. Seeing her regenerates the ice in my stomach.

I stagger to a standing position, shucking off the blanket and balancing myself on the arm of the couch. "I am glad that you aren't wandering around the streets of Juneau. But what's all this nonsense about me kicking you off the boat when you—"

"Is that what you thought? That I was scurrying around the Juneau alleyways, shooting up?"

My face flushes, from the whiskey or because that is exactly what I thought. I put my hand on Sitka's shoulder. "Honey, why don't you go on up and run me that hot bath after all?"

Sitka looks from me to her mother and back again, and her right eyebrow arches, the way it does when she's trying to figure out her geometry homework.

"It's okay," I encourage her. "You go on. Your mom and I just need to sort a couple of things out."

"Yeah, whatever." Sitka's voice is tight, the words squeezed at the end. She walks up the stairs, brushing past her mother. At the corner she looks down at me one more time before turning down the hall.

"It wouldn't have occurred to you that I would have gone to church." Jenny takes the last steps down to the landing and stations herself right in front of me. "It wouldn't have occurred to you that I needed some reassurance that I was still a worthwhile human being."

Above us I hear the faucets squeak on and water run into the porcelain tub. "You went to church? Why didn't you return to the boat when you were supposed to?"

Jenny focuses over my shoulder, as if someone were standing behind me. Checking in with Almighty God, no doubt. "Thank the Lord the preacher was there. Reverend Scott and I had a very long talk. He's never even met me before, but he at least understands me."

"If he understands you so well, why didn't you just stay in Juneau?"

Jenny snaps her eyes back to me, full of venom and vinegar. "Reverend Scott was right. You made me afraid to go back to the boat. All those years of your disapproval, of your contempt, kept me from returning."

"Let me get this straight." I tick off the events on my swollen fingers, my heart pounding fast and unrelenting. I don't want to be doing this now. Not after what we just went through. "You go AWOL from the ship. You're chatting up some minister, but you don't even bother to let any of us know. We're in the harbor waiting around like idiots. You leave your crewmates holding the bag and let them do your work for you. We're out there in the worst conditions I've seen in years, trying to not get sunk by ice, and you have the absolute gall to stand there and accuse me? What kind of person does that?"

"A meth head, Dad." Jenny folds her arms over her chest and gives me a half-smile. "Isn't that what you tell everyone? How you still see me? That way you can blame me for what happened with that winch, just like you blame me for Mom's death."

"Did I say I blamed you?" In those uneasy months when Jenny lived with me after Sitka's birth, we never once talked about Donna's death. I was too angry. Too afraid if I exploded on her, she'd leave with the baby.

"It's what you didn't say." Jenny keeps her arms tucked close, like she's protecting herself. "It's how the rest of the crew looked at me. How you looked at me, like I was a barnacle hanging on the underside of the boat. You might as well have been waving a flag. Here's my addict daughter screwing things up yet again. It's her fault if we come home empty-handed."

My right shoulder's contracting into a spasm. All that mallet banging must've messed something up. I try rotating it back and forth, but this only encourages the muscles in my neck to seize up as well. I should go soak in the hot water, drink my whiskey, listen to some Bruce Springsteen. That's what I should do.

"All those years doing drugs have made you paranoid. For God's sake, grow up and take some responsibility."

"The same old record since I was a teenager. Yes, I used drugs. But did it ever occur to you that I was acting out because you ignored me, because I couldn't get your attention any other way?" Jenny spits the words out at me, and they land with force, wearing me down beyond my exhaustion.

"Enough," I tell her. "We almost lost the boat and you weren't there to help us save her." My head is pounding now and all I want Jenny to do is to stop plowing through with her excuses and accusations.

"When I turned thirteen you wanted nothing to do with me. I used to ask Mom what I did to make myself invisible to you. Sitka's almost a teenager, Dad. You're not going to do to her what you did to me. I swear to God I won't let you, not even if I have to take her out of this house."

Before I can stop myself, before I even know what's happening, the back of my hand strikes against her face, as if it's not even part of my body. Her head jerks sideways. She staggers and loses her balance, spinning a half-turn before landing seated on the carpet, looking up at me. Blood trickles from the side of her mouth, her cheek already turning a dark plum. She must have bitten her lip. I hear sobbing but it's not Jenny. Sitka is standing at the top of the staircase, her fist to her mouth, her back flattened against the wall.

Chapter 14

THE HOUSE HASN'T BEEN this desolate since Donna died. Squeaks in the stair treads, crackling and popping from the oil heater, drone of the refrigerator compressor—every sound is amplified in the absence of Sitka. It's been a week since she's been gone. A lifetime.

After I slapped Jenny, it took all of twenty minutes for her to pack two bags, one for her and one for Sitka. She told Sitka that she was taking her to a Christian home. She knew someone from her church would put them up, which makes me wonder if she had been planning to leave all along.

Sitka didn't want to go at first.

"We'll be safe there," Jenny told her.

"Safe? You're the problem around here," Sitka said. "Not Ray. He would never do anything to hurt me."

"He loves you, does he?" Jenny narrowed her eyes at Sitka as if she had just told her that God didn't exist. "Did you know, my dear daughter, that if it were up to him, you wouldn't ever have been born? Did he tell you that?" Jenny turned her gaze on me like a wolf on a rabbit. "Go ahead, Dad. Tell her. Tell Sitka how you wanted me to have an abortion."

Sitka scrunched up her face. Her jaw trembled and she dug

her fingers into her thighs. It was true. I did suggest that Jenny end her pregnancy. Jenny was a child herself back then. A child on meth, unmarried, and totally incapable of taking care of another human being. If a drug-damaged baby came out of her, who was going to take care of her? Me and Donna. And I was so pissed at Jenny for getting pregnant. But I didn't insist on an abortion. I just brought it up as a rational option.

The same look Sitka gave me—mouth dropped open, almost like she couldn't possibly understand—was on Donna's face when I brought up the possibility of abortion twelve years ago. Her outrage surprised me, because we had always supported a woman's right to choose, had voted against any restrictions.

"I never meant my own grandchild," Donna had said. "How could you think I ever meant my own grandchild?"

And the memory of this shocked me as well, because I had buried it, forgotten it had ever happened. And that was how Jenny was able to take Sitka by the hand, take her upstairs and get her to pick out some clothes and leave, without me blocking the door, without me holding her back. Whatever neurons that were supposed to fire up and move my body to keep Sitka from leaving remained quiet, dumb as iron.

It's difficult to sleep. I'm pretty much living on coffee and cigarettes. I've gone out crabbing twice with Felix. I thought the work would distract me, get my mind off Sitka. But it didn't, and that's a dangerous situation. When I nearly lost my hand in the latch of a crab pot, Felix insisted we call it a day.

"We need the money," I told him.

"Then let's take on another crew member and you keep your butt in the pilothouse. The last thing Sitka needs is for you to wind up in the hospital. You talk to that lawyer of yours yet?"

"Of course." But it hadn't given me much hope.

As soon as Jenny left, I called Ben Sato, who informed me that if I had filed for guardianship of Sitka when she was a baby, Jenny wouldn't be entitled to take her away.

"I'm sorry Ray, but you aren't Sitka's legal guardian," Ben

said. "Even though you have been fulfilling those obligations all her life, Jenny still has full parental rights and can legally make decisions for her daughter. Including where she's going to live. The best thing you can do is file for adoption and fight it out in court. It's a long, expensive process, and I'm guessing there's no way Jenny will sign off on a guardianship request now that she's out of prison."

I meant to follow through when Sitka was a baby, but paperwork isn't my strong suit, and besides, I was reeling from Donna's death, changing diapers, making bottles, and dealing with the fact that our only daughter had just been sent to prison. As the years passed, I just thought of Sitka as mine.

Ben agreed to file for adoption on my behalf, citing Jenny's past drug use and previous abandonments as reasons for her being an unfit mother. Turns out, Ben discovered Jenny had filed a complaint with the Office of Children's Services, claiming that I have been putting my granddaughter in peril by taking her out on the boat. That's crazy. Parents and guardians of minors are allowed to bring them on commercial fishing outings. Everyone does it. State law says you can do it.

So here we are, battling over my granddaughter. The first step is going to court to decide Sitka's temporary living situation. Ben says the judge may want to hear testimony from Nicole, since she is Jenny's counselor. I don't know how the counseling's going, or even if Jenny has been showing up, and I haven't seen Nicole since that night. What am I supposed to do? Show up at her door and say, *Hi, remember me? I'm the guy who slept with you, then broke up with you so you could treat my daughter, and now I want you to tell the court that she's unfit.*

That is exactly what I need her to do. And to make that happen, I have to show Nicole that Jenny cannot possibly be responsible for Sitka, that she is morally unfit, certainly more unfit than me. It goes beyond the drugs. Jenny caused Donna's death. And if I can get Nicole to understand what kind of person Jenny really is, then she'll have to support me in court.

It's a little after 7 p.m., so I'm assuming Nicole is home from work. I don't phone her to check. I don't want her refusing to see me. She has to hear me out.

I get into my pickup and drive over to her apartment. An afternoon drizzle has turned into a steady nighttime rain. The steady swoosh-swoosh of the windshield wipers does little to steady my thoughts. The closer I get to Nicole's the itchier my palms feel on the steering wheel. When I get there, her lights are on. I shut off the engine. The wipers stutter to a halt halfway down the windshield. Nicole isn't going to talk to me about Jenny. Not counselor to patient's father, not this close to the hearing. But Jenny isn't who I'm thinking about tonight. I roll down the window, wanting to breathe in some fresh air, but the whole night smells like gutted, rotting fish. I should go home. But to what?

I get out of the truck and walk over to the entry. Twice I place my finger on the buzzer to Nicole's apartment, twice I let it drop. Just as I'm ready to turn away, an older man appears, adjusting the shoulder of his raincoat before venturing out. He holds the door open for me. Small island trust. I mumble a thanks and head upstairs.

I close my eyes in front of Nicole's door. The image of Donna dying in the mudflats makes my hands shake. It edges across my chest like a dull gill knife. A couple of minutes pass before I'm ready to knock.

"It's me," I say. "I have to talk with you."

Nicole doesn't open the door. "What do you want, Ray?" she asks, her voice close but quiet. "I know Jenny moved out with Sitka. I'm sorry, Ray, but I can't talk to you about this."

"It's not about Jenny. I just need someone to listen."

"Then go have a beer with Felix," Nicole says.

"I need you to listen to me. I'm not asking you to tell me anything. I'm asking you to listen. You don't have to say anything about this to anyone else. You don't even have to say anything to me. I just need you to know."

"What, Ray? What is it that I don't already know?"

"How Donna died."

There's a long pause. The door doesn't open. I thought for sure she'd let me in. But she doesn't tell me to go away, either. I lean my forearm on her door, get my face as close as I can, and begin.

After Jenny and Diesel Kurtz and the other kids stole the truck from the Moose Market and smashed it up on Greenbay Mountain, Donna and I thought Jenny would change her life around. After all, two of her friends had died and she nearly went to jail. We forbade her to see Diesel of course. I guess everyone says that their kids are running with a bad pack—not that the kids themselves make up the pack.

Jenny's attitude seemed to change during the six months she was under house arrest. She was cheerful when she got up in the morning. She didn't talk back. She volunteered to do chores. After she was done with the ankle bracelet, Donna and I made sure she went to school and did her homework. We gave her a curfew, all that kind of stuff. By the time she started her senior year, we thought we were well on our way to having her graduate. We even talked about her going to Sheldon Jackson College to study marine biology.

Then in early May, just a few weeks before graduation, she didn't come home for an entire weekend. Donna had me out all night driving all around the island, looking for her. We called all of her friends. We called the hospital. I knocked on doors at midnight. We had the sheriff out patrolling the roads for her, although I could tell he pretty much assumed she had run away. It's not that unusual. Small island like this—teens start getting antsy, want to check out the scene in Juneau or Anchorage. Every now and then one of them tries to stow away on one of the cruise ships headed to Vancouver or Seattle. I thought that was what Jenny had done. But Sunday night she came waltzing through the front door like she was coming home from the movies.

She stood in the middle of the living room and announced she was two months pregnant. Just like that. She's pregnant and screw us if we have anything to say about it. I'll never forget the look on her face, proud, as if she were telling us she had just won a scholarship. It wasn't her having sex that really upset us. Hell, we grew up in the seventies. We had done it by the time we were seventeen and had our baby at nineteen, but we were married, and I had a steady job, and we weren't addicts.

Donna had given Jenny the talk, even offered to go with her to get birth control. But Jenny had refused, said we didn't trust her and that she knew how to take care of herself. And that's what Jenny wanted to throw in our faces—not the sex, but the absolute lack of responsibility, the total disregard for all the lessons her mother and I had given her. She wanted us to know that in spite of how we tried to help her pull her life together, she'd just as soon get high and chuck it into the dumpster.

That's when I suggested an abortion. Jenny and Donna both threw it back in my face. So pregnant teenager it was going to be. Jenny promised us no more drugs. That she'd quit tomorrow, cold turkey, for the baby's sake. I wanted to know who the father was and of course Jenny refused to tell us, except to say he was someone who loved her and understood her, and blah, blah, blah.

Jenny and Donna and I went at each other until midnight or so, when I finally called a halt to it. I had to get the boat out in the morning and a few hours rest would do us all some good. I went upstairs and fell asleep. Donna stayed awake, tossing and turning. She kept pulling the blankets off me and sighing, as if that was going to wake me to talk some more. Sometime before five, Jenny got up, swiped $200 and the keys to her mother's 1989 Ford Taurus, and lit out.

I called the sheriff and let him know that Jenny had stolen our car and that if he or the highway patrol found her, they should pull her over and throw her butt in jail for a day or two. I couldn't waste time dogging after her. I had fishing to do. Donna drove me down to the pier in our pickup truck. I told her to go home and wait. Jenny would call or come back or the sheriff would pull her over.

But Donna wouldn't let it go. She called every last one of Jenny's friends. She finally got one of them to tell her that Jenny was on her way to Anchorage, that Diesel Kurtz was the baby's father. They must have gotten together as soon as he was released. He went up there to try and sign on as a crew member on one of the big boats and Jenny had decided to follow him. And Donna couldn't let things be. She had to go after Jenny. She wanted me to go with her, but I had to be out on the boat. Someone had to earn a living.

I stop talking, worried that Nicole might have gone away. But there's an intake of breath, quick and sharp, and I can't stop now or I won't get through it. This is the part I dread telling. Twelve years and the words are rough chunks of gravel that roll and churn, scraping my insides, making my throat raw. But I have to tell her. I have to get it out of me.

If you don't have a plane, the only way to get from here to Anchorage is to take a ferry to Cook Inlet and drive from there. You have to go across Turnagain Arm, alongside this vast stretch of mudflats. When the tide is out, the mudflats are exposed. Everyone around here knows you never, ever drive or walk out onto those flats. We call them mudflats, but they're glacial silt mixed with water. If you step out on them, you dislodge the water from the powdered rock, and those millions of tiny grains come together and suck you into place. Like quicksand. Worse. Like wet concrete.

Donna was racing across Turnagain in our pickup truck when the brakes started to go out. The deputies could tell from the tire marks that she swerved pretty hard. The truck careened off the road and onto the exposed mud. She knew enough not to pump the brakes hard, but somehow the truck still spun. Donna must have hit her head against the steering wheel when she lost control. She was bleeding and apparently disoriented. She opened the door and jumped out of the cab and immediately sank into the mud. A retired couple in an RV saw what had happened. They stopped and radioed in for help. By the time the highway patrol showed up, Donna was knee deep in the muck.

The officers were desperate to pull her out, because a ten-foot high tide was due. But they didn't dare walk out to her and she was too far out for them to throw a rope. They called in a Medevac helicopter. The chopper circled overhead and dropped a cable to her. Donna tied the end around her waist but she was so embedded, they couldn't lift her out without ripping her body in half.

The tide surged in and within minutes flowed up and around her hips. As it continued to rise, someone finally thought to patch a radio call to my boat. I was out by the Wrangells, running the spring salmon. The highway patrol cop described what was going on. I yelled to Felix to pull up anchor and as soon as we were free, I turned the boat toward Cook Inlet, opening the motor to full throttle. Meanwhile the helicopter dropped a handset to Donna. So I'm on the radio to her, even as the mud is settling around her waist and the cold tidewater is rushing in, now up to her chest. I'm racing the *Jenny-Sais-Pas* across the straits, the boat jumping as it smacks the top of the crosscurrents.

But the closer I come the more Donna recedes from me. She is about to drown, and she knows she is going to drown, and I know it, and the cops know it, and the couple in the RV knows it. The helicopter crew knows it and there's not a damn thing anyone can do about it. And I'm stuck on the *Jenny-Sais-Pas*, telling Donna how much I love her over and over, the same few words, loud and insistent, because I couldn't think of anything else to say, anything more important than those words, and she's telling me to take care of Jenny and the baby. Her soft, soothing voice, the same voice she used whenever Jenny had a fever, as if I were the one needing comfort, as if I were the one dying. That's all she keeps repeating is to take care of Jenny and our grandson. She says she knows it's a boy, she is sure of it. It takes another fourteen minutes for her to disappear, fourteen minutes for the icy waters to climb up her body and overpower her, closing over her mouth and nose.

I can't say the final part out loud, can't stop the goddamn tears. I lean against my arm, choking out inarticulate sounds.

The doorknob turns and the door opens slightly, the chain

still fastened. Nicole's fingers reach for the outer edge of the door. "Oh, Ray."

I touch her fingers with mine. She hesitates before pulling away.

"I'm so sorry, Ray. I wish I could say or do something, but I can't."

"You don't have to do anything," I tell her. "Now you know what happened. That's all I wanted."

I drop my hand and turn away, and Nicole latches the door shut. I'm relieved I told her what happened, how it was all Jenny's fault. I don't know what Nicole will say in court, or if I made a difference in coming here. I just want Sitka back. She belongs with me. But as Felix says, life doesn't give you guarantees, no matter how many gods and goddesses you think you've got on your side.

Chapter 15

I'M A MENACE, A dim-witted brute. Senseless as a slimy sculpin. I should spend the rest of my days skulking under the rocks of shallow streams, waiting to ambush anything foolish enough to crisscross my brackish shoals.

This is pretty much the portrait that Jenny's lawyer is painting of me, and she's doing a damn good job, even though, as the Honorable Judge Harold S. Morrison has pointed out, this is just a hearing, the first of many. Right. Just a hearing inside of a courtroom, with lawyers on both sides. They've already taken depositions from all of us, including Sitka and the Children's Services people. Now Judge Harry will determine if Sitka stays with me or goes with her mom until her future is permanently decided. Adoption proceedings, especially contested ones, apparently can take years.

Sitka's listening from one row back, closer to her mother's side of the courtroom than mine, wearing dark green pants I haven't seen before and her favorite yellow turtleneck sweater. Muskeg has her arm over Sitka's shoulder. I am so glad she offered to come with us. On the other side of Sitka, a woman in a beige skirt studies a manila folder. Must be the guardian ad litem Ben told me about. She's supposed to look out for Sitka during this process. I don't get it, though. Who knows what's better for Sitka than I do?

It's been three weeks since Jenny took Sitka away. There's not a ton of court cases on Yatki Island, so hearings get slotted when the visiting judge comes down from Juneau four times a year. I'm itching to get this over with, so my granddaughter can come back home where she belongs, where she's always been. It's absurd that we're even here. I'm the negligent grandfather because I take Sitka out on the boat like all the local fathers take their kids out? Just because I didn't sign some papers to be her legal guardian? Who would ever think that Sitka would be better off with her meth-head mother than with me?

And here's an extra kick in the behind. Jenny's suing me for possession of the boat. Okay, so technically she owns it. When I first got it all those years ago, I put it in my wife's name. Then Donna leased it to me for a dollar a year. That way if someone wanted to sue me, it would be harder for them to take the boat. At the time it seemed like a pretty clever thing to do. Donna left the boat to Jenny in her will. Now my dear daughter not only wants to take away my grandchild, she wants to take away my living.

And just when the season was turning around for us. The weather cleared the day after Jenny and Sitka left. We had three strong days of crabbing, me and Felix, the twins, and Green. Hoyt didn't sign on again, still pissed at me for wasting time when Jenny went AWOL. But we did well, even without him. Every pot we hoisted teemed with tanner crabs, most of them adults. We netted fifteen tons. With a haul like that, I figured I'd be able to pay Ben to take care of that damned lawsuit from Walt Francke. Then I'd have enough to replace my pots and pay for the rental ones I had to jettison, and still have enough left make the boat repairs over the winter. I could maybe even get Sitka's college fund back on track. But Jenny's dead-set on torpedoing those plans.

I must be scowling, because Ben elbows me, which is his subtle reminder to maintain a pleasant, caring demeanor. I sit up straight and smile, but I have to keep flexing my feet and toes to keep myself from making fists. I'm not prepared for this. I never thought any sensible person would question my fitness to raise Sitka, so maybe Jenny's lawyer is right about me being thickheaded. My brain cells might as well be made of seaweed.

I've only seen Sitka once a week since her mother took her. The people at Children's Services said I should get her half the week, until everything's decided, as long as I don't take her out on the boat, but it's winter anyway, so I wouldn't, but besides all that, Sitka hasn't wanted to come home yet, so I haven't pushed for more days. Our last visit was four days ago. I treated her to dinner at the Burger Chalet. We sat in a booth with red plastic seats and our food came in woven, red plastic baskets, and our sodas in red plastic glasses. I waited until she unwrapped her straw and plunged it into her Coke.

"How are things going?"

"Okay." Splatting ketchup over her fries.

"Don't you miss the house? Your room?" What I wanted to ask was whether she missed me. "It must be strange to be in someone else's house."

"We moved into our own apartment. It has satellite TV," Sitka answered, but without the enthusiasm of someone who had always claimed how deprived she was without HBO and Showtime. "You should have done all the legal stuff they say you didn't do, Ray."

"I know," I tell her. "I was busy with the boat, and with you, and I thought your mom would come back clean and sober, and be your mom again, and I wanted to believe that, but then more years passed, and I never got around to filing for legal guardianship. It seemed more important to drive you to the Marine Museum and things like that. I'm sorry."

"I want to try things out with Mom." Sitka swirled a french fry around in the ketchup. "But I don't like being in the middle between you two. You're both being stupid."

"You probably got that right. We're trying to work things out. I just wish you were back home."

Sitka dropped the french fry and put her hands under the table. "I don't know where home is anymore. I wish I was staying at Sarah's." She scooted herself out of the booth. "You should take me back now. I have a lot of homework."

I drove her over to Jenny's new apartment. We didn't say much, but Sitka did let me give her a hug before she went inside, and I told her again that I would try to work things out with her mom. So here we are. In court. Working things out.

My attorney is on his feet talking to the judge. He's in a three-piece suit, while I'm wearing a pair of dark blue Dockers, a button-down white shirt, and the maroon sweater Sitka got me for Christmas last year. It's as dressy as I know how to be. With his round glasses sliding down his nose, and the light from the window illuminating his balding head, Ben appears smart and professional. At least I want to believe that desperately. He's thirty-eight. That's the right age for a lawyer, right? Okay, his voice is a bit nasally and it goes up at the end of sentences. I wish he wouldn't scratch the top of his head so much when he talks. I mutter another prayer to Themis, the Greek goddess of justice. My statue was too big to fit in my pocket, but I wish I had brought her all the same.

"My client has raised his granddaughter since she was an infant. In all that time he has provided a loving, nurturing, and stable environment. The child is a straight-A student and participates in school sports. There is absolutely no indication that he should not continue to be the primary custodial parent. He and his granddaughter love each other. To separate them would be cruel and not in the best interest of the child. The fact that he takes her out on fishing trips only demonstrates that they are an integral part of each other's lives."

I turn around to look at Sitka, hoping she's nodding in agreement. She studies her lap, trembling, while pulling at the ends of her ponytail. Muskeg squeezes her shoulder and whispers something in her ear. I wish I were sitting there next to them, and I wish I hadn't been so insistent about Felix catching up on boat maintenance this afternoon. It would have been nice to have him here too. Not one of the gods, but a real flesh and blood friend on my side—and who knows, maybe he has a special ritual for keeping a family together.

"Your Honor." Jenny's attorney interrupts mine. Her voice is confident, sarcastic without stridence. Her blue suit seems to fit her a bit more naturally than Ben's does. She's my age or thereabouts, slim and poised. "Since Mr. Sato has raised the primary issue in this case, I would like to ask Captain Bancroft a couple of questions to clarify the answers he gave in deposition."

Judge Harry taps and holds his middle finger on the bench. "As long as they are relevant, clarifying questions." He looks at me. "Captain Bancroft, I'm not going to make you take the stand. You can answer from where you are sitting. But you are bound to answer truthfully. You can proceed, Ms. Crowley."

Jenny's lawyer reads over something on a pad of paper before speaking. "Captain Bancroft, you noted that you are often away for several days at a time when you go out crabbing. Who takes care of Sitka when you are gone?"

"She usually spends those nights either at a friend's house or with her godmother."

"And how does she get to her friend's house?"

"She bikes. It's not that far."

"Even in winter, when it's raining hard or even when there's ice on the roads, is that right?"

"Well, if it's that bad, her friend's mom will bring them home from school. Or else her godmother will pick her up and she'll stay with her."

"Yes, her godmother. At her house you mean?"

"Of course at her house. Where else would she be?"

Crowley looks like she just caught a hundred-pound halibut. "For the first four hours after school, she's at a saloon, isn't that right? The Blind Dog Tavern?"

My toes cramp against the soles of my shoes. "Sitka waits in the kitchen and does her homework. It's not like she's out in the bar."

"I see." Crowley flips through her legal pad, rustling the

pages. "You also stated that your eleven-year-old granddaughter helps on some of your fishing trips. Is she a crew member?"

My head pulls back, twinging the muscles in my neck. "No, she isn't crew. She's family. She likes being onboard. She likes to help out."

"Help out. What exactly does she do?"

"Cut bait. Help clean up. Things like that."

Crowley picks up what looks like an official report. "What about working with the pots? Emptying them? Stacking them?"

I dig my right thumb into the palm of my left hand. "The small ones for shrimp, yeah. Not the crab pots. I don't let her go near those."

"Every year the Bureau of Labor Statistics documents the jobs with the most fatalities, and every year commercial fishing tops the list."

"Sitka's always safe out there with me," I tell the judge. "I make sure of that. I only take her out in good weather, never in the winter, just as any other parent on this island."

"And crabbing in Alaska is by far the most lethal form of fishing." Jenny's lawyer jabs her forefinger against the report. "You are providing anything but a safe environment for your granddaughter, Captain Bancroft. Isn't that right?"

Ben stands up before I can explain how I don't let her come crabbing. "Your Honor."

Judge Harry raises his hand. "That's enough, Ms. Crowley. I said clarifying questions only."

Ben continues before Jenny's attorney can say more. "Your Honor, what Ms. Crowley is not telling us is that ninety-five percent of the fatalities in that report occur up in the Bering Sea, with the very large commercial operations, when crews are out for weeks and pushed to exhaustion. As to this business with the godmother, the Blind Dog is a pub that serves food as well as drinks, but there is absolutely no indication that my client's granddaughter has ever been exposed to alcohol. The danger to the child is not with her grandfather. The simple fact of the matter is that the plaintiff, although she is the child's biological mother, is a drug addict. She has been since she was a teenager."

Judge Harry raises his hand. "Folks, we've been through this. We have already established that Ms. Bancroft has been in recovery from her addiction for three years and nine months." He reaches his hand over to the laptop he brought out with him and taps the keyboard. I don't have a clue if he's checking legal precedent or looking up the tide tables. "We've heard from each side. And I've met with the young lady in question." He nods to Sitka, and then looks at me. "My congratulations to you, Captain Bancroft, on raising a bright, articulate, and well-balanced granddaughter. She seems very well-adjusted. It's clear she loves you."

I turn to smile at Sitka, but at the same time Jenny extends her arm back, even though she's too far away to reach her. Sitka buries her head against Muskeg.

"However," the judge continues, and my stomach contracts. "It's also clear that she is beginning to develop a relationship with her mother. The court places a child with her biological parent whenever possible. So my job is to decide if her mother, in spite of her previous troubles, is now capable of raising her daughter, or if we should allow Captain Bancroft, who has in fact been acting as her legal guardian for the past eleven years, to continue to have temporary custody until his adoption petition is resolved. To that end," and he motions to the bailiff, "I have one more person I want to hear from."

Nicole gets up from the back row of the courtroom and approaches us. Dark gray skirt. Matching jacket. White blouse. I try to catch her eye, to exchange a heartening smile. But she walks straight ahead without looking at me or Jenny. The judge reminds her that she is bound to be truthful.

"Ms. Harris, you serve as an addiction counselor to Ms. Jennifer Bancroft, correct?"

"For the past month or so, Your Honor."

"And what is your assessment of her ability to be a competent, full-time mother to her daughter?"

I watch Nicole shift her weight from one heel to the other. "Ms. Bancroft appears well-adjusted to her new life."

"Drug use?" the judge asks.

"Her regular tests have all come back clean. And the reports I've received from the New Ways House in Kalispell and the prison's addiction counselor confirm she has been clean for nearly four years now."

The judge waits a moment for her to continue. "And is she getting the support she needs to stay off drugs?"

"She attends a twelve-step program twice weekly." Nicole's voice remains even and clipped. Professional.

"So, to the best of your knowledge, she is clean and sober," the judge says.

"To the best of my knowledge, yes."

The judge scribbles some notes on his pad. "And what is your assessment of her relationship with her daughter?"

"Your Honor?"

As the judge tilts his head to look at Nicole, his glasses slide down the bridge of his nose. "Ms. Harris. I don't like having to pull information from you one syllable at a time. You are here as an expert. So, I am going to ask this as clearly as I can and I want a full, straight answer. In your assessment, is there anything that suggests Ms. Bancroft would be an unfit parent?"

Nicole takes an audible inhale, then slowly lets the breath out. "No, Your Honor."

The judge glances at the screen of the laptop. "No, as in you won't annoy me, or no, as in you see no reason why Ms. Bancroft should not have primary custody of her daughter until the adoption is resolved?"

"She has not had custody of her daughter," Nicole says. "Only on paper, not in practice. Ray has been—"

"Ms. Harris." The judge peers over his lowered glasses. "Please answer my question."

Nicole's hand is trembling. "There is no reason to separate Sitka from her mother."

Her words sear my chest like a firebrand. This isn't what she should be saying. After all I've told her about Jenny's drug use, about how she's been manipulating things to get Sitka away from me, about how she was responsible for Donna's death. I turn and look at Ben. "Goddammit, object or something." He ignores me.

"Thank you, Ms. Harris," the judge says. "You may step back."

"I'd also like to add, Your Honor." The judge frowns, but Nicole rushes on. "Ray Bancroft is an integral part of Sitka's life. Any successful reunification of Ms. Bancroft and Sitka must include significant visitation time and involvement between Sitka and her grandfather."

The judge waves his hand, dismissing Nicole. Her eyes are wide, her mouth turned down. I stare at my feet and shake my head. When I look up, she's gone.

"Before you rule, Your Honor," Ben says, "I must point out that Ms. Bancroft has no visible means of support. How is she going to provide for her daughter? Is the child to go on welfare?"

"Your Honor." Jenny's attorney is quick on her feet. "Regarding the issue my colleague has raised, we point you to the adjoining petition and ask that you grant that motion as well."

Judge Harry holds up his hand. "Normally I'm not inclined to mix apples and oranges in one session. But in this case, the corresponding petition is in order, and it does have bearing on my decision. Captain Bancroft?"

Ben pulls on my sleeve so I stand up. "What?"

The judge ignores my lack of manners. "I've read over your late wife's will. You do realize that she had named your daughter Jennifer as the sole beneficiary of the boat, the *Jenny-Sais-Pas*?"

"Your Honor. She did that for the same reason lots of spouses do, to protect us in case someone sued my business. The whole point was for me to keep the boat. And she did that before we knew Jenny was on drugs. She didn't mean to—"

"Unfortunately, Captain Bancroft, we cannot debate her

intent. We have the will to go by, and according to it, the *Jenny-Sais-Pas* is the rightful property of Jennifer Bancroft. And I hereby order that to be carried out."

"You can't do this!" I'm not sure who I'm yelling this to—the judge, Jenny, Ben, or Themis.

"Mr. Sato, control your client."

Ben pushes on my shoulder and I collapse in my chair. I'm shaking like I have a fever. I feel like throwing up on Ben's polished shoes.

The judge raps his gavel. "Okay, here's how it's going to play out, folks. Until the question of permanent adoption is resolved, I am granting primary custody of Sitka to her mother. In addition I am granting visiting rights to her grandfather. He is to see her at least once every week for a period of at least forty-eight hours. They have a deep bond and I do not want that interrupted. Is that clear, Ms. Bancroft?"

Jenny nods her head, all smiles. "Yes, Your Honor."

"I want to reiterate that this is a temporary ruling, effective only until Captain Bancroft's adoption petition reaches this courtroom." He points the handle of his gavel at Jenny. "And if I ever catch you in here on anything vaguely resembling drug or alcohol charges, Ms. Bancroft, then I will immediately rescind this order and your daughter will go back to her grandfather faster than you can blink."

"Yes, Your Honor."

"Good. Then I wish you all the best of luck."

I have only a vague sense of standing as the judge departs. Ben gathers his papers. "I'll look into appealing the boat ruling," he says, but it is half-hearted.

Jenny waits for Sitka to give Muskeg one last hug, and then they follow Crowley through the oak doors, the guardian ad litem trailing behind them. Muskeg starts toward me, but I rush out into the hallway, Ben on my heels, and Muskeg calling out for me to slow down. They're all standing at the far end, near the elevators, Jenny's arm around Sitka's shoulders. My family.

I bolt from Ben, running toward them. Muskeg cries out

something about not making things worse, but I ignore her. "There's no reason you have to do this!" The words echo down the hallway.

"Grandpa!" Sitka holds her hand out toward me. "I'm sorry. This is my fault. I told the judge I wanted to spend time with Mom but—"

Her words fracture my heart. "Sitka, it's okay. You didn't do anything wrong. Everything will be all right."

I stop a few feet from them, wanting so much to take my granddaughter's hand, but Crowley places herself between us, holding up her briefcase. As if I were going to pull a gun out of my pocket and start shooting. Sitka's sobbing beside her mother, loud wet gasps, and I want to bend down and let her run into my arms like she used to every afternoon when I picked her up from school.

"My client has nothing to discuss with you at this time, Captain Bancroft. We will call you within the next two days regarding visitation."

I take a step sideways to appeal directly to Jenny. "You made your point. You've punished me for all the wrong I've done you. We can all go home now, all right? We can live in the same house, Jenny. We've done it before."

"Mr. Bancroft," the guardian-whatever-she-is says, "you'll have a chance to discuss visiting—"

"Fuck the visiting hours," I say. "Be reasonable, Jenny. You really think you can take care of Sitka on your own?"

Muskeg's voice is at the back of my neck. "Don't, Ray."

"You don't have a job, Jenny. I don't know what you're getting for assistance, but how long do you think you and Sitka can survive on that? Are you thinking of selling the boat? Nobody buys a boat this time of year. Just come on home with me, both of you."

Jenny presses the elevator button. It dings almost immediately and the doors whoosh open. She steps in and holds the door, motioning for Sitka to follow. I want to grab Jenny's shoulder, make her turn and respond to me, but her attorney is still between us and Ben and Muskeg are right behind me.

"Jenny, I need Sitka and she needs me!"

"Goodbye, Dad." As if she were taking leave of her dentist. Sitka's hair is sticking to her face from the tears, but she's quiet now and lets her mom lead her away.

The elevator doors close and I'm left staring at the scratched beige metal, the light disappearing down the shaft.

Chapter 16

STANDING ON THE BACK porch of Felix's cabin, I listen to a chorus of redpolls hunkered down in the branches of the hemlocks and silver spruce. You can barely hear their chirping above the heavy rainfall. There's probably some pine siskins in there as well. The air is thick with rainwater. The trunks of the cedars look like towers of mud. In spite of the downpour, I hiked two miles down to Beaver Gulch and back again, trying to get my thoughts straightened out. They're about as clear as the muck on the bottom of my boots. I scrape the soles against the green-black shingles nailed onto the steps, trying to dislodge the thickest chunks of mud. As I dig in harder, one of the shingles rips apart. I scuff the broken piece back and forth like sandpaper under the toe of my boot, before flicking it into the air. It sails on its side like a wounded duck before plummeting into a puddle of mud under the winter daphne.

That bush isn't looking so good. Another day or two of this rain and the roots are going to suffocate and the branches will turn black like they have the plague. I remember helping Felix plant that daphne when Sitka was a toddler. She always loved that plant. She'd waddle over to it and bury her nostrils in the lilac-colored blossoms. She'd pinwheel her arms in the air, letting out a loud "ahh" as she inhaled the sweet odor. If she reached for the red berries, I'd snatch her back. She couldn't understand that while sniffing the blossoms was fine, eating the berries or bark was poisonous. It's a wonder why nature sometimes attracts you to the very things that can just plain kill you.

I feel the buzz of my cell phone in my jacket pocket. I reach in and flip it open without even checking the caller ID, praying that it's Sitka.

"Ray?" Her voice has as much hope as I did a second ago.

"It's you," I say.

Nicole waits a few seconds before continuing. "I know I'm probably the last person you want to talk to."

"Not exactly the last, but close."

She gives a long sigh. "I understand if you feel betrayed, but I didn't have any choice. I had to give my honest assessment of Jenny to the judge, no matter how I felt about you. You can see that, can't you?"

It's getting dark rapidly. Somewhere in the distance a pack of Malamutes starts howling. "Yeah, okay. The judge had you in a headlock and you were just doing your job. I get it. Anything else?"

"You must be feeling pretty alone right now. I can't change what happened in the courtroom, but I can be there with you. I can come over and we can talk."

"I'm not at my place." My voice biting back, daring her to keep trying. "Besides, doesn't that go against those rules of professional conduct?"

"I'm not seeing your daughter," she says. "The rules no longer apply."

"I'm not surprised. She never could stick with anything very long, especially once she's gotten what she wanted."

"She didn't end the sessions, Ray. I did. She wanted to continue. I referred her to a family counselor. I was wrong to ever start this. I should never have agreed to see Jenny, since I have such strong feelings for you."

It was a mistake on my part, one of many. I'm the one who

asked Nicole to help Jenny. I'm the one who didn't file for guardianship. If Donna had been alive, she would have done it. I should just keep my mouth shut at this point, but I press Nicole.

"Why did you agree to work with Jenny, then?"

She answers without hesitation. "Because I thought it was what you wanted. That it was the best way to help you at the time. I should have known better. If a colleague had asked for my advice in a similar situation, I would have pointed out the dangers."

"Just so you know, I'm not blaming you for the judge's ruling. Or for any of it. This has been a long time coming. Jenny and I have had unfinished business ever since her mother's death."

"I'd like to see you again." Her voice ends on an upswing, hesitancy and hope mixed together. "I think you could use a friend right now. I'd like to be that friend."

Is this what I want? I can't decide right now, not while everything is up in the air about Sitka. "Maybe, but not for a while yet."

"I'm not going anywhere," she says. "Can I check in with you in a few days? As a friend?"

The hinges of the porch door squawk as Muskeg opens it and pokes her head out. She sees the cell phone against my ear. "Sitka?" she mouths.

"I gotta go," I tell Nicole. "I'll call you, okay? I'm not sure when, but I will."

"You know where to find me."

I turn off the phone and slide it into my jacket.

"Was that your attorney?" Muskeg asks.

"Just a friend." I reach inside my raincoat and fish a Camel out of my front shirt pocket. I flick open my butane lighter, the one with the grinning moose wearing a hunter's cap on it. Felix took Sitka shopping Christmas before last and she picked it out for me. I thumb the scroll wheel, sparking a small flame. I have to cup my hand over it to light up. Filling my throat with the acrid taste of tobacco does little to calm me. I exhale and the blue-tinted smoke is immediately battered down by the rain droplets.

Muskeg steps all the way out onto the porch, placing her hand on my shoulder. "Cigarettes, coffee, and a couple of beers is all you've had all day. Dinner's ready. What you need is a bowl of my famous cabin fever stew."

I pitch the butt into the air. It lands a few yards away in the mud, and is immediately sucked down and extinguished.

"What I need is to be fixing dinner for my granddaughter at home where she belongs. Then I need to be on my boat, catching crab."

"Well, Sitka isn't home and you don't have your boat," Muskeg says. "They're both terrible things, but there's nothing you can do about it tonight, so you might as well come in and get some decent food into you."

She goes back inside the cabin, but I stay outside. If I had acted differently toward Jenny when she was a teenager, if I had been a better father, would she have stayed at home instead of running away to Anchorage? Would she not have even gotten pregnant in the first place? And why did those damn brakes have to go out on the truck when Donna was driving across Turnagain Arm? I knew they needed work, but I was so busy with the boat, and we were tight on money.

It's so wet out here, I can barely breathe the thick air. I wander through the mudroom and into the small kitchen. The A-frame cabin is made up of the kitchen, a bathroom, and one large open room with a futon sofa, leather-bound mission chairs, and a television-audio setup. There's a bedroom loft and separate bathroom above the open living room. Felix carved just about every piece of furniture in here. Double-paned windows let in what little winter daylight there is. The white drywall that we put up a few years ago helps to deflect the grayness of the day. It's warm enough that I take off my coat and my sweatshirt as well as my boots.

In the great room, Felix is sitting down at the small pine table that holds his computer and printer. He's wearing a flannel shirt identical to Muskeg's, checkered patterns of green and blue. Felix pokes his finger at the screen.

"Ray, take a look. Here's a Navy sub moving north just outside Holkham Bay. I wonder where she's headed to. Oh, and here's an oil tanker that registered in Macao. Hell, I hope she's seaworthy."

"Felix, will you please shut that thing off?" Muskeg asks. "Stew's ready. How many times do I have to tell you?"

"In a minute, Peach Lips." But he keeps his focus on the screen. "I could look at ShipMates all day," he says to me.

Felix bought the software program for himself last Christmas, since he knew that Muskeg was getting him a new hunting knife. The program uses a real-time GPS system to monitor the coordinates of any registered ship, including commercial fishing boats. Ships show up as icons on the screen. The triangular points move in the direction indicated by the GPS signal. You click on a ship icon and a dialog box pops up and shows you the name of the ship, its owner, where it's registered, and so on. The first time Muskeg saw the name of the program she thought it was an illicit dating site and nearly smashed in the computer screen. Now she says that it might as well be porn, given how much time Felix spends on it.

"You can use it after dinner," he offers. "I'll be doing the dishes anyway."

"No thanks," I say.

"I'm not going to tell you again, Felix." Muskeg's voice is as strong as the aromas from the kitchen. "You think I'm Suzy Homemaker, here to dish up dinner at your convenience?"

"Of course not, Honey Pot. After all, who cooked dinner the last three nights running? Yours truly, that's who," he adds, as if Muskeg were actually going to debate him.

"Oh, just sit down," she says. "No one's saying you don't make good husband material."

"Like she would ever actually consider marrying anyone," Felix says to me.

I sit down at the far end of the kitchen table. Muskeg ladles stew from a cast iron pot into our bowls. The dish smells thick and rich, large chunks of beef mixed with potatoes and vegetables.

"Thanks, Muskeg." I don't mean to sound unappreciative.

"Just a minute, my sweet nectar." Felix gets up and goes to the kitchen counter, where he snaps off three sprigs of rosemary from a large branch sitting in a pitcher of water. With a bit of a flourish, he drops a sprig into each bowl. They look like miniature redwood trees floating in a muddy river.

"I saw this in a restaurant when I was in Juneau," he says. "There's no reason you can't add a little class to anything you cook, even your cabin fever stew."

"Lord, have mercy." Muskeg rolls her eyes as she sets down three open bottles of Alaskan Amber.

I grunt over the bowl, grab a slice of bread, rip it in half, and dunk it around in the gravy until it's coated and dripping brown. I pop it into my mouth and move it between my cheeks. It tastes pretty damn good, like pot roast.

"I was about to say a little prayer of thanks," Felix says.

I dip another piece of bread in. "I'm not feeling very grateful to the gods right now."

Felix tears off a sheet of paper towel and swipes his mouth. "All right, be that way. You're the one who wanted to stay over here for a few days. But keeping company with you is like hanging out with a hibernating bear who just got poked with a stick."

"Enough, Felix," Muskeg says. "Leave him be a bit. He's going through a pretty rough time. He doesn't need you harping on him."

I put down my spoon. "What if Sitka thinks I don't want her anymore? What if she thinks I've given her up?"

Muskeg pats my hand. "She's not stupid, Ray. She knows it was a judge's order. She knows you love her. And she loves you. And you'll get to see her this weekend."

I get up from the table and go into the main room and look out the windows. It's already dark. Everything is reflected back at me. I keep picturing when Sitka packed up the rest of her be-longings. Two days after the hearing, a woman from Children's Services ferried in from Juneau to meet with me and Sitka. She assured us we'd still have plenty of time together, and then she spent an hour with Sitka up in her room. When they came down, Sitka had her suitcases in hand. With a little nudge from the social worker, she came over and hugged me. I could feel her tears through my shirt.

"I don't want to leave you, Grandpa," she sobbed. It was like she was a little kid again.

"I know." I hugged her tight against me. "I'm so sorry. I should have handled things differently."

Sitka pulled back from me, studying my face. She ran her hand under her cheeks, removing any trace of her crying. The mature pre-teen emerged. "Yes," she admonished. "You should have."

If the social worker hadn't been there, ready to take Sitka back to the apartment, I would have begged her to stay a little longer. "I'll see you next weekend, kiddo," I told her. "I love you. You can call me anytime before then. You know that."

Sitka joined the social worker at the front door, each of them carrying a few bags. Then, just like that, as if the last eleven years didn't mean a thing, she was gone.

Muskeg and Felix follow me into the main room. Felix hands me another beer. "It'll work itself out. You'll see. Now, why don't we enjoy the evening. I rented that new James Bond movie."

"Jenny's going to do everything she can to turn Sitka against me. I swear, she's been nothing but a pain in the ass since she walked in the door."

Muskeg sits in a mission chair, eyeing me. "It seems to me that you share some of the blame for what's going on."

"Seems to me you never had a problem with Sitka coming out on the boat with us." My jaw tightens. Muskeg's getting on my case? These are supposed to be my best friends, the ones on my side. "You never said anything before."

"That part I figured was your business. But Ray," she says,

her voice suddenly chilled. "You hit your daughter. I know she's been a handful ever since she was a teenager. I know she pushes all your buttons—"

"You don't know the half of it."

"That's still no excuse for you hitting a woman, any woman. We put up with too much of that crap."

My face flushes like the breast of a redpoll. I look down at the cabin floor. "Yeah, okay. You're right. I had no excuse for doing that." I raise my head back up, evening my line of sight with Muskeg. "But dammit, that's no reason for you to start taking Jenny's side!"

Felix steps between us. "Now, Ray. Don't you be yelling at Muskeg. She's been a good friend to you. Who lent us the money for the new winch and the boat repair, huh? Muskeg, that's who." He turns to her. "And you haven't asked for one penny back, have you, Honey Bunches?"

Muskeg shakes her head. "Oh, Felix. You're missing the point, as usual. This ain't about the money. Although things have been a little slow at the Blind Dog."

"You see there, Ray?" Felix says. "She ain't rolling in dough, but she loaned us the money anyway. And a damned good thing she did. A crab boat ain't much use if you can't pull up the pots."

Muskeg leans toward me. "There's no rush to repay me. I know you don't have the money right now. That's not the important thing here."

But something that Felix said has clicked in my muddled brain. I sit on the sofa next to the mission chair. "Felix is absolutely right, Muskeg. You do need to be paid back. You need to be paid back immediately. And if you aren't, why then you're going to have to take some drastic action."

Muskeg tilts her head at me. "Have you not heard a word I said, Ray?"

"Don't you get it? I'm no longer the owner of the boat. Jenny is," I announce, as if I had just won a prize. "Any debt associated with the boat is now hers. As far as I know, she only gets welfare money. Without income from crabbing, there's no way that she could pay you back $7,000. In the meantime, you have a perfect- ly legal right to take the winch back."

"I'm not getting where you're going at all." Muskeg scratch- es her cheek. "Why would I want to take the winch back?"

"Like Felix said, without a winch, Jenny can hire a crew, but they're not going to pull up any crab pots. She'd be sunk for the season." I rub my palms together. "Oh, and the tools. They're mine. She doesn't get them. I can use those to dismantle the winch. No, this is perfect. Why didn't I think of this before?"

Felix frowns. "Some people," he says, shifting his gaze briefly to Muskeg, "might call this extortion."

"Bullshit. It gives me back control is all," I answer. "Jenny's convinced the court that she has the ability to earn enough mon- ey to have primary custody of Sitka. She thinks she has what it takes to fish and crab and shrimp. But what if she doesn't? She'll have to come to terms with me."

Muskeg folds her arms across her chest. "How is Jenny sup- posed to take care of Sitka if she can't hire a crew and make a catch? Raymond Bancroft, if you for one minute think that I am going to do anything to put my godchild in jeopardy, then you've got the brains of salmon roe. The very idea that you would let your granddaughter go hungry and be out on the street—"

"No one's going to be out on the street," I tell her. "I'm going to cut a deal with Jenny. She hires me to captain the boat. I bring in her catch and take a captain's share of it. That still leaves her enough to support herself on. But in return, she sends Sitka home to live with me and doesn't contest my adoption petition. End of story."

Muskeg leans back into the chair. "And why wouldn't Jenny just sell the boat? Or hire someone else to be the captain?"

"Sell that old boat? In this economy? Do you know how many boats are for sale around here? Too much glut in the market. Jenny won't have a choice, I'm telling you. Hell, where would she find a licensed captain this late in the season?"

Muskeg drums her fingers on the armrests. "Let's just say this scheme of yours might work. There are legal ways to go about it. We meet with your attorney. He helps file an injunction, and we see where it goes from there."

"My attorney." I stand up and grab my heavy raincoat off the coat rack next to the front door. "He's done me a lot of good."

"Now where you going?" Felix asks.

"I'm going down to the boat to get my tools and take out the winch cable and motor."

Muskeg jumps up and tries to get between me and the door. "You can't just walk on that boat. You'd be trespassing. You don't even have keys anymore. What are you going to do? Bust the hatch open to get your tools?"

"Jenny's been trespassing in my life since she's been back." I fish out the ring with the truck and boat keys attached and jingle them in front of her. "And if you think I was stupid enough to hand over the only set of keys to her, you're the one who has the eel brains." I give her a quick peck on the cheek. "I know you're watching out for me, Muskeg. Don't worry. I'm not going to do anything half-cocked."

Felix takes my arm for a minute. "You've got a couple of beers in you, Ray. Don't be getting yourself arrested or anything stupid like that."

"I'm not drunk, I promise. You two enjoy the Bond movie."

Felix looks back at the television. "Shoot. If I had known it was just going to be me and Muskeg, I would have rented something steamier."

I'M DOING A MENTAL inventory of tools when I pull up to the dock. How many pipe wrenches are onboard? How many drills? The rain has let up just a little, the silver drops slanted sideways in the yellow dock lights. The wind's up from the north. There are a few cars and trucks parked in the lot, but I'm not worried about being seen. Anyone here will be minding their own business. Besides, who's going to stop me from getting my own tools? I unlock the gate that leads down to the pier where the *Jenny-Sais-Pas* is docked. Halfway down the planks, something seems wrong. There's a light on somewhere on my boat. Jenny's boat. It's not the pilothouse or the deck lights. A wide beam sweeps across the aft deck. Must be a flashlight.

Why would Jenny be here? She doesn't know beans about maintenance yet. There's nothing particularly fun to do on a boat when it's docked, unless she wants to revel in her new property. But why do that on a rainy night? Crouching down, I scuttle along the other boats until I'm next to the *Jenny-Sais-Pas*. I poke my head up like a harbor seal. The dock lights illuminate the foredeck and starboard side. No one seems to be near the bow. Carefully, very carefully, I hoist myself onto the bulwark and lie flat on the foredeck until I catch my breath.

The trick is to keep my body low and flat and not make a lot of noise. Fortunately the wind and rain work in my favor. I hunch over to the wheelhouse and peer around to the aft deck. The light is coming from below. Whoever's here has opened the hatch to the aft hold. I wish I had one of my pipe wrenches, but they're stored below. Then I remember the fire hatchet hanging on the inside bulkhead of the pilothouse. I crouch along for another few feet and reach the door. My hand turns the knob and the door hinges groan like a sheet of ice. Damn. I kept meaning to lubricate those. I turn my head but don't see anyone. Just in case I lay flat for a couple of minutes. I'm getting too old to be skulking around like this.

When it seems all clear, I put one knee inside and stretch my hand up and wrap my fingers around the handle of the ax. I try to lift it off its pegs, but the leverage is all wrong. I have to get up on one knee and slide it up along the wall. Once it's free, I pull back and almost drop the damn thing. The handle slips in my grip and the blunt edge of the blade smacks the fleshy crotch of my right hand. I muffle a curse.

I back out of the pilothouse and move to the stern. There's still light coming from below, though it's not moving around. I crawl to the hatch and look down. A flicker of shadow and the barest whoosh make me turn just in time to see the flash of met-al pipe coming at my head. I dodge away but the pipe whacks me on the shoulder. The pain explodes all the way to my right hand. I have to consciously grip the hatchet to hang onto it. Through instinct more than anything else I kick out and man-age to knock the attacker's legs out from under him. I see a face with a scruffy goatee as he goes down. But even as he's falling he swings the pipe again. I hold up the ax handle and manage to deflect the blow, but the reverberation sends a searing arrow of pain back through my arm and shoulder.

The guy stands up, hovering over me, his upper body bathed in the mercurial harbor light. He's breathing hard, his chest moving up and down like a bellows. I have a hint of rec-ognition, but can't place him.

"What are you doing here?" he demands. "This ain't your boat."

"Hell it isn't. Who are you and what are you doing here?"

He's in his late twenties or early thirties. His watchman's cap has fallen off, revealing brown hair with a deep receding hairline. I scan the rest of him: a long angular nose, high cheek-bones that form a ridge between the nostrils and ears. The goa-tee has a bit of gray in it. Blue tattoos mark his knuckles and his left wrist, where one might expect to find a wristwatch.

"I ought to call the harbor police," he says.

"Go ahead, dipshit. They're going to wonder what the hell you're storing in my hold."

He narrows his eyes at me. "I told you. It ain't your . . ." He stops. "Fuck. Of course. Jenny's old man."

When he says Jenny's name I finally realize who it is.

Diesel Kurtz.

Chapter 17

THERE'S A TAUT MEMBRANE of pain stretching across my chest and right shoulder. My right hand is sore and puffy, as if a jellyfish has taken up residence under my skin. I can flex my fingers, so my hand's not broken, but it hurts like hell when I do. My thoughts have scattered like chum tossed to a sea lion. To focus, I stare at Diesel, my expression as stony as I can make it. We're in the pilothouse. Diesel's stretched out on the bench against the starboard bulkhead. You'd think he was in his own living room, the way he has his arm draped over the top of the cushions. His flannel shirt peeks out from the holes in his gray sweatshirt. His jeans have a greasy cast, as if they haven't been washed in months.

I'm at the counter on the port side, the captain's chair between us. We've reached a truce of sorts, neither one of us wanting to have the harbor police onboard. I've flipped on the interior lights, but that shouldn't be a problem. Nothing unusual about a couple of guys chewing the fat late at night on a boat.

"You're a bigger pain in the ass than I remember." Diesel rubs his left knee. His voice has a stuffy nasal quality to it, like his nostrils are all plugged up. His nose bends to the right side of his face. The inner bone and cartilage seem like they've been knocked off track more than once. He looks around the pilot-house like there's a hidden treasure somewhere. "Life's been good for you over these last dozen years, hasn't it, Ray? You sorry to be giving up the romantic life of a sea captain?"

He's trying to goad me, so I goad right back. "I heard you were getting out. What were you in for this time?"

Diesel scratches his ear and doesn't respond.

"I wish I had known earlier. I could have testified at your parole hearing."

"I bet." He gives me an open-mouthed grin. The overhead light glimmers off the dental fillings that stagger across his mouth, one end to the other. "I doubt that would have mattered. Our prisons are overcrowded, haven't you heard?" He stretches his arms, fighting back a yawn. "They had to let me out to make room for the really dangerous criminals."

"You going to tell me what you're doing here?"

Diesel holds up a set of keys and shakes them. "I'm here all legal-like. I came at the request of the boat owner, my very own beloved."

"I thought Jenny was trying to make a new start." I move a few steps toward the starboard side, trying to hold my ground so he knows I'm not intimidated. "I don't want you anywhere near Sitka, do you hear me?"

"Ah, Ray, I've been clean almost as long as Jenny." Diesel puts the keys back in his jeans pocket. "Or should I call you Dad?"

My hands turn to fists, and it's a good thing the captain's chair is still between us.

"She didn't call you? I moved in with them. We're getting married soon, probably before Christmas, just like we always planned. How's that for a present from your daughter to you?"

"Look, asshole. You and Jenny want the boat, fine. I'll manage somehow. Just leave Sitka out of it. She stays with me."

Diesel takes one of the bench cushions and tosses it up into the air. Just as he's about to catch it, he opens his hands and lets it plop to the deck. He picks it up and tosses it again. But he does it patiently, like someone who's learned to amuse himself for long periods of time. When he picks the cushion up again, he holds it toward me. "You don't get it, Ray. Jenny, me, Sitka— we're one big family now."

That does it. I lunge toward Diesel, even though I'm likely to hurt myself more than him. But I don't get the chance. His left hand pops out from under the cushion, holding an eight-inch boning knife. I stop well short of his reach.

"Paroled felon with a weapon, not very smart, Diesel."

He cocks a smile. "Self-defense is always a good idea. Can't arrest a guy for defending himself with a knife that he just happened to find on a boat." His metallic sneer disappears. "Now back the fuck off."

I settle into the captain's chair. My chair. "Just what is it you do want? I don't think it's Sitka, even if you are her father."

"You don't get it, do you? Jenny said you wouldn't."

"Why don't you explain it to me since I'm so damn dense?"

Diesel lets his arm relax and lays the knife across his thigh. "Look, old man, you've had things your way for the past dozen years. While Jenny and I sat in jail without one finger of help from you, you got to be out in the open every day. Every single day, you could walk down to the ocean and smell clean air. You could walk or drive or go wherever you pleased. You got to go to bed at night when you wanted to. You got to walk around without worrying about getting a knife stuck in you, without worrying about getting gang-raped. You got to live life. You got to play parent with our daughter."

The image of Diesel as Sitka's father makes me want to heave, but that's the last thing I want him to see. "You a born-again Christian as well?"

"Everyone who gets paroled has found Jesus Christ." His eyes gaze forward and downward, as if he were trying to bore a hole into the deck three feet in front of him. Then he lifts his head, a ragged grin drifting back across his face.

"I thought as much."

"But you're wrong if you think Jenny ain't dead serious about her religion. Hell, she even surprised me with that holy roller heaven-and-hell stuff." He wipes the blade of the knife across his oily jeans, then points the tip my way. Too far to do any damage, too close to ignore. "Walk away, old man. People have been fucking with me my entire life and I'm not going to take their crap any more. Got it?"

"Oh, so you're just the poor victim here."

He gives a small shake of his head. "No, I'm the guy whose day has finally come. It's my turn to have the wife and the kid and the boat. My turn to have a life."

He sounds sincere and I wonder, for a moment, if I can reason with him. "No one's saying you shouldn't get your share. But what kind of a life does Sitka get out of this? Have you thought about that?"

This seems to stop him for a second. "That's up to Jenny." He puts the knife on a cushion and looks out the window, or maybe at his own reflection. I wonder how much of it he sees. "It's a package deal," he says. "Jenny, the boat, the kid."

"How do you expect to make this work? You've never captained a vessel before. You think you just point this thing out into the water and go?"

Diesel snorts and turns around slowly. "Running this tub ain't that hard, Ray. Besides, Jenny's been getting in some practice. It was mighty nice of you to teach her a thing or two about crabbing. She appreciates it."

"Like I said, Diesel, you and Jenny can take the boat. Go start a new life for yourselves. But do you really need a pre-teen in tow? A few months of her ups and downs and you'll be going crazy. It'll be hard enough just for the two of you. You'll have a much better chance if you leave Sitka with me. Come on, what do you say?"

Diesel tightens his fists. "People like you think you can pull other people's strings. But you don't own me."

"You're going to support your wife and daughter with an honest day's work, is that right, Diesel?" He doesn't answer, so I press on. "Got a full-time job or some investment funds? 'Cause it's going to take a while to make a decent living crab-bing, especially if you've never done it before."

"You know what? Shut up and get the fuck off our boat."

I step forward and put my face within inches of his. "You're a loser and you know it, Diesel. Always have been. Always will be. What have you been doing down in that hold, anyway? Inspecting the fuel lines? Maybe you wanted to make sure you had the right ballast. Tell you what. I'll go get the harbor police and they—"

The quick pressure of steel against my right cheekbone tells me that maybe I'm not going about this the right way. I could have sworn he left the boning knife on the cushions.

"How'd you like your granddaughter not to recognize you the next time she sees you?" He presses the blade and I feel a dab of blood, like warm thick paint, seep out onto my face.

"Put it down, you little toad."

I don't know who's more surprised to hear Muskeg's voice—me or Diesel. From the corner of my eye, I see a piece of metal. It's the muzzle end of her hunting rifle. Diesel lowers the knife and steps back. She lowers the barrel just a little.

"You okay, Ray?" Felix asks. "Muskeg thought we—"

Before he can finish, her voice runs over all of us like a tank. "I knew it, Ray. I knew it in my bones you'd come down here and start up something you shouldn't."

Just what I need right now, a critique of my battle strategy. "Allow me to introduce my future son-in-law Diesel Kurtz."

"I remember him well enough," Muskeg says. "Felix, why don't you go fetch the cops while I keep an eye on Mr. Kurtz?"

"That's not necessary," I say quickly. "Diesel and I were just having a little chat, a family disagreement. We'll work things out, won't we Diesel?"

Diesel grunts a "Sure, man."

I walk over to Muskeg and gently push the rifle barrel so it's pointing all the way downward. "I've got this, Muskeg. Let him go. I just came down here to get my tools, remember?"

"You got a problem with this man getting his tools?" Muskeg asks Diesel.

Diesel opens his arms, then lets them fall at his sides. "Like I give a fuck." He nods at me. "Get them and don't come back."

"I'll help you." Felix turns to Muskeg. "This won't take long."

"Don't you worry about Sitka, now," Diesel says, getting in one last dig.

Muskeg walks straight to him, the gun barrel pointed at his gut. "Whatever problems you and Ray have, we'll settle through the lawyers. But that little girl is mighty important to me. You and me understand one another?"

Diesel glares at her, but keeps his fists at his sides. "Sitka's my kid. You think I would do anything to hurt her?"

"See that you don't," Muskeg tells him. "Go on and get your tools then, Ray. And you," she says to Felix. "Well, what are you waiting for? Go on and help him."

"Right you are," Felix says. "Right you are."

He steps out to the deck and I follow him, Muskeg behind us. I almost expect Diesel to come out as well, but he stays in the pilothouse, his face close to the window, watching us, or maybe staring at his reflection again. It's stopped raining. But the air is cold with the dampness that still clings to it.

"Should we yank out the winch?" Felix whispers. "I mean, we're here and all."

"Haven't you heard a word I've said?" Muskeg answers in a hushed voice. "That's my winch and you'll get it only after I get a court order tomorrow. I leave this to you two and I'll be the one arrested for stealing."

The tools are stowed in the aft hold, so Felix and I clamber down the rear hatch. I flip on the light switch, hoping to find drugs, or illegal immigrant stowaways, or anything that would be evidence of the criminal crap I know Diesel must be up to. But it's all pretty much as Felix and I left it, with the exception of four wooden crates stacked against the port bulkhead. Ah-ha, I think, as I open them up, but they're just full of pots and pans, towels, and blankets. While Felix carries up my welding torch and one of our toolboxes, I run a flashlight over the deck and bulkheads, looking for any signs of Diesel making a secret compartment. Nothing.

"I don't remember signing up to do one hundred percent of the work here," Felix says.

I stow away the flashlight and pick up a six-foot wrench. The solid pull of its weight feels good. But with my right arm and shoulder still smarting, I'm limited as to how much I can carry, and it takes us another twenty minutes to get all the tools up, offloaded, and into the bed of the pickup. When I close the tailgate, I take out a pack of cigarettes and give one to Felix and one to Muskeg. We all light up, staying quiet for a few minutes. The town is quiet too, most lights out. The dark water laps against the seawall with a low, gurgling sound as it churns over and under itself.

Finishing my smoke, I crush the stub under my boot. "I should come back here after he's gone and just tear the whole boat apart."

"Jeez, Ray," Felix says. "What if you don't find anything? What if he really is only getting the boat ready for him and Jenny to go crabbing?"

"Yeah, right," I argue. "What you and I should do is take turns watching his every move. Maybe he's got drugs stashed in their apartment. We could wait until he and Jenny are gone, when Sitka's in school, and tear that place apart. Then we could take the drugs to the cops, and I could get Sitka back."

"I don't know how many ways to tell you what I've already told you," Muskeg says. "Be patient. Work through your lawyer. Anything you do now could influence the adoption proceeding."

I kick the toe of my boot against the rear tire of my truck. "Fine. You made your point. I'm going home."

Muskeg looks up at the gray night sky. "Men," she says, as if she can't fathom what kind of leftover scrap pieces the gods were using when they fashioned us.

Chapter 18

WHEN I WAKE UP the next morning, the taste of blood is thick as fish roe on my tongue. The left side of my mouth is swollen and my jaw feels like someone's yanked it with a pair of pliers. I go into the bathroom and switch on the light. My left cheekbone is underlined with a purple and blue discoloration. Beyond that, and three-day beard stubble, I don't look as pummeled as I thought I might. I run my tongue over my teeth, feeling stringy tissue under the back molar. The punch that Diesel hammered me with last night must have loosened the tooth. It's not completely out and I wonder if it can be saved or if I'll need a dental implant. Jesus, how much do those things cost?

I remember from the Coast Guard first aid training class that rinsing with warm salt water should help with this kind of thing, maybe keep it from getting infected. The morning air is chilly. There's an icy breeze slipping in under the windowsill. I put on some sweatpants and a flannel shirt without bothering to button it up, then stumble my feet into some dry socks.

There must be a way to use some leverage against Jenny and Diesel. The good news is that after last night's confrontation, Muskeg will be bent on keeping them from using the boat. The bad news is that she is just as insistent on going through the lawyers and courts to make it happen. Keep it legal. All nice and proper, tied up with a pretty pink bow. Look where that's gotten me so far. And now that Diesel knows we're checking up on him, he'll keep his plans under wraps. And what about Jenny? Is she going to use my little escapade on the boat last night to keep me from seeing Sitka? I don't think she could, but then again, I never thought anyone in their right mind would give her custody. Even temporarily.

I head downstairs and flip on the light switch, wanting a strong cup of coffee more than the salt water. A figure hunches over the kitchen table.

"For fuck's sake!"

It's Sitka. Her head cradled in her arms, breathing in and out like a napping seal pup. Her rain jacket has slid off her shoulders and halfway down the back of the kitchen chair. Her school backpack is crumpled on the floor. My shouting doesn't wake her, which isn't a surprise since she's been known to sleep through nuclear-level blasts of hip-hop music from her alarm clock. But the light does. She twists her head toward the door-way and squints open one eye.

"Turn those off. Can't you see I'm sleeping?" She pulls up her jacket and nestles her head back into her arms.

"What are you doing here?" I walk over to her and tap her shoulder. "Sitka?"

"Hmm?"

I prod her again. "Sitka, wake up. Come on."

The seal pup arches her back and lifts her head, before stretching her arms and yawning. "It's cold in here. Don't you have the heat on?"

I take out a chair and sit down next to her. "Did something happen at your mother's?" I have this immediate picture of the inevitable clash between them. I don't care what the court says. I have zero faith in Jenny's ability to be any kind of mother. "Did she send you here? Did she kick you out?"

"No, it's not that."

There was this show on the History Channel once. It came

on just before *Ice Road Truckers*. It was about how the human brain evolved and this scientist said we all have this part of our brain that's at the base of our skull. It's like a lizard's brain and it gets all fired up when we feel threatened. Right now mine must be lit up like the Northern Lights in February.

"Sitka, has your dad done anything to you?"

"Nothing like that," she insists. "He and my mom argue a lot but he's okay with me. Why do you have to treat everyone like a criminal?"

"Okay," I concede. "But you can't blame me for suspecting something. Does your mother even know you're here?"

"Yeah." She pulls her arm close to her mouth, biting her sleeve.

I don't believe her, but decide not to press her on that. "It's awfully early. Just when did you get here?"

She shrugs. "I don't know. Maybe an hour ago?" Like I'm one of her teachers throwing out a pop quiz.

"An hour ago was 5 a.m." I should call Jenny and check in, but knowing her, she'd make this my fault somehow. "And just how did you get here?"

"Rode my bike." Her tone is one big duh.

I rub my fingers against my forehead. "I love you, Sitka, but that was a stupid thing to do. Some nutcase could have dragged you off into the bushes. I don't ever want you doing something like that again. You got me?"

"Yeah." She traces nondescript shapes on the tabletop.

I watch her face, trying to see the little girl I've been missing, the child who comes and goes. "How come you didn't go up to your bedroom?"

Her finger zigzags to the middle of the table and back to her left forearm. "'Cause."

"Because why?"

She turns her head, and her bangs get in her eyes. She tries pushing them aside, but they wind up sticking up in the air. "I didn't know if it was still going to be my room. I mean, maybe you turned it into a workshop or something."

"For heaven's sake, Sitka. You slept there just last weekend. And, I may add, it's just as messy as when you left it."

She sits up straighter in her chair but doesn't look at me. "When Sarah's sister Jackie went off to college in Portland, her mom turned her bedroom into a sewing room."

I come close to making a joke about renting the room out to tourists during the summer, but the way Sitka's mouth has etched itself into a straight line stops me.

"Your room will be there as long as you want."

"Even though I told that counselor I wanted to try living with my mom?" Sitka delivers this to the linoleum.

"Oh, honey."

"That's why the judge took me away from you. I didn't know I was choosing between you and my mom." Big tears drip down her cheeks and make round wet spots on her jacket. "I didn't want to choose. I just wanted to spend some time with her. Are you mad?"

"No, of course not, Sitka. Of course you want to spend time with your mom. Get to know her." So that explains why the judge ruled the way he did, and it's also good news for the adoption. If Sitka tells the powers that be that she wants to be with me, maybe it won't be much of a fight. I walk behind her and put both hands on her shoulders, which are shaking with her full-out sobs. "I've filed some papers so I can adopt you, and you can live here permanently, the way we've always done, and you'll see your mom as often as you want. Unless you'd rather live with her?"

Sitka stares at me without answering. She lets the tears keep coming down her cheeks. Not wiping them.

"Honey? Are you okay?"

"Don't ask me to choose between you and my mom. I'm only eleven. I have a new favorite band every month. I don't want to choose where to live."

"Fair enough." I give her shoulders a squeeze and step back from the chair. Hell of a thing, asking a young girl to decide who she loves more, who would take better care of her. She's never known her mom as an addict. How little it takes for Jenny to turn.

I can't lose her. Not to her mother, not to anyone.

"You okay, Ray? You get hurt? Your mouth looks funny."

"Nah," I lie. "Caught the wrong side of a boom, that's all. But let this be a reminder for you to pay attention when you're on the boat."

She cocks her head at me. "You still want me on the boat?"

"Of course I do. Once we have all the legal stuff cleared up, the weather will be better." I run my finger under my eye. Still tender. "You hungry? Want some breakfast or something?"

"In a minute," she says. "I feel all gross. I'm going to take a shower."

"Go on up and I'll fix you some oatmeal. Aren't you glad I made you keep some of your clothes here?"

Sitka fails to acknowledge this act of extreme foresight on my part. She stands up and takes her jacket off, hanging it on the back of the chair. "I don't have to go to school today, do I?"

"Uh, yeah, you do," I tell her. "You don't get a free pass on that one."

"Why is everyone trying to make my life so miserable?" She throws the protest over her shoulder as she exits the kitchen and plods up the stairs.

I put on some coffee. While that's going, I run warm water in a glass, stir in some salt, and rinse my mouth, spitting out pink liquid into the kitchen sink. I run my tongue over the tender, puffy gum tissue, coaxing that back molar back into place. The phone chirps unexpectedly, making me jump for the second time this morning. I pick it up on the fifth ring and say hello.

"Ray, it's Hank O'Neill." From his tone I'm guessing my insurance agent isn't bearing good news. "I know it's early but I wanted to catch you before you went out on the boat. Not to mention the call from Chicago that woke me up thirty minutes ago."

I don't have a boat any more. But I don't want to talk about it, either. At least not before coffee. "What's up?"

"We've been trying, with Ben Sato's help, to negotiate a settlement with Walt Francke's insurance company. I thought we were all on the same page." Hank is normally a mellow guy, but his words ratchet through the phone like they were driven by a torque wrench. "Only they tell me that Mr. Francke had a certain visitor at his hospital room."

"I guess I should have told you or Ben about that."

"Any settlement deal is off. They're going for a full-blown personal injury suit. Complete with judge and jury, if they have their way. They're going to be looking for punitive damages. I have to tell you, Ray. In all the years I've practiced up here, I've never had something like this go all the way to court. Never."

"Walt's being an ass. Do you really think they have a case?"

"I'm hoping a judge will encourage them to settle. The deposition that Nicole Harris gave Ben certainly helps our case. She was very detailed and comes off like an expert. You're lucky she was onboard."

"What happens now?"

Hank rustles some papers on his end. "I'll talk to Ben and have him send you over a statement summarizing why we do not believe you were responsible for the injuries. I want you to look it over as soon as possible and get copies back to both of us with any comments or concerns. I'm flying up to Anchorage later today, but you can reach me on my cell phone."

"You always know how to make my day, Hank," I tell him.

"Just don't do anything stupid. Do me that favor, please." With that parting shot, he hangs up.

I hear the shower turn off upstairs. Sitka comes downstairs, puts her arms around my waist, and gives me an extended hug. There's not a lot I can do about this lawsuit. I can hug Sitka right back, though, hug her and love her and try to be normal so she remembers what it's like to live with me.

"Feeling better?"

She lets go of me and nods. "Is breakfast ready? I'm starving."

"In a minute."

I dump a packet of instant oatmeal into some boiling water, swirl it around with a wooden spoon, then pour it into two bowls. Sitka watches me, her right arm propped up on the table, her ear cradled in the palm of her hand. She follows each movement, as if this were the first time she's ever seen me fix breakfast. I slice half a banana into each bowl, sprinkle on some cinnamon and sugar, and set one in front of Sitka. The steam from the oatmeal rises up to her bangs. I sit down and put my bowl in front of me but leave it alone.

Sitka spoons some more sugar onto her hot cereal. "What about milk?"

"Do I look like a waiter to you?"

Groaning, she slides out of her chair and over to the refrigerator to retrieve the milk. She splashes some onto the oatmeal, a gray puddle forming near the top. I wait until she swallows a spoonful.

"What made you bike over here this early in the morning, Sitka? And I want answers that contain more than one syllable."

She slurps another spoonful, watching me, trying to read my expression. "I want to stay here for a while."

"And you're sure your mom knows you're here and she's perfectly okay with that?"

Sitka drops her hand, hitting the rim of her bowl with the spoon, tipping it over sideways. The oatmeal runs freely onto the tabletop and the milky part soaks into the edge of an old newspaper. Neither of us moves to clean up the spill. I have to admit that Jenny kept the place a little neater when she was here. But now that it's just me most of the time, I've found comfort in my old habits.

"So maybe I didn't exactly tell her in person that I was leaving, but I wrote her a note, not that she'll even read it, because she's probably still in bed with him, and they're never up until way late, and I have to fix my own breakfast, and they probably wouldn't even know if I was like gone for ten days, because they're so moony-eyed, except when they're yelling at each other, and then she's dishing out all that Bible crap and playing holier than a TV preacher, as if I didn't know what they were doing in there, and I have to put on my iPod just to do my homework, and he's like trying to act like he's my long-lost dad, especially when she's looking, and when I try to talk to Mom about it, she's like, 'You're not giving him a chance,' like I'm the one stopping everyone from being one big happy reality show family." Her words roll into sobs and she swipes at the tears running down her cheeks.

I scoot over and put my arms around her, letting her bury her face into my chest, feeling my shirt get wet.

"Kiddo, kiddo, it's okay," I say, stroking the back of her hair.

She pushes my hand away. "I'm not a baby. Leave me alone."

Why am I suddenly the bad guy? I scoot my chair back just a little to give her space. "Sitka, listen to me. I'm really glad you're here. But you can't be taking off from your mom's like that."

"I don't want to go back. There. I've made my choice. I want to stay here."

"You and me both." I probably shouldn't say what I'm thinking, but I do. "Of course it would be easier for you to stay here if we could show that your mom and dad weren't treating you right. Are they using drugs? If they are, or even if you've seen anything that looks like drug stuff, then you could stay here all the time."

"I told you it's nothing like that," Sitka says. "It's you."

"What do you mean?"

Sitka focuses on the spilled oatmeal and keeps her voice calm and even. "Mom says you won't want me around after I become a teenager. I'm almost twelve, so that's only like a year away."

"Nonsense," I say.

She looks up at me, searching my face, as if she wants to separate fact from fiction. "You didn't even want me to be born, remember? You wanted my mom to get rid of me."

Her words are razor clam sharp. I sit there, looking down at my ape thumbs, breathing hard. The silence between us swells like toxins in a red tide.

"It's like this." I rub my unshaven face, the scratch of stubble loud in my ears. "When your mom was pregnant with you, I thought she should end the pregnancy. But for chrissakes, she was seventeen, on drugs, failing school again, and already in trouble with the law. Obviously I'm glad things turned out differently. I love you. I can't imagine my life without you. Yes, I should have done whatever was needed to be your legal guardian, but that was a mistake, not because I didn't want you. I'm not the most organized person. You know that. But I always have wanted you here with me."

Sitka nods without smiling, as if she's already thought this through herself, and I'm just confirming her conclusions. Or maybe that's wishful thinking on my part.

"Why didn't you want me born? Because I'd be a meth baby?"

I consider this for a minute before answering her. "I didn't even know that term back then. Look, this was about your mom. It wasn't until she was well along that the social workers said there might be some problems with you."

"What was I like?" she asks.

"What do you mean?"

"As a baby. What was I like as a baby?"

My first thought is to tell her that she was the sweetest baby in the whole world, the best baby anyone could ever hope for. But I know the last thing she needs to hear right now is some fairy tale version of her early childhood.

"You were a real handful the first year," I tell her. "Cranky. All day, all night, crabby. Your mom must have cut down on her drug use once she knew you were coming along. She said she stopped using, and she probably did. Otherwise, you'd have been born with convulsions and God knows what else."

It surprised me when Jenny knocked on my door, nine months pregnant, begging for a place to stay. She didn't have anything to go back to in Anchorage after Donna's funeral, since Diesel got himself arrested again. Maybe it was the Yatki Island myth that kept Jenny here during the rest of her pregnancy—how the children born here are protected. I heard she had an apartment for a little bit, and then Diesel's mom Becky took her in, seeing as it was her grandbaby, too. But Becky couldn't afford to support her, let alone a baby, even with Jenny's pizza delivery job.

When she came back home to me, she swore she was clean and sober, swore she was through with meth, through with selling it too, and swore she wanted to be a good mom and had nowhere else to go. Donna would have taken her in. Looking at her swollen belly, I knew I had to help her, for our grandbaby's sake. So I gave her another chance. Gave her a room, paid her hospital bills. It went really well, until the day Jenny called from Juneau, saying she had been arrested for possession with intent to sell, and that I should keep Sitka so she wouldn't get shuttled into foster care.

"Tell me more about me as a baby, Ray." Sitka's looking at me as if this is the most important request she's ever asked me, and maybe it is. I never wanted to tell her any of this, turn her against her mother, or worry her, but she's dealt with a lot since her mom came home, and if she wants to know what her mother's drug use did, I'll tell her.

"You had two modes: listless and wailing. You were really underweight. You didn't want to eat the first few weeks. Your mother and I stayed up with you night after night, trying to get you to take the bottle. There was no way she could have breast-fed you. Jenny slept a lot. I remember that. I'd take you and sit in the rocking chair or walk you up and down the hallway for hours while you yowled like an orphaned wolf pup. When your mom got arrested, you were eleven months old, and after that, Muskeg came over every morning to help watch you. Felix helped at night. I think I ran on three or four hours of sleep, tops, until you were about eighteen months old. Then whatever effects the drugs had on you began to wear off. Still, even when you were kindergarten age, there were small things I noticed. Do you remember when I would try to take you to the hardware store?"

She shakes her head.

"We'd be going down the aisle looking for nuts or screws or bolts or whatever. When you saw a bin of open parts—didn't matter what it was—it would set you off. You'd have to stop and reach out your little hands and try to put all the individual pieces in some kind of order. Up near the register they'd have a mesh wire basket with all kinds of little knick-knacks on sale. That one really got to you, because everything was just thrown in helter-skelter. I'd have to wait an extra fifteen minutes so you could try to arrange all those items. Got so I didn't take you in there at all until you were eight or nine."

Sitka raises an eyebrow. "I guess I was a pain in the butt, huh?"

I move my chair right next to hers again. "A little bit, just like anyone else. You turned out to be one amazing kid. And here you are, and here I am, and we've been doing pretty well, I think."

She sinks against me, rubbing her head against my shoulder. I give her a good squeeze.

"If you want to come back here to live, I'm sure we can go back to the judge, and you can tell him. That'll change this temporary arrangement, get you back to your own room, and then you can testify in the adoption proceedings."

"It's too late," Sitka says.

"No, honey. It's not. I'll promise the judge that I won't take you out on the boat again—at least not until I'm your official guardian. Besides, I'm going to have to sign on as a crew member with somebody else for a while. We'll get someone to be here when I'm out for more than a day. The judge won't have any reason to say no to us."

She pushes away from me and stands up. "It's too late!"

My jaw tightens, sending a little shock of pain back to my left ear. "What do you mean it's too late? What's going on?"

She bites her lip before answering me. "They're taking me away."

"Your mom and dad? Where?"

Sitka steps back from me. "I don't know. Not exactly. They

said something about Kodiak Island, but I don't know for sure."

"What the devil do they want to do on Kodiak Island?"

"They want to build a wonderful new life together." Sitka rolls her eyes. "As if."

I run my fingers through my hair. "Just what did they tell you, exactly?"

"They didn't tell me anything. I overheard them talking in the bedroom yesterday. They think it's so lovey-dovey cozy and private in there, when I can—"

"Did they say when all of this was going to happen?"

She shakes her head. "Not exactly. In a few weeks, I guess. Mom was saying something about being there for my birthday."

"But you're still in school," I protest.

"Like they really care about that. Mom wants to homeschool me so I can learn in an environment with Christian values."

The lizard part of my brain starts throwing off lightning bolts again. "They can't do that!"

Sitka looks at me like I'm a child who needs the world explained.

"They can do anything they want. They're my parents."

Chapter 19

"YOU'VE GOT TO STOP them. That's what I'm paying you for."

Ben Sato settles his backside further into the seat of a maroon leather chair. We're in an office that Ben's firm pays to have available when they do business on the island. He's wearing khaki Dockers and a blue, button-down dress shirt. Ben taps a pencil on the manila folder that holds my case files.

"First of all, let me remind you that except for the small retainer, you haven't paid me."

"You mean two small retainers," I remind him. "I'll pay more as soon as I get hired onto another boat."

"Now have a seat. You look like hell, by the way."

I'd be insulted, but I didn't shave or shower this morning. Didn't brush my teeth either. My mouth tastes like salty cotton soaked with cold coffee and cigarettes. Since Sitka came over on a day that wasn't an official visitation day, she went back to her mother's apartment after school, at Ben's insistence. I haven't been able to focus on anything other than how to get her back. How she wants to live with me. How this all was a terrible mistake, and somehow Sitka's paying for it.

"Sitka living with them is more than I can handle." I slump

into the alder wood visitor's chair. I still have on my parka and Ben's office feels uncomfortably warm. "I should have hired an attorney who specializes in custody."

"You would have had a hard time finding one you could afford around here." Ben settles his left hand on his chin, cocks his head, and raises his eyebrow. I bet it's a gesture he's practiced for excitable juries and agitated clients. "She had to go back today. Your daughter could have had the sheriff after you for interference."

"You don't get it." My armpits and waistband are soaked with sweat. "Jenny and that asshole are going to take Sitka off this island to God knows where and to do God knows what."

Ben lifts his fingers off his chin. "They are Sitka's parents. They do have a right to move to another residence, as long as it doesn't interfere with your visitation rights." The fingers land again, brushing his cheek like it was the skin of a peach. "Unless you can prove that this move will violate the judge's order by keeping Sitka from seeing you, there isn't much I can do."

"What about what Sitka wants? She wants to stay with me. She told me."

"Judges don't like to change rulings," Ben informs me, "just because a teenager decides she doesn't like her parents. Hell, my kids are always telling me how much better life is at any of their friends' homes." His little joke falls flat and he sits up straighter in his chair. "You don't know when they might move or where, right?"

"Sitka said it might be Kodiak Island."

"Might be Kodiak. Might be down the street." He shakes his head. "By law, they can't take Sitka out of state without the court's permission, at least until the adoption process rolls through court, and if you lose, they'll be able to take her anywhere they want. But right now, if we're talking about a move within the state, it's up to the discretion of the judge, and only after you file a complaint. They could, for example, arrange for Sitka to stay with you for a month every three months or so."

He drums the pencil on the desk. "It would be helpful to have something more specific to go on. Did you ask Jenny?"

"She denied it. She said that she and Diesel had talked in general terms about what they would do after they were married, but nothing definite was in the works."

"And you don't believe her?"

"Jenny's life has been one big lie since she was fifteen. I can hear it in her voice, the way her sentences have question marks at the end. There's no way she was telling me the truth."

"Hardly the kind of evidence that would convince a judge to change his ruling." Ben flips open the manila folder and scratches something with the pencil tip, then looks up at me. "I really can't do much at this point. My advice is to make sure you talk with Sitka every day. If her mother tells her to start packing or gives her anything more specific on a move location, then we can go back to the judge and say that Jenny is placing an undue burden on your right to see your granddaughter."

"Why is everyone ready to give an ex-addict the benefit of the doubt? Don't I have any rights as a grandfather? And Diesel. Did I tell you that he was scoping out the hold on the boat? I bet he's running drugs." I stop when I see Ben examining a file folder on his desk. "Am I boring you?"

Ben sets his arm down and opens up the file folder. "While you're here, I want to review our statement to Walt Francke's lawyers."

I cut him off. "I'm not done talking about Sitka. As far as that lawsuit goes, Walt can go kiss my—"

Ben puts his hand up. "Calm down and hear me out." He leafs through the documents and removes a sheet of paper, scanning from top to bottom. "Walt Francke's suit isn't against you personally."

"What do you mean? My name is front and center, as I remember."

Ben hands me the sheet. "Not your name, your title. They're going after the owner of the *Jenny-Sais-Pas*. They just happen to assume that you are the owner."

I look at the sheet and confirm what Ben is telling me. "And since that judge gave the ownership to Jenny . . ."

"It's Jenny they should be suing. As your attorney, I can inform both your insurance company and Walt's of that."

I rub my hands through my hair. "I doubt Jenny has taken out any liability insurance. I don't want Walt's attorneys to come down so hard on her that Sitka suffers."

"Let me worry about that," Ben says. "I'll set up a meeting with Hank. We'll get our strategy in place."

"He's in Anchorage for a few days."

"Not a problem," Ben assures me. "I'll get something on his calendar for when he gets back. Once Walt's attorneys find out that there's a possibility that the boat might be moved to an as-yet-undisclosed location, they'll seek an injunction to keep the boat here and Hank will agree. Meanwhile, if we find out that Jenny and Diesel have some concrete plans to move, I can talk to the judge and see what we can do about your visitation rights. You'll see. It will all work out. Just leave it to the legal system."

"How long is this all going to take?"

"Once I meet with Hank, two, three days at most." Ben shuffles the papers together and puts them back in the case file. "You'll have Sitka this weekend, right?"

"Starting Friday afternoon."

"Good. Bring her into the office on Saturday morning, say about ten. I'll want to get a statement from her saying that she wants to stay with you permanently." He steps from behind his desk and gives me a pat on the shoulder. "Stop worrying, Ray. We'll sort this out."

"So what do I do in the meantime?"

"Nothing stupid," Ben says.

"Okay." I turn to leave.

"One more thing, Ray. That woman who was on the boat." He opens up his folder for a second. "Nicole Harris. The same one who testified at the custody hearing, right?"

"That's right."

"She's been a good champion for you with Francke's

lawsuit. If she's got anything additional to report that could support your adoption of Sitka, it wouldn't hurt to get that on the record."

"I'll see what I can do."

NICOLE'S APARTMENT ISN'T THAT far from Ben's office. After parking on the street, I tramp up to her apartment and press the small round button next to Harris. It makes the zzpp-zzpp sound. Without asking who it is, Nicole buzzes me in. And when I walk up the three flights of stairs to her floor, her door is already open. I rap the brass knocker once for politeness, and go in. The apartment has a lemony smell, maybe from one of those scented candles or some kind of furniture polish.

Nicole steps into the living room to greet me. "I'm glad to see you, Ray. How are you? You look a bit frazzled."

"Things seem to keep sliding out from under me."

"Take off your coat," she suggests. "I'm having tea. You want some? Or something cold? I've got mineral water."

"Nothing, thanks."

I shuck off my rain parka and my sweatshirt. It's warm in her apartment, same as last time. Overheated and dry as parchment paper. If Nicole's not careful, she'll have nosebleeds by Christmas.

She returns from the kitchen and, in spite of what I said, hands me a glass of mineral water. She's wearing a long-sleeved white pullover shirt and a partially buttoned black sweater. As she sits on her couch, the bottom of her shirt rises just above the metal button on her jeans. She's not showing any skin, just that little rise of white cotton over the fly button.

My mouth is suddenly dry, so I drink half the glass of water and put it down on a coaster on the coffee table. I sit in a chair facing her, with my extra layers draped over the armrest. "Thanks for letting me in."

"What's going on?"

I tell her about Jenny and Diesel's plan to take Sitka

off-island, to homeschool her, and how Sitka really feels about all of it.

"I don't trust Diesel and I don't see how he can be a good influence. My lawyer might want you to talk with Sitka and, you know, see if it changes your opinion, and if you would make a different recommendation to the judge when the adoption proceedings roll around. I bet they'll ask you to testify again."

Nicole shifts her weight and the bottom of her shirt falls into place, covering the button of her jeans. "Ray," she says, as if my name contained five syllables. "I thought we already went through this."

"Look, I'm just asking you to talk with her is all. See if things have changed. And maybe you should talk with Diesel. He wasn't in the cards when you testified. He just conveniently showed up right afterwards. Doesn't that tell you he must be up to no good?"

"No," Nicole says. "I can't say that he isn't a good father or shouldn't be in your granddaughter's life. I don't have any basis for that."

I stand up. "Great. Thanks a lot." I grab my sweatshirt and parka.

"Hang on a minute, Ray," Nicole says. "I didn't say I wouldn't talk with Sitka, but—"

"But what?"

"I thought we were going to try to be friends. For my part, I'm more than willing to be your friend, to support you. But you can't use me like you'd use a screwdriver to repair an engine."

"I'm not trying to use you. I'm desperate here."

Nicole lays her hand on my sleeve. "Don't you see, Ray? That's the same language, the same justification that addicts use. They're desperate, so that somehow justifies them in using people to get what they need."

"I'm not the addict," I insist. "If you don't want to help me, just say so."

She drops her hand. "I don't know if I can do it. You can't force Sitka, or for that matter your daughter or her boyfriend, to talk to me. Maybe your attorney knows some way to make it happen. Even so, I can't guarantee that I would recommend that the temporary arrangements be changed or that your adoption should proceed. Jenny is Sitka's mother, and she's been working really hard to change her life."

I catch that compelling scent of hers, and I smile, even though I can't believe she's still taking Jenny's side in this. "Then let's take it one step at a time."

"I want to be absolutely clear." Nicole looks at me and nods once, businesslike. "If I do this, then it really is over between us. There's nothing more I'd like to see than you and your granddaughter reunited. But I can't flit between being your friend and being a counselor. If I testify again on your behalf, then you'd just be another client. And I'd be sorry to have that happen."

"Yeah, me too." The nerve endings in my fingers want to retrace the curve of her body, the softness of her skin, the crease at the back of her knee. "But Sitka comes first in my life, and if there is something my attorney wants to set up, I'll have him call you."

Nicole opens the door for me. "Good night, then."

I turn back to face her in the hallway. "Thanks, Nicole. I do like you tremendously, you know that, right?"

"I know." She places her arm on the vertical edge of the door. She watches as I turn and walk away. She hasn't shut the door by the time I descend the steps.

I'T'S AFTER SIX BY the time I leave Nicole's. The last thing I want to do is go home to an empty house. I drive over to the Blind Dog Tavern for some of Muskeg's cooking and company.

"Waa sa iyatee, ya yaa koosge daakeit, Ray."

"Hey, Muskeg."

"You look like a moose that's been wandering the woods, rubbing its hide against the trees." She swipes the counter with a rag as I sit down at the bar, so close I can feel the breeze. "Earl went hunting up at Delta Junction when he was in Fairbanks last week. So we've got some fresh bison steaks in the big fridge.

Comes with fries and my special coleslaw, of course."

"That and a pint of amber, I guess."

"You want that steak dead or alive?"

I shrug. "Doesn't matter. Somewhere in between."

"One wounded buffalo," Muskeg yells to the kitchen window behind her. She draws the beer, and sets it down in front of me. She leans over the bar, making sure no one else is eavesdropping. "I signed an official complaint against Jenny this morning. My attorney says he can get an injunction within five days."

I spread my elbows on the bar. Feeling dizzy. "Thank you, but it's too little, too late." I fill her in on my meeting with Ben, leaving Nicole out. I don't want to get into that whole thing.

"Well, don't that beat all? We could have two injunctions on your boat in the next week or so." Muskeg considers me for a minute, nodding her head. "At least you had the sense to see your attorney this time."

"Oh, yeah. I feel so much better now." I take two gulps of ale.

"Men," she mutters. Placing both hands on the bar, she leans into my face. "Ray, you miss that little girl so much right now, why don't you call her? I'm sure she'd love to hear your voice. I'll have your dinner up by the time you're finished."

I have to hand it to Muskeg. It's the most sensible thing anyone's said all day, including me. I lumber off the bar stool and step outside where my cell phone can get better reception. The early November wind picks up speed and whips the collar of my parka. I punch in Sitka's name from my call list. The phone rings four times before her voice answers.

"This is Sitka."

"Hi, sweetie—"

"Thanks for trying to get hold of me. Say who it is and I might just call you back."

I push the end call button. Okay, she's probably studying or watching TV. I take out my wallet and lift out the slip of paper that I've written Jenny's number on. I punch in the numbers. It rings eight times before going to voice mail.

From the edge of the Blind Dog parking lot I can look down

on the harbor. Out at sea, six or seven boats are returning along the horizon line, their lights rising and falling on the waves, illuminating the dark water and a thick mass of charcoal-colored clouds. If I checked a barometer right now, it'd show the atmospheric pressure dropping. I try Sitka's phone number again, and this time I leave a message for her to call me.

There's no reason to panic, but I need some reassurance. Muskeg will understand. I abandon my beer and meal inside the tavern, get into my truck, and drive over to Jenny and Diesel's apartment. When I get there, the lights are out. I jump out of the truck and run up to their door. I press on the doorbell. No answer. My stomach muscles start to tighten and my intestines feel like I've swallowed sandpaper.

I get back into my truck and head down Hemlock Street toward the harbor. Within a hundred yards pellets of rain and sleet start dancing in the headlights. I punch the button on the truck radio and switch from Fleetwood Mac on the classic rock station to the weather channel. Sure enough, an early winter storm is bearing down on our little island. I can smell the air going cold through the air vents. It's going to go to ice before long.

I'm going too fast as I make the turn onto Harbor Drive, and nearly take out a parked Chevy. I lift my foot off the pedal a little and correct my steering. Finally I skew into the harbor lot and switch off the engine. I buck the door open and try to jump out fast. The key gets stuck halfway out of the ignition. Cursing, I lean back in and jiggle it out.

The air smells like gray slush. I still have a key to the pier gate. I unlock it and push it open. The hinges squeak for lack of lubricant. I jog to where the *Jenny-Sais-Pas* is usually docked. A larger craft is blocking my view. Slivers of rain, turned silver by the dock lights, cascade across the slickened wood underfoot. I run faster, lose my footing, and nearly fall. I'm nearly out of breath when I reach the berth. It's a punch in the stomach when the only thing the lights from the harbor lamps reveal are patches of fuel skimming the dark green water.

Chapter 20

FELIX MOVES HIS MOUSE back to the ShipMates menu options. "No sign of them here, either."

The wind rages outside as I squint at his computer screen, willing one of the little ship icons to be the *Jenny-Sais-Pas*. "Let's try Yakutat Bay. That's about as far as they could get, even if they left first thing this morning. We can work our way back down."

"Jesus, Ray." Felix pushes his chair away from the desk. "We've been at this for the last four hours."

"So? Any other time you're on this damn thing all night long. You want me to give up trying to find Sitka?"

Felix rubs his fingers over his bloodshot eyes. "What I want to tell you is what you already know. There are hundreds of little islands between here and Yakutat. Talk about your needle in a haystack. We've already searched half a dozen straits and channels, and identified a hundred boats. It's time to stop for the night."

"But we—"

"Look, Ray. There's a grand total of three ships in Chatham Strait. Three! Those two in front are big cruise ships and that one is an oil tanker. Do you need me to show you again?"

He rolls the cursor over each of the ship icons. "See? It's the *Holland Statendam* from Vancouver. And the one behind it is the *Sea Princess* out of San Francisco. And you wanna know why we're only seeing big cruise ships and oil tankers, Ray?" His voice is sounding testy. I could answer him because I already know what he's going to say. "Because it's one o'clock in the morning and there's a heavy storm! Anything smaller is docked or anchored for the night. And my eyes are so tired, I couldn't see a boat on this screen even if it was parked in the damn kitchen."

Felix puts his hands on the arms of the chair and pushes himself up so quickly that the wheels shudder. "Keep at this if you want, but I'm going to bed."

"All right." We're not going to get anywhere tonight, he's correct. "But do me a favor and leave your computer on so I can look at it myself in the morning. I'll probably be up before you."

"Yeah, you probably will." He looks over at the couch, my bed for the night. "You know where the pillows and blankets are. I see you didn't bring your overnight beauty bag."

I shake my head. "You got an alarm clock?"

"There's one on the kitchen counter," he says. "But I only got one extra toothbrush and that's for Muskeg, so you'll just have to smear some toothpaste on your fingers or whatever."

I scratch my hand over my stubble. Two days since I shaved. "I'm so worked up over this, Felix. I can't think straight."

"We'll find her." He puts his hand on my shoulder. "But you need to get some sleep, brother."

"Why do the two of them need Sitka anyway? They have each other."

"Parenthood is a powerful force of nature. But I don't think that's the real question you have." With that, he turns and heads toward his bedroom.

"Felix, wait. What is this supposed question?"

He goes over to the fireplace and puts two more logs on the fire. Red and yellow sparks fly up. "This should keep you toasty through the night." He settles himself into his armchair.

"Your real question is in the story of the woman who was taken by the frog people."

"The frog people?" I sit down on the couch. "I suppose there's a Tlingit story and moral somewhere in there."

"A story, anyway." Felix leans back in the armchair, rubbing his eyes. "Takes place up by Yakutat Bay, by the way. There was a village near a big lake. And the lake was teeming with frogs. The village chief's daughter was both fascinated and repulsed by the frogs. She made fun of them, picking one up and saying to it, 'There are so many of you! I wonder if you get married like people? Hmm, little frog? Do people come and live with you?' She tossed the frog back into the lake and went home. The next day a very handsome man came to her house and proposed marriage. She was smitten with him and followed him to his father's house, which was, of course, the lake. So she became part frog, lived among the frog people, and learned how to eat bugs and swallow mud."

"And she lived happily ever after?"

Felix shakes his head no. "Her family mourned her for two years, but one day, one of the men from the village was bathing in the lake and recognized her among the frogs. He went back and all of the people came and drained the lake. As the frog king saw the lake water disappear, he asked the woman to tell the village chief to have pity on them. The woman did so, and her father the chief left a little water in the lake so the frogs could survive. The chief took his daughter home, but she could not eat food because of all the black mud she had swallowed when she lived with the frogs. They tried and tried to get her to eat and be like the humans again, but she couldn't."

"If there's a point here, Felix, I'm not getting it."

"The question you've been asking yourself for years, but have never really wanted to answer, is why did Jenny go to live among the frog people? And even when she came home, why could she no longer live with her tribe?" He stands up and raises his arms above his head, yawning. "That's all the brilliant insight I'm providing. This old body needs its beauty rest. Good night."

Hmmph, frog people. What am I supposed to do with that? No wonder people prefer the Greek myths and German fairy tales, "The Tortoise and the Hare" and "Jack and the Beanstalk," stuff like that. Good versus evil. Easy to wrap your arms around. Still, Felix is right. Why did Jenny go to live with the frog people? Why couldn't her mother and I keep her home?

I grab the blankets and pillow from the closet and fix up the couch, set the alarm for 5 a.m., and lie down. I have to bend my knees and scrunch my neck to fit. My body and my brain start fighting, the first exhausted, the second still wide awake, listing things I could have done differently, stacking them like Lincoln Logs. But a whirlwind of what-ifs knocks them down just as quickly as I build them. Finally I slide into sleep.

The frog woman appears in my dream, standing knee deep in a mudflat. She's wearing a flowered dress and I shiver to think how cold she must be. Big splotches of sludge cover her arms and dress. It's even in her hair. I can see her face. It's not Jenny, and it's not Sitka. It's Donna, but younger, when she was pregnant with Jenny. She reaches down, scooping up gobs of mud in her hand. The mud is so wet that it oozes from her fingers. She lifts the black muck up to her face, looks directly at me, and stuffs it into her mouth. I want to tell her to stop, but my mouth refuses to open.

I JOLT AWAKE TEN minutes before the alarm goes off. I roll off the couch, my back and thighs stiff and sore. I don't want to think about, or try to interpret, the dream. I use the bathroom, get dressed, make coffee, and sit down at Felix's computer. When I move the mouse, the screen asks me for a password. I'm about to wake Felix up, but instead I enter Muskeg into the dialog box. It's wrong. I think for minute and type in "Honeybuns." The box disappears and the screen with the ship locator software comes up. There are dozens more ships in the northern half of Chatham Strait. The first one I click is a Coast Guard patrol boat, the *Anacapa*. I check the others, but none is the *Jenny-Sais-Pas*. Felix is right. This isn't just a needle in the haystack. It's more like *Where's Waldo*, with hundreds of haystacks.

I try to figure out how to change the location from Chatham to Yakutat. I click on the main menu. Scrolling down I see an item that says Search Parameters. I click that open, hoping it will tell me how to change locations. The second-to-last option says Ship Locator. When I select that, a dialog box asks me to enter a ship's registry number.

"Felix!" I shout up toward the loft. "Wake up! Felix! Get down here!"

I hear a groan and in a moment Felix climbs down the steep stairs from his bedroom, scratching the top of his head. "Be a little quiet, will you? Muskeg's still asleep."

I point to the screen. "Why didn't you tell me this thing could locate a specific ship?"

Felix yawns. "Didn't know it could. You know I never read directions."

"All we need is the registry number."

"So enter the number," Felix says.

"I don't have it memorized." My fingers rub the tight muscles in my neck. "Do you have anything here? Any of our insurance papers or fishing licenses, anything like that?"

Felix scratches his head. "Shoot, Ray. You keep all that stuff at your house."

A few weeks ago, after Jenny pointed out that storing important papers under the passenger seat of my truck wasn't such a hot idea, I actually did some filing. Now I wish I hadn't. "I hate to have to go all the way back there, but I guess—"

"What about the loan papers Muskeg made us fill out for her attorney?" Felix says. "Maybe they had the registration number on it."

I want to kiss him, stubbly beard and all. "Well, get them."

"Let me see. I know they're around here somewhere." He roots around in his desk drawer. "Hmm, maybe in the kitchen."

While he searches, I open the drawers underneath his

bookcase. Phone book. Phone bills. Church bulletin. Book of coupons for Heidi's Kjokken Buffet. Copy of the *Yatki Island Visitor's Guide.* Fish chowder recipe. Cutout newspaper article. Installation and warranty manual for the satellite dish. Utility bill. Expired two-for-one massage certificate from Kathy's House of Healing Hands.

"Isn't anything around here organized?"

"Got it!" Felix runs in from the kitchen and hands me a crumpled sheet of paper. "I used the back of it to write my grocery list."

I unfold and scan the document. There at the bottom of the second page is the name and registry number for the *Jenny-Sais-Pas.* For once, I appreciate the anal-retentive quality of legal documents. Back at the computer, I enter in the numbers and click OK. An hourglass icon fills the screen. And stays there. And stays there.

"Shit. How far a range does this have?" I ask Felix.

"Dunno." He shrugs.

I hold up my hand as the hourglass disappears. On the screen is a single icon of a boat. I move the cursor over the image and up pops *Jenny-Sais-Pas. Seiner. U.S. Owner: Jennifer Bancroft. Yatki Island.*

"Is that her?" Felix asks. "Where is she?"

"Tracy Arm."

Felix squints his right eye. "On the Canadian border? I thought you said they wanted to go to Kodiak Island."

"That's what I thought. That's what Sitka told me."

The icon moves a fraction. "They must be headed to Williams Cove," Felix observes. "But why there?"

"Who knows." I drum my fingers on the desk. "If it were summer, there might be a few smaller tourist ships, one or two Zodiacs, and some kayakers. This late in the year? Nothing. Nothing but trees and bears."

Chapter 21

THE CESSNA 182 FLOATPLANE zips up Stephens Passage and bears northwest toward Tracy Arm. The remote fjord is about forty-five miles south of Juneau. Multiple waterfalls channel the melting water of glaciers off the tree-lined ridges into the salty water below. Through my set of hunting binoculars I can see a gathering of tufted puffins nesting on the sheer rock cliffs. Below them, mew gulls lift off the rocks and soar over the icy inlet. I keep scanning for a boat among the hundreds of baby berg ice chunks floating in the water. The only dark shapes I see are a few bearded seals popping up and around the ice. Nothing human.

"I can set down right in Williams Cove," Bloor Helse yells over the hum of the single-piston engine. "But I'll have to swing around for a fast approach."

I give him a thumbs up, knowing from previous flights that this model of Cessna is a bit underpowered and needs extra attention with takeoffs and landings. Bloor owns an air charter outfit and he and I have sent each other customers over the years. I called him from Felix's cabin and even though it was six in the morning, he agreed to fly us up here first thing. When I told Bloor the trip was a personal emergency, he did what I would have done for him: brought us up here free of charge and without asking questions. It was after nine by the time Bloor could get everything ready and we could take off. Fortunately, the weather has improved, and while it's still cold, it's only partly cloudy.

Bloor brings the plane down, making the gray-green waves below us rise up and fall over. I scan the curved, wind-pruned shoreline, best I can, since it's still pretty dark. The outer edge is stripped of trees, and the surrounding terrain is steep and heavily forested. At the very end a silver waterfall has formed a gravel pan. On the east side of that pan I spot the *Jenny-Sais-Pas*. I hold up my hand to Bloor and draw a circle. He nods and comes in for a slow pass above the boat. I peer through the binoculars. No sign that anyone is aboard. Close to where the boat is anchored, I see the Zodiac inflatable raft that we use for shallow water transport. It's tied up to a beached log just above the shoreline. Someone must have gone to shore.

I point my index finger downward, and Bloor steers a 360 to bring the plane into its descent, skimming over the cove. When the floats touch down, the plane bounces four times as the skis displace the surface water. Bloor throttles back and we coast to the shoreline near where the boat is anchored. After he switches off the engines, I open my door and move out onto the strut. Bloor does the same on his side. We plunge into water that comes up just below the top of our boots. Despite the rubber insulation, I can feel how frigid the glacial cove is.

Bloor and I nudge the plane to a sandy section of the beach, about twenty yards from where the Zodiac is tied up. Once Bloor secures the tie rope, Felix leans out from the back seat and hands me two backpacks and a pouch that holds his hunting rifle. He clambers out of the plane and joins us on the small strip of beach.

"Door-to-shore-by-Bloor service," Felix chants, readjusting his Greek fisherman's cap as a breeze stirs over the sand and gravel.

"Thanks, man." I shake hands with Bloor. "I owe you."

The bush pilot looks around at the heavily wooded

landscape. "You sure you don't want me to fly back here later and get you guys?"

I tell him no. "If all goes as planned, we'll be coming back on the boat with my granddaughter."

Felix looks at me with a raised eyebrow, but I motion to him to help me and Bloor release the rope and push the plane backward. As the plane drifts into deeper water, Bloor clambers back inside the cockpit and starts the engine. Two minutes later the Cessna lifts itself from the cove, banks up and left, and disappears from view.

"Maybe it's my old age," Felix says, picking up his backpack, "but I can't for the life of me remember you spelling out any kind of plan."

"Hmm," I answer, taking off my binoculars and putting them in my backpack.

"What I do remember is you pounding on the bathroom door and telling me to haul my butt out of a nice hot shower, and next thing I know I'm stuffed into the back of Bloor's Cessna, munching a peanut butter granola bar for breakfast." He slings his rifle pouch onto his right shoulder. "Suppose Diesel is armed? What are you going to do? Please tell me you've thought this out."

"We'll take things step by step."

"One step at a time, huh? If you skippered our crabbing business like that, we'd be broke." He turns to me and smiles. "Oh, I forgot. We are."

I swing my backpack onto my shoulders and ignore Felix. "Let's check out the boat."

As we walk to the Zodiac, I scan the beach and woods, but still don't see anyone. Our boots make a crunching sound as we trudge over the wet gravel and sand. Each time we take a step, the impression fills with a mixture of the salt and fresh water. Small white crabs scurry away from us. As we near the inflatable raft, the smell of the rubberized tubes mixes with that of the sea. The eight-foot-long craft is empty, except for the four paddles. We throw our gear into the raft, untie it, push it into the water, then jump in. Felix and I paddle to the port side of the *Jenny-Sais-Pas*, hitch our line to a cleat, and climb aboard.

"You check the pilothouse and I'll go below," I decide.

"What if they see us?"

"If they do, they do. They'll need us to come back to the beach and get them, won't they?"

While Felix ducks inside the pilothouse, I check out the aft hold. The hatch has a new lock on it. "Careful fellow, aren't you, Diesel?" I rummage around for something to break it open with. "But not careful enough."

He's left a toolbox against the bulkhead, in plain sight and unlocked. I lift up the lid, take out a hammer, and bust open the lock. As soon as I lift up the hatch, a pungent, gamey smell assaults my nose. I go down the ladder into the hold, switching on the lights. I open up a locker, finding only ropes and fenders. That animal odor seems to be coming from somewhere near it. I check the rest of the hold, but everything seems fairly normal. I hear footsteps and instinctively start to hide, but it's just Felix coming down.

"Someone should tell Jenny and Diesel that they need to keep a proper log. There ain't but a few scribbles in the logbook." He looks around. "Phew! What's that smell?"

"I don't know yet. Help me shove this out of the way."

We push the storage locker so it slides across the deck. I kneel down. There's a thin line, no wider than an eighth of an inch, in the shape of a rectangle. "He's gone and made a false bottom. And not a very good one, at that. Any harbor patrolman or Coast Guard officer would spot it in a second."

Felix sniffs, then jerks his head back. "That's where the stink is coming from all right."

"Find me something to pry this open with. And a flashlight."

Felix hands me a small crowbar. I stand back up and set the tool edge down into the crack. Diesel has probably fastened a hidden latch, but I'm not going to take the time to figure it out.

"Hey, Ray. You don't think it's dead Russian or Laotian immigrants or something like that down there, do you?"

"Doubt it. Whatever it is, it reeks more of animal than human. Got that flashlight ready?"

As I crack open the false hold, the stench becomes strong enough that I have to put my arm over my mouth and nostrils. Felix shines the flashlight into the hole. "Well I'll be. Would you take a look at that?"

I reach down and pull out the severed paw of a grizzly bear. The brown fur is matted and stiff, the six-inch claws still sharp. Felix takes the paw from me and cups it in his palm, murmuring to it.

"Such a waste," he tells me. "It's a crime against nature. Makes me want to feed Diesel Kurtz to the wolves."

"These things are worth a lot of money in China," I tell him. "I hear they sell for $1,000 or more on the black market."

"Apiece?"

When I nod yes, he adds, "Poor brother bear."

I take the flashlight from Felix and peer down into the hold again. Another eight or so paws are piled next to each other. I reach past them and pull out a dark brown pouch in the shape of a parachute. "Here's the real treasure."

Felix picks up the pouch, holding it by the darker, open end of the parachute. "Oh, that's just plain disgusting, Ray." He drops the pouch to the deck. "He's selling the gall bladders, too."

"So someone can extract the bile," I say. "I hear it goes for thousands an ounce. Our friend Walt Francke wanted to know where he could get some of this stuff. I bet he's not the only middle-aged guy out there willing to shell out big bucks for these." I pick up the bear gall bladder and turn it over in my hand. It feels dry on the outside, but pliable with the thick liquid inside the sac. "Diesel doesn't strike me as someone who would go out hunting bears."

"At least he ain't selling drugs," Felix says. "Seems like he and Jenny really are clean."

"It's still illegal, and I'll be damned if I'm going to let them get Sitka involved."

"You want me to radio the rangers over at the Forest Service?" Felix offers. "They could send somebody over and have Diesel arrested."

"No. If you're right about him having a gun, I don't want him getting spooked and shooting at the cops. Too much chance of Sitka getting hurt in any crossfire."

I can't think with this stench, so we put the false cover back as best we can, kicking the splintered pieces of wood against the bulkhead. Then we finagle the storage locker back over the cover. Felix follows me back up to the aft deck.

"I wonder how far they've gone," I say. "You didn't see anything in the pilothouse that would give a clue where they were headed?"

"They have supplies stashed there and their sleeping gear, so I doubt they're aiming to be gone for more than the day."

I point to a narrow, open chute of land on the beach, which zigzags up the ridge. The tall grass has been pushed aside recently.

"Okay," I tell Felix. "There's a path over there. "I'll take the Zodiac and see if I can locate them. You'd better stay onboard in case they come back."

"And what am I supposed to do if they show up without you?" Felix asks.

I think about this for a minute. "You'll see them before they see you. Shoot one of the emergency flares up into the air. That will signal me and may put Diesel on his best behavior if he thinks the Coast Guard has seen it. Unless you've got a better plan."

"Guess I don't. I do wish you could get a decent cell phone signal out here. At least we could communicate." He unzips his rifle pouch and removes the gun. "You better take this."

"I don't want any gun play around Sitka. Safer not to."

"Tell that," Felix says, "to any of the bears you meet along the way."

He extends the rifle and I take it, together with my backpack. I tell him I hope to be back soon, but I don't really know.

"Might as well make myself some coffee. It'll help me keep a lookout," Felix says. "And that's another thing. Doesn't anyone in that family know how to clean up? You should see the mess they've made in my galley. The only thing they bothered to throw into the trashcan was our Billiken! They got no respect."

He takes the statue out of his pocket and holds it out. Without even a second thought, I rub its belly.

"Good," Felix says.

I climb down the short ladder and step into the Zodiac. Felix unties the line, throws it to me, and gives the raft a good shove. I paddle backwards to clear the boat, then head to shore. After tying the Zodiac to the same log as before, I grab the rifle and my backpack and cross the beach.

The first fifty yards of the makeshift trail is bordered by salal bushes, six feet tall or higher. But as the sandy path morphs to rock and dirt, the greenery is mainly deer fern, hemlocks, and Douglas fir trees. After a half hour I stop to catch my breath. I take off my backpack and get out my canteen for a good swig. The water has that metallic taste you get from a canteen, but it's refreshing. I listen for signs of voices or movement, but it's quiet except for some blackbirds and redpolls trilling in the branches. I'm sweating already. Although the air temperature must be below forty, I take off my outer jacket and stuff it into the backpack before closing it up and shouldering it. I sling the rifle over my shoulder and start off again.

The path narrows from a series of wide switchbacks to a steep climb. My progress slows. The days are short now, and there's still only a scant amount of daylight to help me with my footing. There's tightness in my calf muscles. My right hip too. The ground is wet and I slip once, twice, before finding a branch that's long enough and sturdy enough to serve as a walking stick. Using it improves my speed.

At the top of the ridge I stop suddenly, catching the smell of wood smoke. I can't see where it's coming from. I start to jog, going down a slope, then lose my footing again, tripping over an exposed tree root and nearly twisting my ankle. I stop and take a breath. To my left is a large brackish pond, full of black water, fallen trees, and devil's club. The smell of smoke is stronger, and it urges me on to the top of the next rise.

There, in a partially cleared meadow, is a cabin. The welcoming gray plume from a fireplace wafts out of the stone chimney. I move as quietly as I can behind a Douglas fir. The cabin is less than twenty yards away. It's a small dwelling, maybe two rooms, the type used by hunters on weekend outings of drinking and shooting. A half-deck, with a single railing, and two steps down to the ground. There's someone on the deck. And when she turns to look out at the lake on the west side, I can tell for certain that it's Sitka.

I'm about to call out to her when the cabin door opens. Jenny pokes her head outside. She says something I can't hear, and Sitka shrugs her shoulders and goes inside. I take out my binoculars and scan the lake and surrounding woods, but only find foliage and a bald eagle's nest perched at the top of a dying spruce.

I take a big breath as if I'm going to dive under the ocean, hoist myself up, and sprint to the cabin. I'm not nimble or limber enough to stay crouched for that distance. About as invisible as a moose. I take the steps as quietly as I can, but the cabin has obviously been around for a while and the wood has gone soft. The squeak is so loud, there's nothing to do but swing open the unlocked door and walk inside like it's my own home.

The room smells like wood smoke and cedar until the aroma of chicken soup breaks through. Jenny and Sitka are sitting at a table with two bowls of steaming broth in front of them, as though they were on a little weekend getaway. They're wearing matching sweaters, dark blue with the Alaskan state flag on the front. Fire licks up and over a pile of logs in the stone fireplace. On the small counter, there's a green Coleman camp stove, with a pot on one of the two burners. Seeing me, Jenny flinches, her eyes wide as a porcelain doll's. Sitka jumps up and surges over to me, wrapping her arms around my waist and snuggling her head into my side.

"Grandpa!" she says. "I knew you wouldn't let them just take me away."

"What in heaven's name are you doing here?" Jenny's voice flares like the wings of a fierce guardian angel.

I let go of Sitka, settle the rifle against the cabin wall, and slip off my backpack. As Jenny watches, I return to Sitka's side, sliding my arm across her shoulder.

"Let me take her home." I press my granddaughter even closer. "I don't care where you and Diesel go or what you do."

Jenny stays seated. A hint of steam rises up to her cheeks from her soup bowl. She looks so much like Donna.

"You really think I'd give up my own daughter?" she asks. "This is what I've been working for, even when I was in prison. I'm building a new life with Sitka, and I have a man who wants to do that with me. Diesel's not perfect, but neither am I. He loves me. We understand each other."

"Do you have to leave Yatki Island to do it?" I pull Sitka closer to me. "She goes to school there. Her friends are there. I'm there."

Jenny looks directly at Sitka, who's winding strands of her hair around her fingers. "Come here, honey."

Sitka lifts my arm off her and slowly crosses the room, her feet dragging on the floor boards. She stops at the opposite side of the table and slumps into a wooden chair. "I'm tired of all this. I just want to go home."

"You see, Jenny? She wants to come back with me."

Jenny shakes her head. "Kids are resilient," she says. "I appreciate that you took care of her for me—"

"I wasn't doing it for you."

"—but a child's home is with her mother and father. You can't throw a mother out of her daughter's life like she's a piece of trash." She reaches over and fusses over Sitka's forearm. I expect Sitka to swat her mother's hand away, and I'm disappointed when she doesn't.

"There's nothing stronger than the bond between a mother and her child," Jenny intones. She squeezes her hand over

Sitka's forearm. "I'm sorry I wasn't there for you before, Baby Doll, but I am now." Her eyes shift up and over to me. "Do you know what I wanted to do before I left for prison this last time? I wanted to visit Mom's gravesite. I wanted to make that connection with her again. Only there wasn't one. You didn't even leave that for me."

My skin goes clammy. It was a nasty business. After Donna drowned and the tide receded, the sheriff and volunteer rangers used saws and shovels to salvage what they could. I was at the site by then, but they wouldn't let me anywhere near her. What they could recover was put into a body bag and sent to a morgue in Anchorage.

Jenny didn't know what happened for another few days until I was finally able to track her down.

"There wasn't any choice but to have your mother's remains cremated."

"But you couldn't keep them in an urn at Jacobsen's Mortuary, some place I could go and just sit with her? Was that too much to ask? You had to go and dump them out in the middle of Glacier Bay?"

"I didn't know you cared where they went. You should have asked. I didn't really think it made much difference where I put her ashes. She loved Glacier Bay."

"Oh, that's rich," Jenny says, "coming from the man who killed her."

I blink several times. "What did you just say?"

"Everyone says it was an accident." Jenny's eyes stay sharp. "But you and I both know that you were the one responsible for Mom dying out in the mudflats."

The only sound is the wind whistling across the meadow and through the small chinks in the cabin wall. Then the cabin door swings open.

Diesel struts in like a war hero, carrying a rifle in one hand and a burlap sack in the other. The sack emanates a distinct gamey odor. He jerks his head back when he sees me. But his yellow teeth widen into a canine smile.

"Well, ain't this just the sweetest thing you ever saw," he says. "Look what a family reunion we got here."

Chapter 22

Diesel's wearing camouflage hunter's pants and a matching jacket. Mud splats cover his boots, and run up and down the pantlegs. His hair is matted with sweat.

"You're persistent, I'll give you that, Ray." He sets a sizeable burlap sack on the cabin floor, keeping an eye on me as he does so. "That float plane I heard before." He nods his head, as if he's having a conversation with himself, the rifle in his right hand.

"My dad thinks he can take our daughter away from us," Jenny says.

Sitka pushes herself away from Jenny and folds her arms. "I don't want to go with you. I don't want to be homeschooled. I want to stay with my friends."

"You heard her." I take a step toward Diesel. "If you really loved her, you'd let her come with me."

"That's rich. I told you before, Ray. You've had your turn." Diesel grips his rifle with both hands. "We're a family unit now. I'd love to stay and debate this with you, but we have to get going. We're on a tight schedule." He tilts his head to the door. "We've got the law on our side, and the law says I'm Sitka's daddy and Jenny is Sitka's mom, and she stays with us."

"I don't think," I say, pointing to the lumps in the burlap

sack, "that the court lets an ex-con commit a felony and still keep his child."

This last statement gets Jenny to stand up. "What are you talking about, Dad?" She goes over to her fiancé and lowers her voice. "What's he talking about, honey? You promised me there wouldn't be any drugs."

"No drugs," Diesel insists. "I promised you and I meant it."

"Care to open up that sack?" I ask.

Sitka nods at me in agreement and then shifts her gaze to Diesel.

"Just bought a bit of leftover elk meat from some hunters up on the ridge over there." He points with his rifle toward the window on the south side of the cabin. "Thought maybe we'd cook something up later on the boat."

Sitka squeezes her nostrils with her fingers, and her words come out nasal. "If that's elk meat, then it's gone bad." She lets her hand drop. "Or else you're a liar."

"Don't let your crazy grandfather put ideas into your head," Diesel tells Sitka. "He'd say anything to turn you against us. He's always been against us, all of us."

"Then you won't mind if we take a look," I venture.

Diesel tightens his grip on the stock of the rifle. "Stay out of this. It's none of your business, old man."

"It is mine." Jenny reaches for the burlap bag, but Diesel grabs it from the ground before she can.

"Jenny, you've got to trust me, babe." He opens his arms wide, the sack in one hand, the rifle in the other, holding them out to her like offerings. "How can we build a life together if you don't trust me?"

Sitka barrels to Diesel's left, snatching the sack from his hand with a two-fisted yank.

"Hey, you little . . ." He twists his lips as he reaches to grab her, but I jump in, blocking him. I'd go for his rifle, but I don't want it discharging and hitting Sitka or Jenny accidentally. I guess Diesel doesn't get how considerate I'm being, or maybe it's just instinct after being locked up for so many years. He swings the rifle butt up toward my head at an awkward angle. Hits my shoulder instead. The blow doesn't pop my shoulder out of its socket, but it hurts like hell.

"Leave him alone!" Sitka shouts. "Grandpa, are you okay?"

I'm breathing hard, wishing I still had Felix's rifle. Sitka opens the burlap sack and screams. She's sprawled on the floor, gagging like crazy, the open burlap bag in front of her, the gall bladder of a bear at her foot.

Jenny's hand flies up to her mouth. "What in God's name is that?" she says from behind her fingers.

"There's a bunch of them in there. It's so nasty!" Sitka says, her fingers clamping her nose again. "And so are you." She addresses the last part to Diesel, whispering, but loud enough for everyone to hear.

As Diesel moves to reclaim his prizes, Sitka backs away toward the door. When she swings it open, the fresh cold air is a relief. I tilt my head at her, urging her to get away, since it's finally full daylight, but she's not wearing enough layers to go very far. Or maybe she's afraid of abandoning me. She stays stationed at the doorway, breathing deep.

"It's our ticket, babe." Diesel kicks the gall bladder back into the bag with the toe of his boot. "The funding for our new start."

I'm finally catching my breath. "I knew you'd be into something like this, Diesel. You just can't do something legit, can you?"

"Hunting bears ain't illegal in Alaska."

"Selling bear parts is, especially paws and bladders," I remind him. "It's a felony."

"Diesel, I don't understand." Jenny's lips pout a little, that half-disappointed, half-angry look I remember from when she was a teenager. "We have the boat. You said if we could just get the boat, that would be enough to start a new life."

"Well, it's not. Fishing's a crapshoot. Just ask your old man." Diesel's voice is sharp, angry at being questioned. He cradles the rifle in the crook of his elbow and counts out the reasons on his fingers. "We need seed money. The boat needs repairs. We need to hire a crew. You think we can go out crabbing by ourselves and suddenly make enough to live on?"

"But how could you do such a thing to those animals?" Jenny puts her hands on her hips as she spits out the words, reminding me of the little girl in the Seattle marketplace, demanding that the fishmongers treat the salmon with respect. "Those bears didn't deserve this. You're not killing them for food."

Diesel takes a deep breath and then smiles at Jenny, nodding reassuringly as he speaks. "Be reasonable, babe. I didn't kill them myself, okay? I'm a, what do you call it, a broker. We'll just sell these the one time, get enough stake to get the business going. Then we'll get a good catch, put a down payment on a house. You said that's what you wanted, right? A little house up in Wrangell. Living the life we want to live. We just need a boost to get us going."

While they're arguing, I casually begin making my way toward Felix's rifle, which is still leaning where I propped it against the wall of the cabin.

"Not so fast, Ray." Diesel raises the barrel of his rifle and points it at me. "Why don't you stand next to Sitka so I can keep an eye on the both of you while Jenny and I finish talking."

It's not a question. While I move over, he gets Felix's rifle. Sitka's leaning against the door frame, looking away from all of us. There are no cuts or bruises on her face, but when I ask her to roll up her sweater sleeves, so I can check her arms, she shakes her head no and twists around to confront me.

"Did you kill Grandma?" Tears are running down her face.

"Of course not." I wrap my arms around her and she lets me. "I would never do anything to hurt your grandmother or you, or your mom. I just want you back home. With me."

Sitka's small arms tighten around my waist. She presses her cheek against my chest. I stroke her hair, twirling a bit of it around my own finger the way she does to comfort herself.

"We can put all this behind us, Jenny," I call over to where she and Diesel are having their little chat. Seems like she's coming to her senses about him, finally. "We can go back. You, me, and Sitka."

"The Lord put us on earth as stewards of his garden," Jenny says to Diesel. "We have to be good custodians. But what's done is done." She points to the bear parts. "I want your solemn vow, your promise, that you will never do anything like this again."

"Sure, babe," Diesel says. "Whatever you say."

Jenny opens her purse, and pulls out a pocket-sized Bible. She holds it out to Diesel.

"Swear to God," she tells him.

Diesel bites his lip like he's resisting an urge to roll his eyes. But he shifts the rifles so he can set three fingers on top of the small book, while tapping the toe of his boot. "My absolute word. I swear, on the Bible."

"We have to build our family on faith and trust. That's the foundation of our future."

"I swore on the Bible, didn't I?" Diesel checks his watch. "We need to get moving or this will all have been for nothing." He's regaining momentum, the command in his voice. "Everybody get their gear. Jenny, put out that fire. We're all going to the boat. And I mean right now."

"Let me and Sitka stay here," I say. "You don't need us."

"Not on your life," Diesel says. "We're all going to the boat. Jenny may trust you not to alert the rangers, but I don't. You can help us get over to Kodiak Island. A guy from Hong Kong is waiting there for us. Once we make the deal, then you can go. By yourself. We keep our daughter."

Sitka breaks away from my hug, stomps over to the table, and plops in one of the chairs. "I'm staying here. I'm not going with any of you."

"Stop acting like a spoiled brat." Diesel knocks the butt of one of the rifles on the floor to emphasize his point. "It's too dangerous for you to be here by yourself. Now put on your backpack."

"I'm not going," Sitka says, with all the authority an eleven-year-old can muster, though her chin is quivering, "until you tell me the truth about Grandma."

"Now's not the time to have this conversation, kiddo." I take a step toward her and tell her I have tried to protect her from the truth all these years. "Let's wait until we're home. Then I promise we'll have hot chocolate and—"

"You think I've never heard you and Felix talking?" Her words are choppy and a bit smothered as if she's doing her best not to cry. "You all think I'm just a stupid kid who can't see what's going on! I'm not going with anyone until I know what really happened."

"It's not like you have a choice," Diesel warns her. "Get your rear in gear right now."

"She's right. She needs to hear the truth." Jenny crosses the room to stand beside Sitka.

Diesel stamps his boot, raising a small cloud of dust. "Babe, we don't have time for this."

Jenny promises it won't take long. "You wait outside."

"Why do I have to wait outside?"

"This is a family matter," she says with complete authority, and for a moment, I see myself in her. That parental tone I used to take with her when she came home drunk and high, past curfew.

"Well, I'm family."

"Diesel, please," she says. "Just wait outside."

"You'd think this was a daytime talk show or something." He puts his hand on the edge of the door. "I'll be right outside. Five minutes, no more! And then everyone comes back to the boat. Got it?"

I wish I had attacked Diesel and taken his weapon when he first showed up. The distance between us, and my bruised shoulder, take that option off the table now. He latches the cabin door closed behind him. The last whole log in the fireplace crackles before it breaks in two, spewing up a small cloud of dust.

"You used to always repeat that old Smokey the Bear saying," Jenny says to me. "'Drown the campfire. Stir the ashes and drown it again.' You always said that when we went camping."

This touch of nostalgia surprises me. I don't know what to do with it. Jenny points to the table and we sit down next to

Sitka, who has pulled the ends of her sweater over her hands. My feet are feeling cold now and I rub one boot over the top of the other, flexing my toes to get some circulation going.

"Sitka," Jenny begins. "It's important you hear both sides of the story."

I slap my hand on the table. "There aren't two sides, Jenny. Your mother died chasing you after you got pregnant and ran away to get high, no matter the cost to you or your baby. She wouldn't have been out there if it hadn't been for your choices."

"You're right. I share that responsibility." Her voice is calm and even. "God knows you had your hand in that, but it was me who ran off. It's taken me a long time to forgive myself for that. But do you remember the sheriff's report?"

"I read it." I stop and look over at Sitka, not wanting to go into those gruesome details.

"It's okay," Jenny says. "I've told her. She knows what happened."

I can't tell what Sitka's thinking. Her mouth is tight, but her lower lip is quivering.

"The sheriff's report said your grandmother died drowning in the mudflats," I tell her.

"But why was Mom on the mudflats?" Jenny asks. "How come she was off the road?"

"Chasing after you, goddammit."

"Her brakes went out," Jenny insists. "Her brakes went out and the front wheel caved under, and the truck went careening into the flats. She hit her head and got disoriented and stepped out of the truck right into the mud. That's what the report said."

"So, that doesn't—"

"They went out because the brake pads and rotors needed to be replaced. The rotors that made that truck shake and shimmy every time you or Mom stepped on the brakes. She was after you for months to replace them, but you were always, 'Oh, they're not that bad. I'll get around to it. I'll get around to it.' But you never did, Dad. You neglected the truck. You didn't pay attention."

Jenny's tears sketch rivulets down her face. Sitka gets up to stand next to her mom, and like someone caught in a riptide, she starts crying again too. Jenny pulls her into a hug. I feel like someone rammed a pipe into my chest. It's difficult to breathe. The rotor and brake pads. The sound of them scraping echoes in my head. Donna did beg me to get them repaired, like she begged me to get the porch steps fixed, and the foundation shored up, and the gutters mended, and the garage cleaned out. I always said I would get around to those chores, but I didn't. There was always so much to do just to keep the boat running and to chase after the crab and shrimp with Felix. And when she begged me to go with her to find Jenny, I refused. I let her go alone.

All these years I've constructed the story that I was blameless in my wife's death. Built it up like a seawall, reinforced it with concrete reasoning. But with Sitka here, the truth smashes against my version like a tidal wave, destroying it in one great surge. Whatever role Jenny may have played, whatever the gods allowed to happen, Donna died because of me, because of what I failed to do, because I let her reach out to our daughter all alone. It's like losing Donna all over again, only this time losing a part of myself as well. Sitka sits there staring at me, wet cheeks, wet eyelashes. Blaming me. I feel gutted, my stomach churning, my hands shaking and clammy. I want to collapse and be swallowed up whole, like Jonah inside the whale, like someone trapped in the mud flats. Don't want to move. Want to sit here until the fire goes out and the ashes go cold and my feet go colder. My lungs feel like they're filled with the blanched remains of the fire. Drown the campfire. Stir the ashes and drown it again.

Sitka disengages from her mom. I must be a pitiful sight, the one who should be sent away to live with the frog people. She moves over next to me, her sleeve rubbing next to mine. "I needed to know."

"I loved your grandmother," I tell her. "I loved her so much you can't believe it."

Sitka puts her arm around my neck and gives me a swift kiss on the cheek. "I know you did. And so did my mom. You both still do."

I lean into her, and speak the words into her sweater. "Yeah, you're right. We both still do."

"There are things we've both done and things we didn't do." Jenny wipes her eyes. She sweeps her hair behind her ears, back to her newly empowered self. The one who doesn't get high. The one who forgives. The one who took her daughter back. "I don't hate you, Dad. But I've got to build my own life now."

"And you honestly think you can do it with him?"

"He's not perfect. I know that. He's not as strong of a Christian as I would like him to be. But he's trying. What kind of breaks do you think people like Diesel and me get?"

I lift my head away from Sitka. "Are you willing to risk your daughter in the process?"

"And you tell me I'm dramatic. Diesel's turning his life around. He's been sober for two years. If I really thought my daughter was in danger, don't you think I'd do anything and everything to protect her?"

Neither Sitka nor I have an answer for that. Jenny marches to the door, lifts up the latch, opens it, and tells Diesel we're done.

"About time," he says, as if he were the boat captain calling his crew back to work. "Let's go, let's go."

Jenny packs the remaining food in her backpack. She wipes out the soup pot with a paper towel and throws it in the fireplace. The stained paper flares when it hits the smoldering ashes, then Jenny pours a bucket of water in. She takes the poker, runs it through the ashes, and dumps a second bucketful onto the gray sludge, turning it hard and cold. Just like I taught her.

Sitka digs her nails into my sleeve. "It'll be okay," I tell her. "I'll figure out something when we get to the boat."

She doesn't look any more comforted than I am by those words. I feel like I should do something, take us on a different course. But my heart is still numbing my brain. That loss. Our loss. My wife. I can't think of what to do but follow along. We put on our coats and packs and start back down the beachhead trail. It only takes twenty minutes to descend. The wet sand splays out under our boots as we cross the beach to where the Zodiac is tied up. The water is calm, flowing onto and receding from the shoreline of the cove with barely a sound.

Before we get in, Diesel surveys the *Jenny-Sais-Pas.*

"You here all alone, Ray? I heard that plane take off. You didn't bring anybody else with you, did you?"

"You see anybody else?"

Diesel motions for Jenny and Sitka to board the raft. After they get settled, Diesel unties the Zodiac. The two of us push off and we paddle over to the boat.

"Everybody onboard," Diesel says when we get there. "Ray, you first. Then Sitka and Jenny. I'll follow close behind."

We do as Diesel instructs, and once Jenny is up, he hands her the two rifles before climbing aboard himself. Right away he takes one back and uses it to point at the broken lock on the hatch.

"No wonder you knew what I had. Well, no matter now." He stops and his nostrils flare. "Why do I smell coffee?"

"Because I felt like a fresh cup." We turn and Felix appears suddenly from the midsection of the deck. He's holding a flare gun, aimed at Diesel. "Now drop that rifle and stand over there like a good boy."

Diesel's mouth drops open.

"Go on, now. Jenny, I'm afraid I'll have to ask you to do the same."

"Don't do it, babe." Diesel shakes his head at her. "That thing only holds one flare. He can only shoot that thing at one of us, then he's done."

Felix straightens his arm, the mouth of the flare gun aimed directly at Diesel's head.

"Don't hurt him." Jenny's voice quivers, but she lays her rifle on the deck and then holds her palms out. "See, Felix? Mine's down. Just don't hurt him."

While I'm wondering how Jenny can still want to protect him, Sitka makes a grab for Diesel's rifle, which places her between him and Felix. I lunge at Diesel, pushing Sitka out of the way, and the gun clatters to the deck. Diesel wraps his arms around me, and then we're going at it like a couple of sumo wrestlers. Screaming and grunting and cursing. He gets one arm free and presses my hurt shoulder with his fist. Pain shoots up to my neck and head. As I try to recover, Diesel whips out that damn boning knife from his boot. He holds it at my throat.

"Drop the flare gun."

The blade is so close, the edge of it digs into my throat as I speak, nicking my skin. "Don't do it, Felix." I take a deep breath and try to keep the shaking out of my voice. "Keep the gun."

"Let him go, son," Felix says calmly.

Diesel backs me up all the way to the port rail. The knife blade presses into my throat as we move. Then he kicks the dropped rifle away with his foot. It skids across the deck toward Jenny.

"Pick it up," he tells her. "Pick them both up. And Sitka, you come over here."

Sitka shakes her head. Doesn't move. She's trembling but holding steady where she is. Good girl.

"Diesel, no!" Jenny shouts. "Leave her alone. Don't do anything to her. She's your daughter!"

"Stay there, Sitka," I say, trying to sound as calm as Felix. "Kiddo, please stay there."

Diesel digs the knife in, warning me. My neck stings, and I can smell the blood now.

"You get over here, Sitka, or I will slice your grandfather's throat and feed him to the fish. It's your choice."

Sitka runs over to us, fingers in her mouth. Her breaths are loud and fast, and I will her to not do anything stupid.

Diesel clasps a hunk of Sitka's sweater to keep her there by his side, and tells Felix to put the flare gun down. "Then you can sit on the deck with your hands under you."

Felix stares at me, waiting for me to tell him what to do. He can't decide, not with his stroke. I try to shake my head no, but the edge of the blade stops me.

"You want to shoot me, Felix? Go ahead." Diesel's mouth opens, showing his yellow teeth and fillings. "But you have to decide which one of these two goes overboard with me."

Felix's arm wavers as he looks at me and Sitka. We've been through so much together, him and me. And now I have to decide for him.

"Put the flare gun down, Felix," I say. "We can't let him hurt Sitka."

I move my leg a little, acting like it has fallen asleep, to see if I can twist around and knee Diesel somehow, but the three of us are too close to the railing, and I can't get the right leverage. Felix lowers his arm and I feel Diesel relax his grip on the knife. He turns to make sure Felix is laying the gun all the way down on the deck. Suddenly Sitka drops to her knees, her sweater stretching away from Diesel's hand, and a whoosh comes from the side. A blur of brown and metal gray, followed by the crack of hardwood against bone and cartilage. Jenny. With one of the rifles. She must have given Sitka a signal that Diesel and I missed.

"You son of a bitch!" she yells, smacking the butt of the gun into Diesel's face again.

He staggers back against the railing and drops the boning knife, his nose bloody and crooked, although somehow he keeps hold of Sitka's sweater. "Christ Almighty, Jenny!"

I reach for Sitka, to pull her away from him, but Diesel makes one final effort to regain his balance by grabbing hold of me. I try to keep us steady, but Sitka contorts her body, throwing a swift right-handed punch at Diesel, and that throws our balance off. The three of us tip over the railing, flailing our arms.

Sitka screams as we spill over the side, arms and legs kicking each other. We plunge into the water, and I swallow mouthfuls before remembering to hold my breath. The salt stings the cuts on my neck. I don't see Sitka. My shoulder refuses to go the way I want it to. My other arm thrashes. I close and reopen my eyes. Having trouble focusing. The green water, all around, looks remarkably calm, almost inviting. Quiet. The cold begins to soothe my aching shoulder. But Sitka—I try to kick, to rise—but that fast, the sea has shocked my body into inaction. My legs are heavy. Useless as severed anchor chain. Brown strands of kelp plants surround me. I try again to move my arms, or at least I think I do. Need to find Sitka. Reach her. Save her. I look for a cone of light to lead me to the surface. Bits and pieces of decaying matter grasp at my legs, pulling me down to the opening mouths of green and yellow anemones. Silt and salt filter into my nostrils. I open my mouth and breathe water. The green starts to turn black. I keep fighting, and will my legs to move, but it won't take all that long to die.

Chapter 23

SITKA SQUINTS AS SHE baits her rigging with a finger mullet, bringing the hook up through the mouth of the small fish. We're anchored at an unnamed cove up near Angoon. It's early May and a warm front has moved up from Vancouver, removing the chill from the mid-morning air. We've taken off our heavy jackets.

"You have your mother's quick hands," I tell her.

She doesn't answer, but when she's done, she straightens up and smiles.

It's a private trip today, a celebration of sorts. Walt Francke's lawsuit finally came to court last week. The district judge in Juneau took about three minutes to dismiss the suit as frivolous. The fact that the judge was an avid fisherman no doubt helped my case. Not to mention that Walt didn't bother to even show up. Seems he and Cindy were on a luxury safari trip in Kenya. The judge told Walt's attorneys that their client obviously didn't have the common sense God gave an eel. I couldn't think of a better way to celebrate than by going fishing with those closest to me.

Sitka casts her line and settles the butt of her reel into its slot on the rail. "Where's Felix? Doesn't he want to fish?"

"You better go get him, honey." Muskeg swaps out a blur lure for a white one. "He's back there spread out on the deck lounge. Last I saw him, he was drinking coffee and scarfing down some of my berry pie. Shoot. It's nowhere near lunch time."

"Good thing you brought two of them." Sitka elbows me and smiles. "Watch my line, will you? I'm going to get some pie myself. Of course I'll have it with Mountain Dew!" She knows I think that stuff is disgusting. She says the same thing about coffee.

Muskeg leans back in her folding deck chair with the extra thick cushion that she likes to bring onboard. I sit down on the cooler seat next to her. "She's doing really well, Ray. Becoming quite the young woman."

As if on cue, Sitka got her first period the week of her twelfth birthday back in December. She didn't make a big fuss about it, certainly not in front of me. It helped that I had the necessary items on hand, thanks to Julie writing a list for me. And now I keep the head stocked with Sitka's favorite brand of tampons and pads. They're not on our official inventory check-off list of course, but they're there just the same. Sarah and her mom went with us to buy Sitka's first bra. We all took the ferry over to Juneau together so they could shop at the bigger stores there. Sitka made me stay outside the lingerie departments, but she was fairly relaxed and talkative when we had lunch afterwards.

"She's coping pretty well," I say. "A lot of days she's doing better than me."

"Give yourself time." Muskeg leans over and pats my knee. "Six months is nothing when you've lost a child, even if she is an adult child. That loss won't ever go away, but it will get better."

I don't know if Muskeg is right or not. I stand up and turn toward the deck railing, watching Sitka's fishing line disappear into the emerald water. The sun sparkles on the surface. My shoulder still aches from that day in Williams Cove. I don't remember all of it, especially after Sitka, Diesel, and I tumbled overboard.

What I remember is being covered with several layers of

orange emergency blankets. The hard wood of the deck under
my back, numb legs, shoulder muscles hot and full of ache, the
skin on my lower back scraped open from being hauled onboard. The only sound I could hear was the rush of water in my
ears. My eyes stung. Hot needles of pain in my feet and fingers
as sensation returned. My shoulder a cold bruise. Gradually
colors started to emerge from the shadows and my eyes sorted
out familiar shapes: the railing, the aft bulkhead, the red cross
on the medical emergency kit, Felix. Who has since filled in the
missing pieces for me.

The first thing I did was mouth "Sitka?" No sound, but Felix
knew what I was asking. He told me that she was safe in the
pilothouse under a heap of blankets. The Medevac helicopter
was already on its way. Despite his inability to make decisions,
following safety protocols came easy to Felix, thank the gods.

"And Jenny?" This time the words came out, sore and raw
in my throat from the seawater I must have swallowed.

"Be quiet, Ray," he said.

But I wouldn't be quiet. I kept asking for Jenny until he
told me.

After we tumbled over the railing, Felix threw the emergency life rings out to us. Diesel grabbed one and started to work
his way back to the boat. Sitka and I were still under water when
the rings hit. Jenny dove in, right where Sitka had begun to
sink. A moment later Jenny sputtered above the surface, looked
around, caught her breath, and dove under again. Twenty, thirty seconds passed. Then she broke the surface and pulled Sitka
onto the life ring, securing her with the straps and hooks.

Felix yelled to Diesel to search for me, but Diesel either
didn't hear him or decided to ignore him. Felix grabbed the
three-pronged boat hook and extended it out toward Sitka, but
she was too far away. Jenny pushed the life ring from behind,
edging it closer to the boat, until Sitka could grab hold of the
polyurethane head of the hook. Felix leaned over and pulled
her onto the boat, Jenny hoisting her up from behind. Once
Felix had Sitka safely on the deck, shivering but conscious, he

turned for Jenny, but something seemed to pull her down. Felix thrust the hook into the water. Jenny tried to reach for it, but her head went under. Felix paddled the water with the boat hook over and over, splashing around to find her, but she sank beyond his reach.

Just then my head broke surface just a few feet away from the boarding ladder. Felix stepped onto the lowest rung, and with one hand clutching the handrail, he used the boat hook to grab the seat of my pants and pull me to the ladder. As he was trying to figure out how to get me onboard, Sitka reached over the railing, grabbed the hook, and kept me from floating away. Felix hoisted himself back on deck and together the two of them pulled me onboard. They searched and searched the water for Jenny, but she had disappeared.

While Felix was rescuing us, Diesel swam to the aft ladder, climbed back onboard, and gathered up his sack of bear parts and some blankets. He took the Zodiac for himself. Felix spotted it beached up on the shoreline. Diesel must have gone back to the cabin, dried himself out, and took off from there at some point. No one's seen or heard from him since. I once asked Sitka if she was at all sorry that her dad was out of her life, and she just rolled her eyes.

While the Medevac copter flew Sitka and me to Bartlett Regional Hospital in Juneau, another Coast Guard crew sailed out to Williams Cove. They sent divers down. It only took them forty minutes to locate Jenny's body and bring it up. She was that close to the boat. That close to Felix's hook. Perhaps it was Jenny's God who gave Sitka and me the blessing of not having to watch her drowned body being hauled up out of the water.

With Jenny's death, and Diesel's disappearance, Ben Sato re-petitioned the court to award temporary custody of Sitka to me. The judge took all of five seconds to approve the request and now the adoption proceedings are rolling along smoothly. Very soon Sitka will legally be my daughter. Ben also asked that ownership of the *Jenny-Sais-Pas* go to Sitka, with me as the official guardian. That petition was also granted, which is how

I ended up going to court over Walt Francke's injury after all. Now I'm taking care of this bucket so when I retire Sitka can sell it and travel somewhere or start a PhD, or whatever she wants to do.

I had Jerry Johnson come out in March and give me a bid on repairing the house foundation. It was too big a job to do by myself, and he and his crew got it done in ten days. It was a chunk of change, but I want Sitka to have the place someday. Whether she wants to live there or sell it and buy a cabin or something will be up to her.

Muskeg lifts herself out of her deck chair and puts her arms on the rail next to mine.

"I wish I could have put things right with Jenny," I say.

Muskeg points to the air and sea. "She's here."

"I really screwed things up."

"Well," she says, "you can stay on that pity pot of yours or you can always make sure you do right by Sitka."

"You sure do know how to cheer a guy up."

"Hmmph. Life's too short. That's all I know. So you better make the best of it with those who love you." Muskeg puts a hand on my sleeve. "Speaking of which, I thought Nicole was going to join us."

"She was, but then they asked her to come in and help out at the hospital. She'll meet us back at the house this evening. She says 'hey,' by the way."

"She better not miss girls' night out at the Blind Dog next Tuesday. I don't want to hear any work excuses."

I didn't think Nicole and I would ever get back together. It was more steadfastness on her part than mine. At least at first. Starting at the funeral service. The minister of the church that Jenny attended offered to have a service there. I agreed and thanked him. I wanted to respect Jenny's religion. And I thought it would be good for Sitka to see that other people cared about her mother.

The day of the funeral was cold and icy, but the sky cleared late in the morning. About thirty people showed up, more than

I had expected. Felix and Muskeg sat with me and Sitka in the front pew. To my surprise, Nicole came in and sat directly behind us. I was glad she was there. We didn't talk, but I turned around and nodded at her. She didn't reach her hand out to me just then. That would come later. Just like her helping me to officially adopt Sitka.

Diesel didn't show up. There's a warrant out for his arrest, but who knows how far away he's run. His mother Becky came. She didn't say a word to me or to anyone else, but she didn't have to. Her being there was enough. The service seemed pretty standard to me, with hymns and readings from St. Paul and other passages. The minister asked if anyone wanted to say anything about Jenny. I knew I couldn't without breaking apart. To my amazement, though, Sitka stood up and walked straight to the pulpit. Her hands shook as she adjusted the microphone. She unfolded a piece of lined notebook paper. I had no idea she had prepared anything.

"I used to," she began. The mike squawked and the minister reached over and quickly readjusted it for her. He patted her on the back. She began again. "When I was a little kid I used to make up stories about my mom. That's because I didn't know her. I didn't even know where she was most of my life, so I mainly made up that she was a soldier fighting overseas on some secret mission. I even drew pictures of her in camouflage uniforms. She was a hero in those stories, always beating the bad guys and saving her troops. I knew she was fighting for me and that one day she would come back with lots of medals. But then she did come home for real. And I thought how stupid I was to make up those stories. My mom was an ex-addict and an ex-con. I hated her for that. At least at first. I used to make fun of her in front of my friends. I would pretend to quote Bible verses in a goofy voice, then my friends and I would all laugh. My mom tried to be really nice to me, but I thought she was full of it. I used to say, 'She's just trying to put on a show,' like we were in a sitcom or something. But I was wrong."

Sitka stopped speaking, her shoulders heaving a bit. She wiped at her eyes and continued. "I was wrong because my mom was a hero. She died saving my life. And I was wrong about things being just for show. She really did want us to be a family. I didn't have a mom before. But I'll always have one now. And it won't be just stories, because she was real and she loved me. And I just hope . . ."

She couldn't finish through her tears. She descended from the pulpit and nearly ran back to the front pew. She buried her face in my shoulder. I squeezed her hard against me.

"Thank you, sweetie," I whispered. "You did real good for both of us."

We had Jenny's body cremated. Sandy Jacobsen, who took over her dad's mortuary business last year, handled the logistics. She asked if we had a recent photo of Jenny to have enlarged and placed in front of the altar. I said we didn't, but Sitka gave her one that she had taken the day after her mom came back home. In it, Jenny is standing in front of the house. There's sunlight on her shoulders. She's smiling and looks more relaxed than I had ever seen her.

Nancy Baker, who teaches ceramic classes at the senior center, made the urn. It sort of looks like a Chinese vase, mint green with little gold veins running through it. Sitka wanted to scatter her mother's ashes in Glacier Bay, so that they could mingle in the currents that carried her grandmother. I told her it was too soon to make that choice yet, that we would keep them here for the next year or so. If she wanted to still take the ashes to Glacier Bay later on, then I would go with her and we would have a ceremony. For now I'm pretty sure Jenny would be happy to be at home with us. I want her to be home with us for a while longer.

Who are the gods of second chances? Maybe all of them. I don't know. But each day, I go into Jenny's bedroom and change the water in the vase of Alaskan forget-me-nots, which have just started blooming. I pick up any of the cornflower blue and yellow petals that have fallen onto the cloth runner. I keep a copy of the photo Sitka took of Jenny and one of Donna on top of the dresser. Jenny's urn is just behind them. I dust the new picture frames and make sure the photos are straight. I clean out the old incense from the small rice bowl before lighting a fresh stick. When I blow gently on the end, the scented smoke drifts upward. It's this ritual that gets me through the day when I feel like the island I'm standing on will split apart. Jenny would probably protest this as unchristian. But the ritual comforts me, and I suppose grieving is for the living. Sitka doesn't join me. She likes to remember her mom by taking long walks along the docks. I tell her that's fine. But I make sure I ask her about her walks, about how she's feeling. She doesn't always want to answer me, but she knows that I'm asking.

The mud and the rain have left my dreams. So has Donna. I guess that's because every morning I sit on the bedroom carpet in front of Jenny's dresser and close my eyes. I let the images of them come to me as they will. Some with fierce accusations. Some with love and forgiveness. Mostly just the small moments that made up our lives together as a family. I don't try to direct them or conjure up one over another. I pay attention. I mourn.

But today is for celebrating.

"Earth to Dad!" Sitka seems to have settled on using that moniker with me. "You were watching my pole, weren't you?"

"Sort of," I admit. "I don't think they're biting yet."

"That's okay. But you promised me you would show me how to operate the winch today."

I put up my arms in mock defense. "We don't need to use the winch right now."

"Dad!" Sitka putting her hands on her hips. "You promised!"

"Ray!" Muskeg says.

"Okay, okay! Come with me, young lady."

Sitka puts her arm around me, just as Felix passes us, his lips outlined in blueberry pie filling.

"Better make sure my honeybuns ain't all alone." When he gets up there, Muskeg spots him a kiss, licks her own lips, and laughs.

Sitka and I kneel by the winch, squinting in the sun. This vibrant, stubborn twelve-year-old.

"The first thing you need to know about operating this equipment—"

"I know. I know," Sitka says. "Always stand behind it and always have your toolbox at hand, because you have to be prepared."

My hand automatically tousles her hair, messing up the sleek lines of her ponytail. She doesn't flinch, but leans into me. I give her a quick squeeze around the shoulders.

"See there, young lady. You're going to make a fine captain of this boat."

"Like you said, I've got my mom's quick hands. And I guess a few of your brains," she teases.

"That should get you by for a little while."

We're surrounded by calm green water, the afternoon light spreading out from the shadows. So reassuring and so temporal. I know there aren't enough gods in the universe to guarantee anything. I'll just have to be there, really be there, for her, as best I can.

About the Illustrator

SINCE A YOUNG AGE Reid Psaltis has been fascinated by animal life and compelled to draw. These interests became correlated, and the natural world has consistently been the subject of his work. Whether for pay or for pleasure he is easily contented drawing anything furred, scaled, or feathered. He is a native of the Pacific Northwest, and currently lives in Portland, Oregon, where he works as a freelance illustrator while also writing and drawing his own comics. Reid's comics and illustrations have been featured on Top Shelf 2.0, Study Group Comics, Trip City, Scout Books' Good Ink Series, and by other independent publishers. More of his work can be seen at reidpsaltis.com.

About the Author

FOR TEN YEARS, DAN Berne has been an active member of a select writing workshop led by bestselling author Karen Karbo. His short stories and poetry have been published in literary magazines and he earned a literary award from the Pacific Northwest Writers Association. Dan owns a market strategy consultancy and is currently writing a book on market transformation. He lives with his wife, Aliza, in Portland, Oregon. *The Gods of Second Chances*, his debut, was chosen to be the first novel in Forest Avenue Press' fiction catalog. Learn more at danberne.com.

Acknowledgments

My dear wife, Aliza, has been a constant advocate and supporter.

I owe so much to my editor and publisher, Laura Stanfill. First-time authors feel fortunate to find someone who will publish them, and when I discovered Forest Avenue Press and its mission to publish and promote quiet novels, rich with character and plot, I knew I had found a home. Laura has been a tireless force, providing wisdom and clarity.

My writing mentor, Karen Karbo, has been an unerring guide. And this novel would not have been written at all without the critiques and support from my fellow writers and authors who gather weekly at her table: Kevin Burke, Charlotte Dixon, Art Edwards, Christine Fletcher, Debbie Guyol, Connie McDowell, Colleen Strohm, Valerie Williamson, and Laura Wood.

Gigi Little is a gifted graphic designer who read a draft of my novel and then captured the essence of it in her wonderful, spot-on cover. I was blown away when I saw what she had fashioned.

When we were looking for an illustrator to render the rhythm and movement of the story, we came across the talented Reid Psaltis, who created the inside illustrations and got them just right.

Annie Denning Hille, Chrysia Watson, and Tracy Stepp offered valuable edits and suggestions.

Finally I'd like to thank the people of Southeast Alaska, and especially the crew and staff at Glacier Bay Lodge and Tours, for helping me discover a truly beautiful and magnificent part of the world.